Star-Scorched Fingertips

Melissa Ferguson

Android Press

Published by Android Press
Eugene, Oregon
www.android-press.com

ISBN: 978-1958121382 (paperback)
ISBN: 978-1958121399 (epub)

Contents

Earth

Prologue

ACESO

Earthyear 2307

Mommy tucked Rae in tight on the top bunk with Cindy, her baby doll. "Time to sleep now. You always wanted bunk beds for sleepovers with your friends."

But Rae had no friends on this new planet with the name like a sneeze.

She smudged the low ceiling with her breath. "I'm not tired." She fancied that if she slept, all the ice crystals still floating around her body from cold-sleep would expand and turn her into a block of ice, like Kay from one of her favourite stories, The Snow Queen.

"Just close your eyes and lie still while I rest," Mommy said from the bunk below. "Lights out now."

Light pained Mommy. Her hand was always clamped to her forehead, pushing at her dreaded headaches. Rae wanted her yellow moon night-light. They had crates and crates bursting with boring grown-up things. But she hadn't been allowed to bring any of her toys except for Cindy doll. Everything was so unfair.

She climbed down from the top bunk and curled up on top of the covers beside Mommy. "Can we interface with Nanna and Poppa?" She missed them even more than she missed her large house on Earth with the staff who had done everything for them.

"No, Rae. How many times do I have to tell you? They've been dead for at least a hundred years and even if they weren't dead, we've no way to contact them."

Mommy rolled away and her shoulders shook. Rae thought she was laughing. She even grinned along with Mommy's joke about Nanna and Poppa. Then she heard sobs, and she curled up into a ball and cried a little too.

Mommy sat up and rattled her pill bottle. Rae reached out to touch the fuzzy bits of hair at the back of Mommy's head. On Earth her hair had been thick and shiny. Every night Rae had brushed it with a polished wood and boar bristle hairbrush. But on Aceso chunks fell away and covered the floor like fluffy weeds.

Father worried about Mommy. She nearly hadn't woken up from the long cold-sleep. But he was more worried about everything else he had to do for the community. It was all he talked about. When Rae had asked Mommy what a community was, she had said in her cranky voice that it was everyone and everything but Father's own wife and child.

When Mommy began to snore, Rae got up. The room smelled like Mommy's rotten breath.

Rae left and closed the door softly behind her. Aceso was bouncier than Earth, so she skipped down the hall. Father liked to say they were in a Goldilocks zone. Rae thought that was his explanation for why they ate boring, porridgey food every day.

Victoria, father's special friend, came around a corner and bumped into her. She flung her long braid over her shoulder and gazed down at Rae from up high.

"Rae! You scared the life out of me."

She didn't look like her life had gone anywhere. "Is it back in you now?"

Victoria screwed up her face. She never did have much of a sense of humour. "Shouldn't you be in bed?"

"I'm going to see Father." Rae rocked Cindy doll in her arms and hoped Victoria couldn't tell she was lying.

"All right. But remember you're not to go outside." She reached down, tapped Rae's nose and walked on.

Rae wiped Victoria's touch away and stopped outside the bridge where there was yet another meeting. The people she had known as Father's friends on Earth were all called Master this or Master that now. If she called them by their old names, everyone scowled at her. She tiptoed past and imagined herself wearing an invisibility cloak.

The metal diamond shapes on the ramp down to the cargo hold pressed into the bottom of her feet. Large crates and boxes covered the lights and made shadows to hide in. Workers moved around, grunting and talking in soft voices. They worked late into the night, every night, setting up the community. Some of them hadn't woken from the cold-sleep. Father had vowed to grow more workers. Rae looked forward to having baby workers to play with and sing to sleep. Father said the new workers wouldn't have names like the workers from Earth, just numbers. But she would give them names and teach them to call her Mommy.

The workers had masks on their faces to protect them from whatever it was in the air that was making everyone giddy. The masks looked like the ones she used to wear at home when the sky filled with smoke. To her the air on Aceso was sweet, and it allowed the Earth to speak to her. When it spoke, it told her that it wanted them back.

Rae slipped outside and stood in the light of the faceless, caramel moons. The sky glowed purply-orange with stars. There were so many that she struggled to pick one out from another. She tried in vain to make out the constellations Poppa had taught her.

Vine crunched under her feet. It was like nothing on Earth, yet it was green like grass and had thorns like the berry brambles that grew under Earth's sky. And it was smooth and tough on the outside, like the seaweeds that grew in Earth's oceans. But when she stepped on the vine, it was spongy, like the mushrooms that Nana and Poppa said kept most of themselves under Earth's soil.

Bugs swarmed and tickled her skin. Her head whirled. She walked around the side of the ship and sat on a sprawling patch of vine. Sap dampened her night dress and she shivered. During the day someone always came to take her back inside before the Earth could talk to her properly, but no one knew where she was now.

She slapped her palms on the leaves and licked the cinnamon-tasting sap off her hand. She was Gretel in the garden of the gingerbread house. The whirly feeling grew stronger. Like when Poppa threw her into the air and she lost her breath from laughing.

Then everything went quiet and peaceful and safe, like Nanna stroking the hair at her temple while she fell asleep. Her bed was in front of her, and Nanna was folding down the edge of the bedcovers as Poppa sat in his rocking chair. Cindy doll and Rae glided forward like they were flying. Her pillow looked fluffy and soft, and her cloud-baby plushie and yellow moon night-light –the moon she could see from her home on Earth – waited for her. Nanna and Poppa grinned wider and wider the closer she came.

Nanna's perfume was sweet and soothing. Rae's feet touched the heated floorboards. Poppa's soft, wrinkled hand gently pinched her cheek.

"Time for sleep now, sweet Rae." Nanna patted the bed.

She climbed in and snuggled down, cosy and safe. Nanna kissed her on the forehead and wiped away the print of her bright red lipstick with her thumb. Rae's eyes drooped and Earth held her tight. The bits of ice inside her melted and oozed like jam in a hot donut.

"Goodnight, sleeping beauty," Poppa said. "When you wake you, and the vine, will heal the Earth."

The vine snuggled her tight tighter and tighter, like Nanna used to hold her when she'd had a nightmare. Thorns pricked her skin. It hurt a little at first, but she soon became numb and so, so sleepy. She yawned and closed her eyes.

Far, far away someone yelled her name.

Part 1

ACESO

Earthyear 2307

1

Centa was extracting RNA from a dozen failed zygotes when the high-pitched beep of an alarm sounded in the gestation laboratory. She held still, a slick of sweat formed between her hands and her latex gloves, her heartbeat almost as loud as the alarm. There was a chance it was just another electrical problem. Or it could be something worse.

"Teacher?" Centa's eight-year-old shadow, who she secretly called Tilter, burst out of the gestation lab and sprinted across the room.

"Worker 517! What have I told you about running in the laboratory?"

"Sorry, it's just..." He gulped and took a big breath.

Centa gripped her pipette and waited for him to tell her that he'd tripped and knocked out a cord or that there was a blockage in a section of tubing. Anything but what she suspected.

"It's a foetus. I've tried everything you taught me." He angled his head to the side and chewed his thin lips.

Centa put down her pipette and stood. She'd been thrown down this hill before. Every single time it ended with her in a broken pile at the bottom.

She peered through the glassware and equipment stacked on the shelves and benches, towards Perpetua's empty bench and the closed door of Master Anton's office beyond. There would be no help coming from either of them while they performed spiritual service. The burden was hers alone yet again. They were ridiculously understaffed. Over and over, they'd requested more workers for the Worker Replenishment Laboratory, but the masters insisted they couldn't be spared. They needed every available worker to fight the carnivorous vine that threatened to engulf the settlement. Where did they think workers to fight the vine came from?

Tilter was looking to her for answers, so she supressed the urge to flee and walked calmly to the gestation lab, past the cold storage chambers and autoclaves.

I am obedient and content. I live only to serve the Spirit, Skyfather, and the masters.

Centa recited the words of faith out of habit. They no longer gave her comfort. Worker 8, who Centa referred to as Perpetua, was scheduled to monitor the incubators. Her every action was irritating. That very morning Perpetua had stood at the long metal washroom sink with toothpaste foaming at the sides of her mouth like a dying lizard-pig. Why didn't she spit?

They'd spent nearly every moment of their lives, all thirty years of them, side by side, sleeping, eating, defecating and, once they were old enough, working. And there was no end in sight. They were linked forever by the sequence of thawed worker zygotes. It was enough to make Centa stab something, someone, herself maybe, with a pipette.

A blue light was strobing above the bubble-shaped glass uterus mid-way down the first row of incubators. The heartbeat of the fist-sized foetus stuttered and slowed. When she was young, every one of the eighteen shiny incubator bubbles had pulsed with life, staggered so that each fortnight a new Sky Human pushed through the outer membranes into waiting hands. But now they implanted no more than one zygote per month, and most of those shrivelled and died within days. Sometimes hours. How had they gotten from that normal to this one? The foetus before her now had been progressing well, showing the beginnings of hair-patterning on the scalp, and the groove of the philtrum beneath the nose.

She tapped the display panel to silence the alarm and scrolled through the values for temperature, dissolved gases, waste products, and nutrients with increasing dismay. Each number was outside of the acceptable range. She sent a bolus of progesterone into the chamber to prevent premature labour. The equivalent of throwing down a bucket of water once a fire front has passed. It was hopeless. Her thoughts strayed to the consequences of the loss of a generation of workers. According to Skyfather and the masters, that was not her concern. All she could do was be the tool through which they worked.

All fate is Aceso's will and Aceso guides us through our Skyfather.

She manually depressed the defib button on the control panel to shock the slowing heart.

"Please, Skyfather and The Spirit of Aceso," she begged. "Lend this Sky Human your strength so that they may grow and serve you."

Tilter stood by, wide-eyed, watching it all.

The heartbeat rallied, and Centa held her breath over the tiny bag of organs, praying it would latch onto life. Watching a foetus die was so familiar it was almost comforting. Like mouthing along to a punishment chant.

As if on cue, the heart slowed again. Couldn't they just have one day when nothing went wrong? It didn't make sense that she kept failing. And it was always her, delivering death. Perpetua was always conveniently indisposed.

Centa didn't want much. If The Spirit of Aceso would grant this cluster of Sky Human cells a steady heartbeat she would worship them for twice as long and with twice as much fervour every single day for the rest of her days.

The heart faltered and ceased beating. Centa initiated another electrical shock. The heart pulsed for a second. She tried three more times. The shimmer of life in amniotic fluid stilled to the dull inertia of death. She couldn't have been more ashamed than if Skyfather himself had blamed her for The Spirit of Aceso's anger.

"We're doing everything right," Tilter said. "Why do they keep dying? It's not fair."

"Don't whine," Centa snapped. She used her anger to halt the tears forming in her eyes. There was no such thing as fair in their work. Just good or bad outcomes. Centa was competent and hard-working—her reputation in the settlement, and a large part of her identity, was based around those very traits—but even she couldn't breathe life back into cells frozen for centuries.

Yet she had little choice but to keep going. The survival of the settlement depended on new lives. She might spend every day of the rest of her life watching zygotes and foetuses die. She was as stuck as a neonate grown too big to fit through the glass delivery channel.

She pressed her fists into the sides of the incubator. The only way out was to smash it all. She visualized glass cracking and liquid gushing as she destroyed them, broken shards slicing her veins. She lowered her hands, thinking of the cleaning up she would have to do, the explanations she would have to give, the disciplinary counselling, and the anger of The Spirit at her disobedience.

Centa flooded the chamber with oxytocin until the inner membranes contracted and expelled the foetus through the delivery canal tubing. It was blue and limp, curling inward with tiny, tight fists. So unlike the full-term infants whose arms and legs starfished once freed and whose blue-grey skin brightened to pink after those first screamed breaths. She'd taken those moments for granted and now all she wanted was to experience it again.

The foetus squelched into the bottom of a biohazard bag, its thin plastic darkening with amniotic fluid, followed by the placenta. They would need to perform a dissection and a genetic analysis.

She wanted to walk out right then, skip ahead through time until she could defy Skyfather's rules and laws, suppress the obedient worker part of herself and think about nothing but Ben and his touch. Disciple Ben was her illicit passion. Workers and disciples were encouraged to share themselves freely, but were prohibited from forming strong, exclusive attachments. Ben, however, was the only one in her heart. He was one of the original settlers, an orphaned child recruited by Skyfather on Earth. Through his stories, the very smell of his skin and the density of his bones, she experienced how it was to have lived on Earth. He was her Earth, with strong gravity that pulled her to him always. And despite all the ways in which she was told that Earth and her emotional attachment to Ben were bad and wrong, both still sounded like home. And tonight, now that it had been thirty years since the day she was expelled from an incubator and the age gap between them no longer troubled him, Ben would finally let her into his bed.

But before she could be with him, she would have to endure the rest of the workday, the evening meal, ablutions, and the pointless chattering in the dormitory. Not until everyone in the settlement was asleep would she be free to be Centa and not just Worker 9.

Perpetua walked into the gestation lab, looking pale as she smoothed her mussed, dark-blonde hair. Her arrival at that time couldn't have been better designed by Skyfather himself to enrage Centa more. Perpetua should have dealt with the loss of the foetus. She should have held open the bag for this ill omen. She should be the one to report the news to Master Anton.

"Excellent timing, Worker 8. As usual."

Centa handed the remains to Tilter. Just this once she overlooked the quivering of his chin and the turned down edges of his mouth. She feared she would lose control of her own emotions if she reprimanded him for his weakness. It was her job to teach him the process of growing new Sky Humans. But the lessons always ended with him holding a biohazard bag. Unless something changed soon, he would never get to hold a newborn in his arms.

Before she could even touch the door handle, blue light filled the gestation lab once again and the cursed alarm blared from an incubator further down the row. Ben may as well have been across the other side of the universe.

· · · ● · ● · ● · · ·

Centa climbed down the vertical bank of hexagonal sleep cells, careful not to step on any heads. The community's surviving workers tended to cluster together, which made it tricky to sneak out. In the cell below her own, Perpetua's eyes were closed and her breathing steady. Not that Perpetua could stop her. She'd give Centa that disapproving look though. Perpetua was perpetually watching. Perpetually disapproving. Centa had named her well.

A lone infant whimpered in the nursery while a carer shushed and paced in front of the door. Centa held her boots in one hand and tiptoed past to the anteroom. There was nothing in Father's Law against moving around the settlement at any time she pleased—but she clicked the latch softly shut behind her to avoid explanations and accusations. Until she and Ben were together, she hadn't committed any transgression.

The air monitor in the antechamber glowed bright green to indicate that the vine dust outside was below tolerance levels. She fitted a mask to her face anyway. The warmth of her own breath against her skin had come to mean safety.

The stars were bright in the cloudless night sky. It wasn't as cold as it had been a week earlier. They were well out of the season known as the freeze and into the thaw. Beyond the perimeter, the vine would be growing with renewed vitality after its semi-hibernation.

Centa stole past the thick hull of their grounded mothership, the central star in the solar system of their settlement. In the early days, detached habs had been erected within its orbit. Over the years, the need to avoid incursions of the vine and exposure to its stupefying dust had led to the bonding of many of the habs, such as the gestation laboratory and dormitories, to the mothership with heavy-duty PVC. The vehicle hab, which was little more than a flat, solar-panelled roof on stilts, was one exception, and to reach it, she had to cross open ground. It was late, and everyone should have been in bed, but still she surveyed the area like a lizard-pig poking its nose out of a burrow. If she were caught it could mean punishment. She had no reason to travel to the outskirts of the settlement at this time of night. But fear of discovery was part of the thrill. And Ben was worth it.

She sprinted over to the two pairs of boxy, white buggies drawing energy from a single charging block, like identical quadruplets sharing a placenta. She yanked the charger from one of the quads and slid into the driver's seat. The engine hummed conspicuously in the still night.

Soon she would be with him. Rebellion washed through her, intoxicating every cell like an intravenous drug. They couldn't control her completely. She wanted to put her foot down on the accelerator and fly all the way to Ben's agronomy hab, a little over two kilometres from the mothership, but she barely made it five hundred metres before the buggy's headlights fell on a leafy lump of lush and bright green vegetation on the ground. She slammed on the brakes and peered over the steering wheel. It was the first time she'd ever encountered vine inside the perimeter.

The masters claimed that the vine spread with runners, yet every now and then a patch sprung up miraculously and Skyfather declared it the embodiment of The Spirit of Aceso's anger. Ben suspected spores. Down the microscope he'd discovered the organism was somewhere between a plant and fungus, with chitinous cell walls. He said the dust was full of spores and they'd been breathing them in for years.

Centa retrieved the flamethrower from a compartment at the rear of her buggy. Incursions were usually the responsibility of agronomy workers, but all Sky Humans underwent training to protect the settlement.

She stood over the verdant patch, her chest fluttering and her mind buzzing in a way that used to only happen in Skyfather's presence. The vine held power, and part of her yearned for destruction it could bring.

Let it grow. Let it take over the whole settlement and kill everyone.

She shook the words from her head, lit the flamethrower and smothered the enemy in flames. Her own thoughts scared her sometimes. The vine was fit only to be feared and hated.

The leaves wilted and charred as she worked, thick clouds of black smoke stung her eyes, and she coughed as tiny particles found breaches in her mask.

For a moment, Centa saw a face in the haze. One she knew better than her own from all the portraits around the settlement. It was Rae, Skyfather's daughter. As a child, Rae had been the first stricken by the dust. Workers had rescued her before the vine had devoured her flesh but not before she'd been elevated to a conduit between The Spirit of Aceso and Skyfather.

The flames died and Rae's image went with them. It was a vine dust hallucination, nothing more.

Centa climbed back into the buggy and took deep breaths of filtered air to clear her head before continuing on her way to Ben.

Beyond the white dome of the agronomy hab, wind turbines turned lazily in the mothermoon's light. Centa parked beside the single buggy already there and quietly pushed open the door of the darkened building. The air inside was fresh and alive with ethylene and chlorophyll, an undertone of soil, and the occasional whiff of decay. She stood by the entrance and whispered *hello* until Disciple Ben, *her* Ben, was suddenly at her side, a hand on her waist and a finger to his lips. She turned her face down to his. He was a full head shorter than her, having grown for the first eleven years of his life on Earth where the gravity was stronger.

"Follow me, Centa," he said quietly. His breath in her ear made her shiver. He was the only one who knew her real name, the one she'd given herself. Everyone else knew her as Worker 9. Finally, they would be together. She'd fantasized about the feel of his naked skin against hers for years, but he'd worried about the imbalance of power. He didn't want to be like the masters, he'd said. And she'd pretended not to know what he meant.

"Here, I picked this for you." He slipped something sweet between her lips. "It's called a berry. Meant for the masters' plates only."

The berry burst boldly on her tongue, and she kissed him with a hint of juice still in her mouth. He took her hand in his and swept her towards his private room at the far end of the hab. She gasped at a cough from the dormitory where the agronomy workers slept.

"Don't worry. They're already dull with vine dust."

Centa bristled at the implication. Despite her best efforts the workers were declining in quality with each generation. It didn't help that only the masters ate enough to keep a soft roundness to their bodies. She let go of his hand.

"This lot are even younger than the last." Ben didn't reach for her again, already more enticed by his worries than spending time with her.

Centa tried to lighten the atmosphere and regain his attention. "I'll be sending you embryos to grow yourself next."

"You start them, and I end them." He pressed his knuckles into his eye sockets. He was in one of *those* moods. Never mind, she had enough passion to clear his mind of all else.

At the threshold of his room he said, "Are you sure about this?"

The portrait of a young Skyfather with his white robes, smooth skin, and intense pale eyes gazed down from the wall. Even he couldn't stop her from feeding the craving that she'd been denied for so long. Defiance only made her ache more intensely. It was no longer enough to share her body with other workers in the dorm and pretend they were Ben. None of them had his scent, the taste of his skin, the voice that vibrated her to the core.

She led him around cloth sacks of potash to his single cot, drew him close and kissed his neck, down his chest, anxious for some response and return of her ardour. She had wanted him for so long. He hardened in response to her caresses and, victorious, she pushed him onto the cot. She was controlled every day of her life, a tool generated and used by Skyfather and the masters, but now she would lose control in the way she wanted. Not in the service of others.

She straddled him and buried her face where his neck met his shoulder, inhaling the smell of the dirt that was as much a part of him as his perfect skin and cells and blood.

I could bite down and rip him open.

What was wrong with her? She sat up and took a moment to still her thoughts as she tore off her shirt. She had everything she wanted, and still violent thoughts appeared as unwelcome and unexpected as patches of vine on settlement ground.

"Did you hear that?" He craned his neck towards the door.

"What? No." She worked on the buttons down the front of his shirt.

"I thought I heard footsteps."

"It's nothing." She had to have him now. They would deal with any consequences afterwards.

She pulled Ben's trousers to his knees and hopped off the cot to remove her own. He looked at her with a bemused, half-smile as they undressed. Was he having doubts? She threw her clothes into the corner of the room and was upon him quickly, before he could start thinking. Then they were warm skin on warm skin, mouth on mouth, until, for a short time at least, troubled thoughts had no power over either of them.

2

Centa hadn't left Ben's room until almost dawn, and by the time he dragged himself to the greenhouse, a small group of workers were already sitting around the table listlessly splitting lettuce seedlings. There was a time when agronomy workers would natter and joke while they worked side by side. He wished this lot would liven up. It might help him stay awake.

This batch had barely been given time for their hair to grow into the ponytails of adulthood before being assigned to agronomy. Once they were done with this morning's seedlings, they would scour the fields and annihilate any invading vine. At least one, maybe more, would be lost by the end of the week. Ben's legs buckled at the thought, and he lowered himself into the chair reserved for him at the table.

He hated them. The way the rich back on Earth must have hated him and all those whose suffering reminded them of their selfish mistakes. He'd never thought that one day he would identify as an oppressor. He hated himself too. If only there were somewhere to escape to. On Earth his parents had been nomads, always in search of a better life. As a child he'd kept himself safe by running from any sign of danger.

Ben's eyes drooped and he stretched his legs out to rest on the empty chair directly across from him. He sat up straight. Why was there an empty chair? And why hadn't he noticed earlier?

He counted the workers. Eight heads bent to their work where there should have been nine.

"Where's Worker—" Ben couldn't remember the child's number. He rarely bothered to learn them anymore. "That one." He pointed to the empty chair. "The one with the red hair."

The workers didn't answer. One of them peeked towards the door to the outside.

"Shit."

The dust was thick, so he grudgingly put on a mask. He hated the claustrophobia of his breath trapped so close to his face. It felt like being gagged. He held a hand to his brow to shield the glare of the rising father star as he searched. He scanned all the way to the dusty horizon. If they were lucky, the worker would still be standing. They weren't.

Behind the beehives, infiltrated and overtaken by vine bugs, the missing worker lay on a fresh patch of vine. Thorns had already pierced their skin and immobilized their muscles. The precise compound remained elusive, but in high enough doses the toxin permanently paralyzed its victims. There was nothing the medics could do once the vine had a grip on a victim, but he had to try.

"INCURSION!" He yelled back to the workers in the hab. "Masks on and bring a flamethrower."

The child's skin squelched as he ripped away the thorns, and blood trickled from the neat holes onto Ben's hands. He hoisted the worker onto his shoulder. They were limp like a wilted plant. How many workers would have to die before the masters understood the utopia Skyfather had sold them was a fantasy? They were unable to adapt and evolve to fit the reality. Instead, he was adapting. He'd become desensitized and callous. If he stayed there long enough, he would eventually be as corrupt as the masters.

Master Helena, a short, round woman with coarse dark-grey hair, watched from the greenhouse entrance, hands clasped behind her back. Ben sent the casualty with two other workers in a buggy to the med hab, and after several deep, juddering breaths, he took his place by the master's side. He pulled his mask below his chin. He'd wanted a moment alone to stand amongst the staked bean stalks, tubs of carrots and hanging tomato plants to collect himself. Growing things calmed him. He'd wanted to join agronomy from the moment they'd landed on Aceso. Working with the soil was a bittersweet reminder of his mom. She'd nurtured life from depleted Earth to supplement their diets. Shoots breaking free of the dirt and leaves unfurling had been a kind of magic to him as a child.

He waited for Master Helena to speak and acknowledge what had just happened.

She pointed to the chickens scratching in their pen outside. "We should get rid of them. Their eggs are green mush now and they stink of dust."

"We just lost another worker." Ben didn't know why he bothered. She never seemed to care.

"Yes. Such a shame." She patted his shoulder. "How are they doing otherwise?"

He breathed through his anger. "Well, they spend most of their time fighting vine incursions and dying like soldiers on a frontline."

She smiled until he got control of his agitation. "Any of them you fancy?" She pushed her glasses up the bridge of her nose.

He didn't know what to say. It wasn't the first time she had dismissed his concerns about the state of the settlement and their work, but never with something so repugnant. The way the masters took advantage of the workers disgusted him. It was no excuse that the younger generations barely seemed to have a thought in their heads.

"You could take one of them or all of them if you wanted to your bed."

"They're barely pubescent."

She sucked in her cheeks and stared at him. He'd been working with her long enough to recognise her look of disapproval. Did she know about Centa? Maybe one of the young workers had been out of bed last night after all.

"I'm giving you some advice because I care about you. I couldn't run the agronomy program without you. You're like a son to me."

Except he wasn't her son. His real mother had disappeared, presumed dead, centuries ago on Earth. His relationship with Helena was close, but she would always be his master. Never his family.

He waited patiently for her to make her meaning clear. She couldn't bear silence for very long.

"The point is, you can have a romp with whoever you want, Ben, but emotional attachments will not be tolerated. I cannot and will not turn the other way indefinitely. Eventually it will reflect badly on me for not having done something. End it and occupy yourself with a selection of young workers. I don't want to have to punish you. That's all I'll say. You're dismissed." She waved him away.

"Thank you, Master," he said through gritted teeth. He replaced his mask over his mouth and headed out to join the workers scouring the fields and torching vine. He wanted to get as far away from her judgements and vile suggestions as possible.

He cared immensely about Centa, but he wasn't in love with her the way she wanted him to be. She felt more like a younger sister. Unfortunately, she didn't understand the concept of family. How could she? She was a worker, and they only knew sex and subservience. But he didn't want to hurt her or lose her by spurning her advances.

And part of him wanted to be punished. He wanted an external stimulus to cause a change. Like a plant that altered its tropism based on the source of light. Punishment could give him the courage he needed to act upon the idea he had been germinating. And Centa might be the only one who would understand.

Ǝ

Perpetua slid in beside Centa at the breakfast table. Couldn't they be apart for five minutes? Centa shifted an inch to the other side. It was her own fault for being so efficient with her morning incubator checks and arriving at the dining hab first. Now it was too late to move.

They stood straight and tall behind their chairs while Disciple Flannery, the head priest, led them through the tenets of Father's Law from the narrow, shin-high platform at the end of the hab.

The Spirit of Aceso is the Supreme Being and Skyfather is his prophet.

Disciples and priests patrolled between the tables, admonishing those who weren't chanting loudly enough. Centa followed Ben's progress around the room. Their evening had been perfect.

The Prophet, the Spirit, and Sky Humanity are the holy trinity.

Ben weaved closer through the tables, touching a shoulder here, whispering in an ear there. Centa flushed with heat as she watched him.

All the love in my heart I reserve for Skyfather and The Spirit of Aceso.

Then he was behind her. He stroked her spine, despite her perfect posture, and electricity shot through her body. His breath tickled her ear. "Master Helena knows."

My mouth and my mind will speak only love and respect for The Prophet, The Spirit and Sky Humanity.

Centa twisted towards him. "Wha—"

"Shh!" Ben moved to the other side of her. "We can't be seen interacting at all."

I will honour the masters, priests, and disciples as they have been chosen by The Spirit, and I live only to serve The Spirit.

Ben glided away down the row of tables and Centa pressed her fingernails into the palms of her hands. Would he want to end it now? He'd always done whatever Master Helena had asked. She should have known. He'd expressed doubts so many times, and she'd refused to accept the possibility his reservations were less about the age gap between them and more about the fact he didn't feel for her as she felt for him. Maybe he'd found an easy way out. Blame it on the masters and their laws and rules.

My body and soul belong to The Spirit as do the bodies and souls of my fellow workers. I will not harm that which belongs to The Spirit.

The Masters trudged in for the weekly gathering. Their grunts and the creaks of their ageing knees sounded through the silent room as they lumbered up onto the platform and ushered Disciple Flannery away. Victoria, the youngest and most mobile of the group, stood proudly at the centre, where Skyfather used to stand. She had taken the place of his wife who had died in the early days of the settlement, and now she presumed to speak for him too.

Through obedience, industry, truth, and harmony I will earn my immortal, Sky Human soul.

Centa angled her body as far as she dared to search for Ben. She'd been stupid. She should have known she couldn't have something for herself. She wanted to gouge her own eyes with her spoon. Then she wouldn't have to see his face every day. She ground her teeth against the violence of the thought.

Everything I am and everything I possess belongs to The Spirit and the Sky Human community. I will not covet goods or attention for myself.

Victoria smiled over them. "Please be seated."

Three hundred chairs scraped back as workers fell upon their breakfast bowls. The savoury smell of algae porridge filled Centa's nose, but her stomach had become small and hard like a newborn's fist.

"The vine draws ever closer," Victoria said, "and still our border maintenance and agronomy workers fight valiantly. We must aid them in their battle by ensuring our behaviour and thoughts are pleasing and helpful to the harmony of the community and thus to The Spirit of Aceso. We must all adhere to Father's Law as it was handed down to Skyfather."

Centa barely heard Victoria's words. Skyfather's proxy had none of his presence and brought her no comfort. Morale had been low since he'd withdrawn from public life to commune with The Spirit. The room closed in on her and sweat rose all over her skin. She wanted to run outside, into the dust where she could hide behind a mask. It was over between her and Ben. She'd thought she could be special, be more than a simple worker. She'd thought she could have something sinful to cut through the numb pain of everyday.

Victoria's clear, sweet voice became sombre and recaptured Centa's attention. "This week we memorialize four Sky Humans—"

A collective gasp filled the room. Four was the most that had ever been sacrificed to the vine in a single week. Centa broke her reverential stance completely and swivelled towards Ben at the back of the room. His head was down, his face red. No wonder he'd been so defeated. Perpetua jostled her to turn back to the platform.

"—taken into The Spirit of Aceso's bosom. One from agronomy, one from water collection, and two who were on root barrier maintenance. Their valiant service has earned them their immortal souls. One day they will be joined by Skyfather and the masters in heaven."

Disciple Flannery read out the worker numbers of the dead. Centa didn't try to recall their faces. The deaths were so frequent now. There was no point in mourning each one.

Victoria's gaze swept the room.

"It has not gone unnoticed that the number of workers claimed by Aceso is increasing. This is why Skyfather has been so long in communion with The Spirit. You must all play your part to restore balance. Do not think your misdeeds are too small to be noticed. The Spirit sees all. You must be vigilant. If your co-worker's behaviour contravenes Father's Law, you must report them. The survival of our settlement depends upon it. All substantiated reports will earn you further merit towards your immortal souls."

Centa no longer believed her behaviour had any real impact on Aceso. For years she'd been perfectly obedient, and the viability of the zygotes she thawed had still decreased. Either there were too many workers doing unlawful things, or it was all a fiction, fabricated by Skyfather and the masters.

"Please commence your breakfast and have a fruitful and industrious day. Skyfather is the light in the darkness of space."

"Skyfather is the light in the darkness of space," the assembled workers responded.

Victoria and the masters left the dining hab, and the priests and disciples took their seats. Quiet conversation spread through the room to accompany the clinking of spoons against bowls.

"Where did you sneak out to last night?" Perpetua asked beneath the clamour.

"Nowhere."

Centa shovelled food into her mouth. She needed to get out of there. The room was too hot and crowded. She pushed back her chair with a screech and hurried over to the washing-up table to deposit her bowl and spoon. She smelt Ben's skin—soil and green things—before she felt the tingle of his body centimetres from hers. He reached around her to deposit his own spoon.

"Meet me again. Tonight. Stay outside in the buggy this time."

She turned to question him—had she misunderstood?—but he was already striding out the door.

· · · • · • • · · ·

Centa wiped her sweaty hands on her thighs as Ben exited the agronomy hab. All day she'd tortured herself with speculation on why he'd wanted to see her. Was he going to end it with her to appease Master Helena? This could be humiliating. He came up to the driver's side window of her buggy, with no mask and one of his disgusting dried-vine cigarettes hanging out the side of his mouth. He'd convinced her to try one once—he insisted they built up resistance to the dust—and it had given her a two-day migraine.

"Slide over. I'll drive." He tossed the cigarette behind him into the dark.

"Dust mask?" She slid across to the passenger side.

"It's fine. You worry too much. The dust isn't as strong at night."

This was true. Without the heat of the father star to dry the sap, the clouds of dust were sparser than during the day. There was still enough to take a person down though.

She tutted. "You should know better." Focussing on his lax safety measures helped ease her fear he was about to end their relationship.

"Don't be cranky with me. What kind of greeting is this?" He leaned over and kissed her on the cheek.

His hair was smoothed down in a dark ponytail, and in the dim light, his eyes were black. She wanted to run her fingertips over the stubble on his jaw. A tuft of chest hair poked out of the top of his shirt. She couldn't continue this familiar banter and pretend nothing was wrong.

"What is this about? Are you ending things with me because of Master Helena?"

"No." He sighed. "Is that what you thought? We'll just have to be more discreet."

She held back a sob of relief. "I've been heartbroken all day, you lizard-pig."

"You let your thoughts run away with you again." He squeezed her knee and eased the buggy away from the agronomy hab.

A headache formed behind her eyes. The bond between them was so fragile, as though she were a leaf clinging to his sturdy trunk by a single stem. The minute the season changed, or a strong wind blew, he could shed her without a single regret. She sat on her shaking hands and took long, slow breaths until she had control over her emotions.

"Where are we going?"

"I can't explain it. You'll have to see for yourself."

He drove through fields of sparse, limp crops, headlights reflecting off the eyes of startled lizard-pigs. She wanted to reach across and hold his hand, but something about the tense muscles in his forearms made her hesitate.

"There's nothing out here. Where are you taking me?"

"Trust me." Ben stopped the buggy at Rae's Bridge, which spanned the root barrier trench that had been dug to keep the vine out of the settlement. "Have a look."

"At what?"

He pointed through the windscreen to where headlights lit the trench. Vine was everywhere. It stretched across the void and snaked along the dirt at the bottom. Roots had broken through the plastic lining. Her heart thudded with dread.

"It's like this all the way around. We don't have enough workers. And it's getting stronger. Evolving. The last batch of workers survived for less than a month. Vine will be all over the settlement before the end of the year. Maybe sooner." His knuckles were white on the steering wheel.

She wasn't surprised. She'd known she wasn't the only one failing at their work. All over the settlement, workers, and disciples struggled to maintain Skyfather's dream. But why did Ben have to burden her with this failure? She had her own failures to contend with. She'd rather remain ignorant. As much as she liked to defy its rules, she couldn't believe the settlement would really fall. And if she believed they would lose control of their perimeter, she also had to believe she would never bring another worker infant into the world.

She fell back to the place of blind faith where she didn't have to think or feel. "Is this due to our disobedience?"

"Come on, Centa. There's just us here. No need to put on an act."

She shook her head. Pretending to believe in Skyfather and the Spirit of Aceso kept her safe and in the masters' good graces. She thought Ben understood that she couldn't question Fathers Law the way a valued disciple could. And at this point, she wasn't sure what she believed any more.

Panic rose in her chest. She couldn't talk or think about the vine or her beliefs or the fate of the settlement any longer. "Let's forget about all this and go back to your room." She rubbed his thigh with her hand.

"I still have something to show you. Outside the settlement. You'll like this."

"Ben! It's too dangerous." She hadn't been out of the settlement for years. Its perimeters kept her safe. She gripped the edges of the seat and swallowed the bile rising in her throat.

He took her face in his hands and kissed her lightly on the lips. "Trust me."

She did trust him. It was everything outside of the settlement that she didn't trust. The thin stem that held her to him bent and strained in this new breeze. She wasn't ready to be let go.

"Fine."

He drove over the bridge and into the domain of the planet's apex predator. Skyfather had always told them they were fortunate. On Earth there were much greater threats than the vine. People who maimed and killed, food and water that filled your body with disease, air that blackened your lungs, animals with sharp teeth and claws, venoms and toxins. Earth was a place of great sin and even greater danger. Still, Centa couldn't think of anything more terrible than these vast expanses of vegetation.

She raised her eyes to the sky so she could pretend they weren't surrounded. The vine was bumpier to drive over than the packed dirt of the settlement. It crunched beneath the wheels and sent up puffs of dust. She imagined particles seeping into the car until they were so overcome that they opened the doors and welcomed the tendrils.

"Is the buggy's air filter strong enough for this concentration of dust?"

"Don't worry I've been out here plenty of times."

"Spirit of Aceso protect me." She rolled her eyes at his recklessness.

The farther they travelled, the more the diversity of life on the planet expanded. They swerved around trees with paisley-patterned bark and flagella-like leaves. These trees were more numerous and vital than the bare, grey trunks closer to the settlement. Small dark shadows of some bird-like creature flitted between their branches. The bony grip of the masters felt looser this far from the community.

"We're here," Ben said half an hour later, halting the buggy at the foot of a mountain range that looked like a carelessly dumped pile of boulders.

"Is this it? The mountains?"

He turned the engine off and cut the lights. "You'll see. Follow me, okay? The dust is weak here. You won't need a mask."

Centa fitted her mask anyway, and followed him to a small, waist-high opening in an exposed outcropping of the grey stone. He handed her a headlamp and disappeared head-first into the tunnel.

"What? Inside? Inside the mountain?" She turned the headlamp over in her hands. "This seems like a bad idea, Ben."

"It's not difficult. Trust me." His voice echoed out from within the dark.

Spirit protect me.

"If it were anyone but you." Centa fitted the headlamp and scrambled in after him.

Tiny, sharp rock edges grazed the palms of her hands, tore through her clothing, and scraped her skin.

"Ouch. Are you sure about this?"

"Not much further," Ben called out from up ahead.

His calm voice gave her the courage to keep crawling forward. Rock pressed in on her from all sides. The tunnel angled gently downwards, beneath the ground. Blood rushed to her head, and she breathed heavily through her mask, both from the exertion and the feeling of being eaten by the planet.

After a minute she reached the end of the tunnel where he waited. She exhaled with relief and wiped tears from the edges of her eyes.

He shielded his own from the shine of her headlamp. "Come on through."

She wriggled forward and he took her by the armpits and helped her down. Their headlamps illuminated bumpy sections of a cavern wall—wet, glossy, and streaked with colours. Ben switched off his light and indicated Centa do the same.

"But I want to look around." Now that she was out of the tunnel, her curiosity was aroused. She wanted to understand why this was so important to Ben.

"It's the only way to properly experience this place."

She turned off her light and he took her hand in his. Warmth radiated through her body from the point of connection between them. Her courage had been worth it. He was sharing something special with her and her alone. He trusted her.

"Give it a moment for your eyes to adapt."

Somewhere below them water trickled, while drops plinked from the ceiling to the floor. Centa wiped a bead of moisture from her temple. Cold settled wetly upon her and she pressed into Ben for warmth.

After a few seconds, every surface glowed pale green with luminescent microbes. The cavern was about the size of two worker dormitories and sloped gradually down to a thin stream. Stalagmites rose from the floor, and stalactites reached down from the ceiling metres above them.

Ben pointed to where the stream disappeared into the rock. "On that side is another tunnel that leads to an underground lake with edible algae."

"Like the one near the settlement?" Something about the cave made her whisper. There was a presence, something spiritual about the place.

"Very similar. You can take your dust mask off. The air's clean in here." He mimed pulling a mask down from his chin.

She scoffed. "You're going to hurt yourself one day." Ben thought he had a unique immunity to vine dust since he'd never been overcome, despite working in agronomy since he'd arrived on Aceso as a child. Centa hypothesized it was because most of the time he was in the greenhouse or inside a buggy, able to retreat whenever reality shone and vibrated towards vine hallucination.

She inspected her bleeding hands, and Ben took a vine leaf out of his pocket and rubbed it gently against the broken skin. In small doses, something in the sap of the puffy leaves repaired superficial abrasions. Neither the medics, nor Centa or Ben in their respective laboratories, had been able to isolate the active component. Skyfather had named it Aceso's Mercy.

Centa brushed the dust from her now smooth palms and turned to stroke a pillar of rock, where a stalactite and stalagmite had met and become one. The luminescence dimmed for a second beneath her finger. She peered back at Ben. He had his head tilted to one side, eyebrow raised.

She lifted her mask a millimetre from her skin and took a shallow breath, ready to put it straight back on if she tasted any of the ominous sweet spiciness of dust. Crisp, clear air chilled her lungs, with the fresh scent of life and growth. No hint of vine dust. It felt slightly obscene to be bare faced, but she draped the mask from her wrist and gave Ben a smile.

"Didn't people on Earth bury their dead underground?" She swivelled around to take it all in.

"Uh huh. There's also evidence that life on Earth began in places like this." He walked over and drew his own squiggles on the column. Their fingertips touched and she giggled softly. His attention was finally on her.

She pulled down the collar of his shirt and kissed his neck. She caressed the side of his face and left a glowing fingerprint on his cheek.

He took her hands between his and stared into her eyes. "We could stay here. Me and you. Forever. We could explore this world beneath the world. There must be more to this planet than the vine."

"What?" Centa shook her head and stepped away. Was this why he'd brought her here? Not to show her a secret place they could share, but to involve her in some blasphemous scheme. Glowing specks scribbled through her pale, blinking reflection in a puddle at her feet.

"I'm going to bring supplies. Bit by bit. We can set up a base."

She dragged her feet as he led her over to a pile of blankets, vacuum sealed food, a dewar of water, and a battery-operated lantern, stacked alongside a curtain of rock that draped in gentle folds from the ceiling.

"We could be together and control our own lives. I wouldn't have to watch batch after batch of workers... just children... dying in my care. We wouldn't have to answer to Skyfather or the masters. There would be no counselling or cleansing. No spiritual service or any of that bullshit."

"You'll be caught and punished if you keep speaking this way." Maybe he would care about the consequences for himself, even if he didn't seem to care about the consequences for her.

"I know how dedicated you are to your work, but the settlement's deteriorating. Soon everyone will have to fend for themselves. Workers are dying, crops are failing, embryos are weakening and, you saw it for yourself, the vine is coming."

It was too terrifying to think about a time when the settlement would fall. A time when she wouldn't go to the lab every day, wouldn't sleep in her cell beside Perpetua every night, and wouldn't follow the rules of Skyfather and the masters. That world was a dream for a future. Not something she wanted to make a reality right now. She wasn't ready for uncertainty or real choices. She wasn't ready to leave the established protocol of her life.

Ben would not be swayed or distracted by her words; she already knew that about him. "Let's spread these blankets on the floor."

He put his hands on her shoulders and stilled her. "I would love to, but not this time. I have an early meeting with Master Helena. I need to get back and get at least a few hours of sleep."

"Oh." He was rejecting her again. Centa wanted to fall from a rock ledge and spear herself on a stalagmite, right through her heart. Ben could make her feel so good. But he could also bring her such pain. Even the pain was something precious the masters would deny her if they could.

She held her pain close, wallowed in it and poked and prodded at its boundaries as they travelled back to the settlement through the wild, dark landscape. Ben made small talk as he drove, but she didn't respond, and he tapered off. She was confused. He wanted her to run away with him, but he'd give up sex with her for a few extra minutes of sleep. It seemed the only way she could have any of him was to take her secret rebellions public and openly defy Father's Law, The Spirit of Aceso, all the masters, the community, and even Skyfather himself. She would be sent to the pyre if they were caught trying to run.

But what if they weren't caught? Would he be different? Warmer? Or would he never want her the same way she wanted him? She'd thought that once they'd finally had sex, they would be equals.

Ben cleared his throat as he parked in front of the agronomy hab. "Take some time to think about it. In the next fortnight master Helena will be taking a group of workers on a foraging trip beyond the borders. They'll be away for a couple of days. That'll be a good time to meet again. You can tell me your decision then."

"So, I won't see you for almost two weeks?" She pouted at this new blow, which on top of all the others she'd taken that night, felt sharper than it should have.

"I think that's best." He got out of the buggy and leant against the door frame.

Centa slid over to the driver's seat, and he kissed her deeply through the open window. She couldn't help feel that he was performing. Like his passion was a gift he gave to her while he felt nothing himself. She would take it anyway.

"Two full weeks," she said. "Will I at least see you at breakfast tomorrow?"

"No. I won't be over to the main settlement until evening meal."

It would be hours before she even caught a glimpse of him again, and that would be from across the other side of the dining hab. She watched until he was through the door of the agronomy building and safe from any stray wafts of vine dust before driving away.

Why couldn't he love her? Was it because she'd been grown inside glass and not inside flesh? Did he believe as the masters claimed, that she had no soul? Did he just want her for company or as a servant, a body to use when it suited him?

The settlement habs appeared ahead, white against the dark. Like ghosts of a civilisation that didn't know it was already dead. None of her questions or feelings mattered. In the end she knew she'd do whatever Ben asked of her if it meant she could be near him.

4

Dining hab workers flicked the overhead lights on and off to indicate they were ready to mop the floor and close the hab for the night. There were only ever a handful of stragglers at this late hour, those who valued a little unscheduled time more than they valued sleep. Ben finished his conversation with Disciple Zenia and stacked his chair on top of the table. As he left, he gave a tiny nod to Centa who had been sneaking looks at him from across the room all evening.

Asking her to leave everything she knew to be with him was unfair and he knew he was taking advantage of her feelings. He feared he'd become an abuser as bad as the masters. He'd been around them for so long he'd forgotten how people treated each other on Earth. Or maybe he was idealising Earth, and all human relationships were transactional, wherever they were in the universe.

The air monitor reported a low particle count outside, so he didn't bother with a dust mask. Night was typically clear, especially within the vine-free borders of the settlement. He'd also built up a resistance to the effects of the dust over the years and suspected the vine saw him as part of the natural environment. He always enjoyed the twenty-five-minute walk, alone and beneath starlight. It gave him uninterrupted time to think.

The lights of the main settlement dulled behind him as he walked, and his eyes adapted to the dark of the moonless night. There was nothing but dirt and the occasional dead tree from here to the agronomy hab. They'd thought this land would be full of orchards and crops by now. Their fertilizers had made no difference. There was no life in the acidic soil. Under the microscope it was devoid of the fungi and bacteria associated with a healthy microbiome. When they'd fought back the vine and cut down the native trees, they'd triggered an environmental death spiral. He would break free of the settlement and find a way to live in harmony with the planet.

Ben squatted to examine the charred patch of vine Centa had destroyed two nights earlier. A lizard-pig sniffed the indentations his shoes left in the barren soil. He had to bring Centa around to his idea. He didn't want to be the last human left on Aceso when the vine inevitably engulfed the settlement. The other disciples couldn't be trusted. Especially Head Priest Flannery, who enjoyed the hierarchy so much she'd become a zealot. They all pretended their lives on Aceso matched the utopia that Skyfather had promised. Ben had known from those first days after thawing, after that first meal of tasteless, chalky paste, after that first slap across the cheek from a master, that they'd been lied to. The masters' parasitic growth over their broken bodies couldn't continue much longer.

The wind picked up and dust devils of dry soil swirled around his feet. A smell came to him on the breeze. Vine dust. Not enough to worry about. He breathed deeply. Small exposures were how he built resistance. But the air ahead was hazier than it had been only seconds before He squinted to see more clearly. Shapes, almost human-like, formed and dissipated all around him like smoke. His heart beat faster. This wasn't right.

He rubbed his eyes and the shapes disappeared. He was just tired and the dark played tricks.

He walked faster and grabbed for the dust mask on his belt, but it wasn't there. Centa would be calling him reckless and arrogant if she knew. The ground ahead of him wobbled from side to side. It was much further to agronomy than back to the settlement, so he turned back, jogging to escape the patch of dust. Once he was through, his mind would clear and he would collect a dust mask from the settlement or even an air-filtered buggy. This would be a cautionary tale he would tell young workers—never get caught outside without a dust mask.

The dust thickened and pulsed, the vaguely humanoid shapes crowded around and rushed him from all sides. He bellowed as they broke upon him and shattered into millions of particles of dust, engulfing him. Dust slid down his throat and coated his tongue, and he coughed and spat, his eyes as large as bowls. He sprinted away, the lights of the settlement skipped and shimmered, dimmed and brightened until he was unsure if they were real or hallucination. All he could do was keep moving and hope that he came to a place with clear air before it was too late. He wasn't supposed to die like this.

The planet turned faster and tried to fling him from the surface. The vine had fooled him into believing he was an exception to its wrath. It had appealed to his vanity the way Victoria had appealed to Skyfather's. But he wasn't like the masters or Skyfather. He wasn't an enemy of the vine or Aceso. He alone had wanted to find a way to share the planet with the vine.

"Mommy, help me," he sobbed.

A word, an idea, a memory blossomed. Earth. He calmed and his heart slowed and steadied. Everything was as it should be. He didn't need to worry. The vine would help him return to Earth. All his life on Aceso, he'd wanted to run away. Now the vine offered him the ultimate escape. Aceso didn't see any of them as an enemy. It cared for the humans who had run away from their home like moody teens and wanted to send them back to the planet that loved them best.

The dust was soft and silky all over his skin and in his lungs. He wanted to make a cocoon of it, sleep and emerge new and happy on Earth. He'd been so wrong. They'd all been so wrong. If only he had time to find Centa and tell her not to fear the dust. Then she could follow him back to Earth.

But there was no more delaying. His parents were waiting. He'd always believed they'd died when he was a child, although he'd never seen their bodies. But now there they were in the distance, laughing as they ran towards him with their arms full of the discarded food they'd liberated from a grocery warehouse. The orange lights of the industrial estate lit their smiles and a new future, a future lived on Earth with his loving parents, became a reality.

His parents faded and he was on Aceso once again.

"No!" he shouted. "Bring them back, please! Take me to them!"

The dust wasn't enough to send him back to Earth. He'd seen how it happened with the workers whose bodies he'd been too late to save. The vine needed to grip him in its thorns, connect with the mycelium it had already planted in his body, devour him and spit him out on the other side of the universe.

Ahead a soft green glow beckoned from beneath the link between the bridge and the mothership. A new, lush patch of vine.

5

All the other workers were settling into their sleep cells, but Centa wandered the dorm, restless after watching Ben from across the dining hab. It had been the first time she'd see him since he'd asked her to abandon her life at the settlement and run away with him. She'd failed to come to any kind of decision yet. There was always a chance they would beat back the vine, as well as be successful in growing new workers and crops. She wasn't ready to give up on the comforts, minor as they were, of the settlement just yet. But the promise of living free from the masters and Father's Law, as well as spending every day with Ben, was enticing.

"Going to bed?" Perpetua hung her toiletry bag from the hook in her sleep cell and climbed up.

"I'm not tired. I think I'll check on the zygotes."

The halls of the mothership and the links between the habs were empty of workers and masters. Centa savoured the dim lights and quiet hum of the laboratory at night. Privacy was hard to come by within the confines of the settlement.

She examined her zygotes beneath the light of the microscope. The cells were already shrivelling, as though the embryo had skipped the in-between years and had progressed straight to old age. She didn't know why she'd expected anything different. One of the zygotes was slightly plumper than the others.

"The weight of the community is on you, little life."

Perhaps a few more hours in the moist warmth and nutrient rich media would stimulate a miraculous recovery. She returned the dishes to the cell culture incubator and headed back to the dormitory.

A blurry shape outside the PVC link between the mothership and the worker dorm caught her eye. Centa pressed against the plastic, clouded by the microscopic scratches of billions of particles of dust, to get a better look. A figure was staggering in a crooked line, arms hanging limp and back bent, the first signs of vine dust intoxication. Whoever they were, they were still upright. If they reached fresh air soon, they might still recover. Centa changed direction to run back into the mothership and alert the priests. The light from the link shone down on the angles of a face without a dust mask. She stopped cold. No. Not him.

"Ben," she yelled and slapped at the plastic. How could he do this to her? He didn't understand that the risks he took with his life put her sanity and happiness at risk also. "Get to the door, Ben, come on!"

There wasn't time to rouse the priests, she would have to save him herself. She ran back through to the dorm, past sleeping workers, and grabbed two masks from the wall of the anteroom.

The air outside was cool and fuzzed with dust. Her panicked breath was loud in her ears as she dashed to where she'd spotted him. But he wasn't there.

"BEN!" she screamed, turning in a confused circle as the dust swirled and clouded her vision.

A groan sounded nearby, and she raced to the dark shape beneath the bridge of the mothership. He'd found a newly sprouted patch of vine, its leaves and stems gripping his body like greedy hands. She dropped to her knees and shook him.

"Get up, Ben." She fitted the mask to his face.

He blinked slowly but didn't make any move to rise. "Centa?"

"We need to get inside."

"Earth wants me. Let me go."

"No! Get up."

She grasped him beneath the armpits and wrestled him into a sitting position. There was a slight resistance and a squelch as thorns ripped from his skin. She pulled him to standing and he flopped against her. Blood dripped from his wounds and left a dark trail in the dirt as they stumbled back to the anteroom. He was so slow. Every second he was outside, the dust did further damage to his brain.

Centa pushed Ben inside ahead of her, and he collapsed to the floor. She ripped off her mask, panting to catch her breath. Stray particles of sweet-tasting dust crunched between her teeth, and the colours of the anteroom brightened and strobed. She put a hand against the door frame to steady herself and took deep breaths of the filtered air until the hallucination faded.

"Can you hear me?" Centa squatted and removed Ben's mask. She manoeuvred him into a sitting position, with his back against the wall. "Take deep breaths to clear out the dust."

He didn't respond. She couldn't believe this was happening. Ben had been part of the community from the beginning. The new workers were the ones taken by the vine. He was too important to the agronomy program and to her. But he was still only a disciple. They wouldn't deify him as they'd done with Rae. He would end up in the recycler with all the other dust-stricken Sky Humans.

His eyes brightened a little and Centa was seized with the hope that clean air would be enough to revive him completely. He murmured something about Earth and reached with one arm for the handle to the outside door.

"You can't go out there." She held his hands and straddled him.

He shook his head forcefully. "I need to go back. I *need* to."

What he needed was a medic. But if she left him alone, he might crawl outside and back to the vine.

"HELP!" she yelled. "HELP!"

She took Ben's face between her palms. "Come back to me, Ben. You can't leave me with Perpetua as my only companion." She kissed him on the lips.

"You two aren't supposed to do that."

Centa reared back, and there was Perpetua, scowling from the doorway of the dormitory, hands on her hips. She didn't care about what she was or wasn't supposed to do. All that mattered was Ben.

"Get a medic," Centa shouted. "He's had a lungful of dust."

"Someone send for the medic," Perpetua called to the workers crowding forward to peer into the anteroom.

Centa put her forehead against Ben's. "I don't care if we're in trouble. I just want you to be okay."

His eyes rolled around, unfocussed in their sockets. Wherever his mind was, it was no longer with her.

6

A sermon by Skyfather's played on a loop in Centa's small, dark cell. She'd lost count of the number of times she'd heard it. At first it had pleased her to hear Skyfather's voice. She found comfort in his account of the founding of their community and the idea she was specially selected and blessed. It had helped distract her from her worries about Ben. She'd last seen him being carried away by Disciple Zenia and her assistants from the med hab. He'd been mumbling and unfocussed and not himself at all. But he'd been more alert than other workers overcome by dust. With some oxygen therapy he was bound to be better by the time she was released. Whenever that would be.

One of the other workers had reported her for inappropriate emotional attachment. She had hoped her punishment for a first offence would be the standard cleansing and spiritual counselling with Disciple Flannery. To waste days examining her confessions of sin and being tutored in meditation and biofeedback techniques that she'd never recall, nor find useful, at the relevant times. Techniques that never tamed her disturbing urges. Instead, punishment was this dark, noisy isolation.

Skyfather's words had lost all meaning with repetition and Centa found that gave her the space and time to think. She had been too busy and exhausted her whole life to just contemplate. Every spare moment had been filled with chanting or sermons.

Now it seemed she had nothing but time. After she'd exhausted every worry that she could possibly have about Ben's health, she began to recall the criticisms he'd made of Father's Law, the masters' and Skyfather's behaviour. And all of them were supported by her own experiences.

Doubts rushed in as though they'd been there all along, waiting for a crack in the wall of her thoughts. In the past she'd turned the doubts away and patched the cracks with her work or thoughts of Ben. But this time they were too many. And more than that, she welcomed them. And when her doubts gave way to fear and then to anger, she suddenly understood it all. Skyfather and the masters had promised to protect them, to safeguard the future of the community. Instead they'd let the workers bear the guilt and responsibility for their failures.

Light burned through the darkness of the isolation cell, bleaching Centa's brain of all other thought. Someone was standing above her. Skyfather's voice ceased, and her ears rang with its absence until another voice filled the quiet. Slowly her brain rehydrated with sensation and memory.

It was Perpetua, hand outstretched. Of course they'd send Perpetua. Her face, even more familiar than Centa's own, was a comfort. She wouldn't know who she was without Perpetua as her mirror.

"I'm taking you to the bridge."

"The... bridge?" Centa's voice croaked with disuse.

"To confirm you've been successfully counselled." Perpetua turned from the doorway and Centa followed her into the hallway. But had she been successfully counselled? Ben had once said that the aim of cleansing and counselling was not rehabilitation, but control. He said cults thrived on using your secrets against you. She hadn't been familiar with the word *cult* and had deflected Ben's attempts to explain. His face resolved out of the mush of her thoughts. Had he recovered from his exposure to the dust? She longed to rest her head on the top of his. Light reflected from every surface and sent spots and flecks floating in her vision. The shapes of workers, priests, and masters streaked past them.

The memorial screen on the wall outside the bridge scrolled through glaringly bright picture of workers lost to the vine. Centa tried to concentrate on her surroundings, to stay with her senses and not let thoughts and emotions take control.

What had she confessed to Disciple Flannery during her cleansing? The vine leaf she'd chewed to open herself to The Spirit had brought a curtain down between herself and reality. She suspected she'd spoken of her feelings for Ben, her doubts about Father's Law, and her unwanted violent thoughts. Or had she turned to the hidden place she only ever glimpsed out of the corner of her eye, her anger and despair at Master Anton's treatment of Perpetua? Even now she couldn't examine it directly and obscured it instead with euphemism. Centa suspected not even the truth-revealing properties of the vine could access that which she suppressed so expertly. Maybe she had told of Ben's secret mountain cache and his plans to flee? Would he ever forgive her?

The bridge door opened and inside was as she'd recalled from her last visit over a year earlier, though maybe looking a little more worn, with even fewer flashing lights on the control panels around the perimeter. The room swayed and Perpetua held her steady. Rae still lay on her platform below the now defunct display screens. She was small for a woman who would be thirty-five years old now. The rumours were that her coma had stunted her growth. Her white-blonde hair lay in a long plait over her shoulder.

Master Anton kneeled before a desiccated figure in a wheelchair. The father. A burst of adrenaline sharpened Centa's mind.

Here he was finally. He looked… not right. Older and faded. Love and power no longer pulsed from his aura. Perhaps it never had.

Master Anton detailed Centa's crimes. The disappointment of the masters and Skyfather injured her pride, despite her doubts about the righteousness of their power. Her ideas of rebellion were so small, contained within the perimeter of the settlement. She was a coward.

"Where's the disciple involved?" Skymother asked from beside the father's wheelchair, her silver-streaked black hair coiled into a bun at the nape of her neck.

"Disciple Benjamin was exposed to the dust. He's not in any state to answer for his behaviour," Master Anton said.

"What do you mean?" Skymother asked.

Centa raised her eyes. Ben hadn't been making any sense when she'd last seen him, but at least he'd been semi-conscious. She'd held on to that fact during her time in the cell.

"He's not exactly comatose, however, he's not coherent. He's in the med hab. Oxygen therapy hasn't helped."

What did *not exactly comatose* mean? No worker who'd been overcome by vine dust had ever returned from the med hab. She'd heard they responded to nothing. But Ben had been aware of his surroundings. He'd been able to stand and walk.

"Worker 9 has undergone an approved spiritual counselling process. We submit her now for the father's evaluation."

"Thank you, Anton. You may stand," Skymother said.

Master Anton staggered to his feet with a grunt. His knees cracked loudly in the quiet room.

"Please." Skymother gestured to the floor where Master Anton had been.

Centa kneeled. She glimpsed the grey pallor of Skyfather's skin and the vacant look in his eyes before bowing her head.

"Come closer to the father, Worker."

Centa shuffled forwards on her knees, eyes on the floor. The frayed and faded tips of a pair of slippers peeped out from beneath the blanket covering his legs.

"Rest your head on his lap."

Centa bent her forehead to the blanket. The smooth fibre smelt faintly of soap, unwashed hair, and urine. She felt a weight on the back of her head as Skymother placed one of Skyfather's skeletal hands upon her. His breath rattled.

"Our father will now reach into your mind and determine if you've had sufficient spiritual counselling."

Centa felt none of the surge of power—a kind of intoxicating giddiness, as though she'd taken a breath of vine dust—that she'd felt at Skyfather's touch in the past. He was nothing more than a sick old man. She ground her teeth against the sudden urge to vomit onto his lap. She wanted to be in his good graces again. She wanted to be pure. She wanted to believe in him.

But nothing of her faith remained.

The weight of Skyfather's hand left her head. "You may now look up." Skymother held Skyfather's hand, her ankles swayed, thick above her bare feet. She hummed tunelessly. "The spiritual counselling was successful," she said at last. "However, you've moved further away from attaining your immortal soul and will need to work diligently to make up the loss. You may now return to your post, Worker 9."

There was never going to be any other outcome. They couldn't banish her or send her to the pyre. They needed all the workers they had left, especially the experienced and skilled ones. It was all a show. Skyfather couldn't even speak for himself anymore let alone assess a Sky Human's spiritual state. A bead of saliva dripped from the edge of his open mouth and onto his chin. He stared blankly above Centa's head. She had been afraid of his power for nothing.

None of it had ever been real. But knowing that now was no help to her. It would be better to have stayed as ignorant and content as the newborns who gratefully guzzled their milk with no concept of their short lives of drudgery. Better to be satisfied with small acts of rebellion, shocking thoughts, and occasional approval from the masters.

Perpetua pulled at Centa to stand and dragged her stumbling into the hallway where Tilter was waiting. She hadn't noticed him on the way in. Everything had been a blur.

"My shadow."

Tilter rushed forward and grasped Centa's waist. She took comfort in the touch for a moment, then pushed the boy away.

"CONTROL YOURSELF, Worker 517," Perpetua and Centa both thundered at the same time.

Tilter fell back and walked the customary two steps behind.

"You've no need to reprimand him," Perpetua said. "Your shadow belongs to me now."

Centa didn't need to ask why. Centa's punishment meant that Perpetua had finally succeeded in replacing her as the senior scientist in the worker replenishment laboratory, despite her incompetence. Master Anton would realize his mistake soon enough. He needed Centa more than she needed him.

"How long was I in there?" They walked two abreast along the narrow link to the dormitory hab.

"A little over eighty hours."

Only eighty hours? It had felt as though an earthweek had passed. "So, Ben has been in the med hab all that time?" Eighty hours was a long time with no sign of improvement.

Perpetua stopped in the middle of the link and stared at her. "Haven't you learned anything? Forget about him or he'll be the ruin of you." She strode away with Tilter in tow but added over her shoulder, "Take some time to recover. Master Anton requires you in the lab in an hour."

Air filters chugged endlessly, high up in the dormitory ceiling as a ten-year-old worker rhythmically scrubbed the floor with a stiff brush. It would have been easy to climb up to her sleep cell and rest, but she needed to reclaim her place in the laboratory. And she needed to find a way to help Ben. So instead, she walked to wake herself up and found herself in the anursery.

Less than a quarter of the metal cots contained infants, peering between the bars. Some of them cried, having not yet learned it was pointless. Others sucked on their empty feeding tubes. The smell of ammonia rose from sodden diapers. Did Skyfather wear a diaper now? At a change table one of the carers reprimanded an infant for wriggling. Centa recognized the child as the last new worker she'd successfully brought to full term, almost ten earthmonths earlier.

The wall screen broadcast a counting song with brightly coloured numbers whooshing across and dancing until it was replaced by a swirled marble image of Earth from orbit. Skyfather's voice boomed from the speakers in prayer, but bile rose in Centa's throat and she rushed from the room. She would never again be able to listen to his voice without nausea. Her counselling had worked. Only not in the way the masters had intended.

· · ● · ● · ● · · ·

Centa made her way back through the mothership. She would concentrate on her work. It was the only thing that made any sense to her. Even if the community was a lie, the lives she grew in the incubators were real. She flattened herself against the curved metal wall near the laboratory link, her head bowed, as a trio of stooped masters lumbered past.

In the laboratory, Perpetua sat at the coveted senior scientist's bench, closest to the cell culture incubator. It had the least damaged laminate surface and the most accurate set of pipettes. It wasn't those facts that upset Centa, though. It was that she would now have to answer to her inferior.

"Master wants you to work there." Perpetua tilted her chin at the bench closest to the door.

The bench near the noisy centrifuges that had been run unbalanced too many times and were now held together with tape and solder. Near the foot traffic of the main door and close to the wash-up sink and cold storage rooms. The bench that everyone left miscellaneous wet and dirty objects all over.

"It's only temporary, until you prove you can control yourself. It was Master Anton's idea. It's not what I wanted."

Every word out of Perpetua's mouth made Centa more and more furious. She took her place and glanced at the closed door of Master Anton's office. She would wait to gauge his state of mind before she made a plea to be reinstated. Once she had regained his respect, she would find a way to help Ben.

Centa struggled to pull latex gloves onto her clammy hands. She cleaned the brittle laminate work surface with eighty percent ethanol, soaking all the cracks and blisters that could shelter innumerable fungal spores and bacteria, and rearranged the pipettes and tips.

She was making her way to the cell culture incubator when Perpetua called out, "Oh, um. The embryos you thawed before spiritual counselling. I changed the media for you. I hope you don't mind. I know you're particular..."

Centa did mind. She didn't like anyone touching her cultures. They would have died without a media change though.

"Thank you," she said in a tone that couldn't be mistaken for gratitude.

Each culture dish in the glass-fronted incubator had a number written in permanent marker on top. She'd sparked to life in a similar dish, swimming in culture media, cells multiplying in a rabid froth.

She stacked the four dishes on top of each other and carried them over to the microscope at the back of the room.

"Two of them didn't look like they were going to make it. I did the best I could."

Centa took a deep breath. As Perpetua had predicted, two of the embryos were dead. The cells were grainy and withered, their perforated membranes spilling cytoplasm and nuclei. Their death likely wasn't Perpetua's fault. Most genetically flawed embryos died in the dishes before they developed little arms, legs, and faces.

The third dish was swarming with bacteria, the tiny organisms seethed busily in the light of the microscope. Centa's technique was perfect. She never contaminated her cultures. Perpetua was incompetent.

The fourth dish contained a fully expanded blastocyst, with an adequately formed trophectoderm that would become the placenta and an inner cell mass that would form the foetus in the fluid-filled centre cavity. The blastocyst was as round and textured as a moon. A world all its own. Another day and it would be ready for transfer to a foetus incubator. Centa turned to hand the failed cultures to Tilter for disposal, but he was no longer a permanent presence behind her in the laboratory. She walked back through the lab to the washing up area, flooded the dishes with bleach and left them to decontaminate.

The door to Anton's office opened. "Welcome back, Worker 9."

"Thank you, Master Anton."

"I'm pleased your counselling was effective."

"Yes, Master." She lowered her eyes. It didn't matter that she no longer believed. She had to find a way to survive and be content.

"I will tolerate no more of your nonsense with Disciple Ben."

"Yes, Master."

"How go the embryos?"

"Only one in four suitable for implantation." Centa refrained from alerting the master to Perpetua's negligence. She wasn't that petty.

"These old embryos are failing at an increasingly alarming rate." Master Anton said.

"What should we do?" Perpetua intruded.

Anton closed his eyes and steepled his fingers. "I remember... back before we left Earth..."

Perpetua rolled her eyes and Centa repressed a smile. They were in for one of his long, meandering accounts of his time on Earth.

After five long minutes the point of his monologue became clear. He pointed below Centa's belly button. They would collect fresh eggs and sperm from the workers. Centa clapped her hands over her abdomen. She was aware she possessed a reproductive system. She, and all the others with uteruses, had been fitted with devices to prevent implantation. According to Father's Law, conception and pregnancy were dangerous because they resulted in surges of hormonally driven emotion that led to erratic behaviour and loss of productivity. Maybe that too was a lie.

"Does Skyfather approve?" Perpetua asked.

Centa pressed her lips together. They were all deluded, believing Skyfather possessed any power or intelligence.

"I'll commune with him on the issue," Master Anton answered, breathing deeply. "First, however, I must boost my spiritual strength. Worker 8?"

"Yes, Master?"

"I require your service." The master stepped back into his office, leaving the door open behind him.

"Yes, Master," Perpetua answered in a wavering voice. She peeled off her latex gloves and followed him inside, clicking the door shit behind her.

Centa visualized jamming the tip of Perpetua's pipette into the master's ear and through into his brain. Then she got to work.

· · · ● · ● · ● ● · · ·

A week later Centa's hand cramped around her pipette. She shook it out and rolled her head around her tight neck. The last embryo that she had transferred to a foetus incubator died after only a day. She and Perpetua kept repeating the same actions, using the same methods and the same equipment, and getting the same dismal results. This was the tenth failed embryo in a row, and laboratory protocol stated she must now perform pointless gene sequencing and protein expression assays that would tell them nothing of practical use.

She'd gone over her methods again and again. The only variables that had changed in the thirty years of the settlement were the age of the zygotes and the introduction of new tissue culture media recycled from dead Sky Humans. They couldn't order new supplies from Earth, and they couldn't undo the cellular damage from years in storage. Her work, the only thing she had left, had become futile. She wanted to sweep everything on her bench onto the floor and walk away.

The voice of Perpetua cut across the lab. "Worker 517, the master needs you to collect samples from the med hab."

Ben was still in the med hab, and Centa had been waiting for an opportunity to look in on him. She'd distracted herself with work because mentally dissecting every possible scenario and overheard conversation for clues about how he was had made her feel like all her internal organs were slowly autolyzing. She came around from her bench as Tilter accepted a cool box from Perpetua.

"I'll go," Centa offered, tossing her gloves onto her bench. "I've been doing extractions all morning. I need a break."

"You can't," Perpetua answered. Everything she said since she'd become senior scientist sounded as though it were a question rather than an order.

"Yes, I can." Centa took the cool box from Tilter's hands and the juvenile stifled a laugh. Ben needed to know that she hadn't abandoned him, and that spiritual counselling hadn't diminished her feelings for him. In fact, it had brought her closer to running away with him.

"You're going to see *him*. You're not supposed to do that." Perpetua sidestepped between Centa and the door.

Logic and good sense suggested Centa should stay away, put an end to her attachment to Ben and her doubts about Father's Law and be the perfect, obedient, and faithful Sky Human the masters wanted. Logic and sense were weak motivators.

"I'm stretching my legs and collecting samples." Centa shoved Perpetua aside.

"What will Master Anton think?"

Centa raised her eyebrows. "Do you want to disturb him?" It was a nasty question. Perpetua's encounters with Master Anton had been leaving her more and more distressed. Still, Ben was Centa's priority.

Perpetua shook her head and returned to her bench. "You think you're so rebellious but you're just selfish. Nothing you do benefits anyone but yourself."

Centa made her way through to the med hab at the end of a link to the mothership. She held the cool box aloft, ready to prove the legitimacy of her errand if anyone tried to turn her back. The clinic waiting area was empty. They too had barely any supplies left and were increasingly turning to vine leaves to treat minor ailments.

She peered through the window in the ward door. Each of the ten beds lined up against the wall contained a juvenile, or barely adult, worker with an intravenous line in their forearm. Ben wasn't amongst them. She pushed her cheek against the glass to see better.

"Worker 9?

"Yes?" Centa swivelled, her cheeks red with guilt.

Disciple Zenia, with flecks of grey at the temples of her short reddish-brown hair, stood at the door of the consultation room. "Can I help you?"

Centa held up the cool box. "I'm here to collect some samples for the Sky Human Replenishment Laboratory." She wasn't entirely certain what samples she was collecting. Gametes for the new method of embryo creation was the most obvious possibility. She should have asked Perpetua some questions before she ran off.

"Ah, right. The ova and sperm from the comatose workers. Master Anton wants to go ahead with that." She frowned for a moment.

Centa handed over the cool box. "That's right."

"I was expecting someone much shorter and younger." Deep wrinkles appeared at the edges of Zenia's eyes and across her forehead as she smiled. She was as short as some of the juveniles herself. "Your lab's shadow perhaps."

"Yes, of course. I decided to come instead. I needed to stretch my legs, and I hadn't been over this way in a while..."

Zenia leaned in and lowered her voice. "He's inside the door, to the right. He's sleeping now. We sedate him to stop him trying to get outside."

"No. I—"

"It's okay. Ben and I keep each other's secrets."

Of course, the disciples were close. Their memories of Earth and what they'd left behind united them. They'd watched a good number of their fellow earthlings die in the early days of the settlement. Those who remained clung together like a pack of lizard-pigs cowering from hunters.

"Will he be all right?" Centa's voice caught in her throat.

"I don't know. We don't understand what's going on with him. We don't understand what's going on with any of them. He's in better shape than the rest though. I suppose that's encouraging." Zenia hesitated. "Actually, on that. There's something I wanted to talk about with you. Just between you and me. Can I trust you?"

Centa swallowed. It was unusual for a disciple, other than Ben, to confide in a worker like her. She didn't know if she wanted to hear what Zenia had to say, but it would be pointless to refuse.

"Okay."

Zenia leaned against the wall and closed her eyes. "All of them, all the vine victims that we've autopsied have fine, almost invisible filaments through their bodies and concentrated in their brains. Ben had a look at them for me once and said it was the same cellular structure as the vine."

Ben hadn't mentioned this to Centa. How many secrets had he been keeping from her?

"He likened it to a mycelial network," Zenia continued. "And now I'm seeing it in the failed foetuses you bring me for autopsy."

"I had no idea." Centa felt giddy. She leaned against the wall opposite Zenia.

"Master Anton's not interested, or he doesn't believe me, and Master Ophelia hasn't been in her right mind for years now."

Centa didn't know what to say. If what Zenia was saying was true, then vine spores had taken root in all of them. There was nothing she could do about this except worry. Why did Ben, and now Zenia, think she was the one to burden her with matters the masters should have been dealing with?

"Why are you telling me this?"

"I don't know." Zenia drooped. "I had to talk to someone who might understand the implications from a biological perspective. Ben and I had been trying to work it out before all this happened to him."

The secret between Ben and Zenia pricked at Centa's pride. It was likely her fault. She always cut Ben off when he tried to tell her about the vine and all the problems with the settlement. She'd forced him to confide in others. She'd pushed him away.

"I'll have to think about all this," Centa said.

Zenia pressed her back against the door of the ward and held the cool box to her chest. "I'll be in the surgery for about twenty minutes, retrieving your samples. Keep yourself entertained during that time." She winked, pushed the door open fully and marched off across the ward.

Unconscious workers breathed shallowly in the otherwise silent room. The air held the slight scent of vine dust until Centa sniffed again and it was gone. Ben lay on his side, curled up as though he were one of her foetuses. His ponytail was full of knots, his skin grey, his lips flaked and cracked. He'd never looked anything other than perfectly groomed before. She wanted to hear his voice and know he was going to be all right, but she knew she shouldn't wake him. Not if rest was what he needed most.

He opened his eyes. "Have you come to take me to the vine?" There was no recognition in his gaze.

"It's me, Centa."

"Centa?"

The sound of her name from his lips gave her hope, but he only frowned and closed his eyes again. She felt invisible, inconsequential. To everyone else, she was no more than a worker, with no thoughts or agency of her own. Ben was the only person she'd been able to be herself with. A look from him was enough for her to feel seen. Now he couldn't even give her that.

It had to be the sedatives. She shook his shoulder. This wasn't good enough.

"Ben? Do you know who I am?" She placed a hand on his cheek.

"Have you come to take me to the vine?"

"No. You need to get better." She kissed his brow. "Please, Ben. It's me. You know me."

He turned his head and searched the air above him. "I need to find the vine."

Centa backed away. She should have spread her sources of happiness into smaller aliquots, as she did with cell culture cytokines, instead of placing it all into one fallible man. Without him she had nothing.

When Zenia returned with the samples, Centa was sitting on the bench in the clinic waiting area with her fingernails cutting into the palms of her hands to hold back her tears.

7

Centa called Master Anton over to the microscope and offered him the eyepiece. She smiled as he discovered the blastocyst, ready for implantation. It was high quality too, with timely development from the zygote stage and no visible abnormalities. Of the ten comatose worker ova she'd fertilized almost a week before—using ten different variations of the vague protocol suggested by Master Anton—only this one had been successful. She was pleasantly surprised. She'd expected to spend months troubleshooting until they got it right.

Master Anton straightened up from his hunched position. "Well done. Transfer it to a foetus incubator and record your protocol for the others to follow." He walked back to his office. "And you can resume your position as senior scientist, Worker 9."

"Yes, Master."

Centa hid her smile from Perpetua and Tilter. She had wisely thrown herself into her work and as a result had been returned to her rightful place. She'd been so busy with the gametes of the comatose workers that there'd been times when she hadn't even thought about Ben or the futility of, well, everything.

Ben. The thought of his illness tainted her fleeting happiness like a single fungal spore in a cell culture dish.

"That's great," Perpetua said. "Quite a relief actually." She turned to Tilter. "I shall no longer be your mentor."

"Would you like me to transfer the blastocyst?" Tilter asked Centa.

"I'll do it myself." Centa flicked off the microscope and pushed her chair away from the bench. "This project is far too fragile right now. You can observe. Then I'll run you through the fertilisation procedure and we can thaw some more gametes."

They had overcome the first obstacle. With hard work and good luck, the foetus incubators could be filled with life within months. With more workers they could expand their crops, get control of the vine again, and maybe even establish a dust-free perimeter around the settlement. The masters could pretend it was all in Skyfather's plan.

That could all happen. *If* the embryo implanted well. *If* the foetus grew to full term. *If* they could repeat this success. The master had renewed faith in her. She had used all her skills and effort to give this potential Sky Human a chance at life. What happened next was dependent upon an intangible ingredient, that mysterious spark of life and fortune that had eluded biologists for millennia. It was now out of her control.

· · · · ● · ● · · ·

Centa had been unable to sleep. The worker-derived embryo she'd implanted only days before wasn't growing properly. Her restless thoughts led her to the gestation lab before the father star's rise. The foetus incubator glowed gently in the early-morning dark. Fluids gurgled quietly in and out of pipes and tubes. The room smelt faintly of cleaning solution.

They'd cursed themselves with too much hope and celebration. By now the embryo should have been the size of a bean, with a discernible head and a lizard-like body. Instead, it was no shape Centa had ever seen an embryo take. There was no genetic mutation or chromosomal abnormality she was aware of that could disrupt the growth program in such a way.

There was nothing else to do. She would have to purge the chamber and perform a genetic analysis. Perhaps look closely at the HOX genes. She hoped Master Anton wouldn't demote her again now that her success had turned.

She had more newly fertilized zygotes in the cell culture incubator. One of them would develop normally. She ran through the protocol in her head for the umpteenth time. It couldn't have been anything she'd done. Could it? No. It had to be an anomaly. A one off. She pinched the back of her hand, hard, to stop her tears. The settlement couldn't fail. She couldn't give in to despair. She would grow new workers and Ben would recover.

The door opened behind her. She steeled herself to face Master Anton. She would rather have informed him of the news when she had a genetic explanation for the failure and had implanted a new blastocyst. He never wanted to know about the problems, only the successes. But it wasn't him. It was Ben, as though her misery had conjured him.

She held out her arms instinctively. He'd come looking for her. He was himself again, and he'd remembered that he loved her.

He staggered forward. His face was unshaven and, as he came into the light from the incubator, she saw grey through his hair where none had been before. His eyes were bloodshot and red-rimmed. He looked almost as old as the masters. He walked past her open arms, his hospital gown flapping about his bare legs, and put his hands on the incubator with the malformed embryo.

"Hey." She touched his forearm. "What's going on?"

"Vine," he murmured.

He was still fixated on the vine. Nothing had changed. She gently removed his hands from the glass and tried to catch his roving gaze.

"Ben? It's me."

He fixed on her. "Centa?"

"Yes. It's me." He was coming back. All he'd needed was her touch. No one else had a connection like theirs.

She embraced him. "I knew you'd come back."

He didn't embrace her in return. Just reached out to the glass with a blank look in his eyes.

"No. Forget about that." She put a hand on each of his cheeks. "Focus on me."

The door to the gestation lab opened again and Disciple Zenia entered, her face pale and her white coat rumpled.

"HE'S HERE!" she called out behind her and advanced with a syringe in her hand. "Come now, Ben. Time for another little sleep."

"Don't hurt him." Centa held onto Ben's arm.

"Sedating him is the only way I can keep him from wandering or dragging comatose workers from their beds." Ben didn't resist as she slid the syringe into his neck and depressed the plunger. "It's for his protection as much as everyone else's."

He collapsed into Centa's arms. Helpless as newborn. She held him tight and breathed in his scent. He didn't smell the same anymore. He reeked of vine. Zenia helped her lower him gently to the ground.

Disciple Flannery and a lower priest ran in. "You need to get Ben under control," Flannery fumed, glaring at Zenia. Flannery took hold of Ben's feet while the younger priest took him by his armpits, and they carried him from the room. To Centa, he looked dead.

"Is he getting any better?" she asked Zenia, who still lingered in the doorway.

Zenia shook her head. "I don't think so. It's nothing we know how to deal with. All our energy's going into keeping him calm. It's likely that eventually he'll be recycled like the others."

Centa felt sick. Recycling was nothing more than a Father's Law term for murder. "But surely he'll get better, given time."

"I'm not seeing it. He does have moments, but there's no progression towards a more present state." Zenia rubbed her eyes. "I'm as gutted to lose him as you are." She closed the door behind her.

Centa turned back to the incubator. There had to be something she could do. If they would only let her spend more time with him. After all, he had come looking for her, hadn't he? Why else would he have come to the lab?

She reached around to turn off the incubator light and suddenly saw it. The embryo wasn't in a random, malformed shape. The shape was of a stem and leaves, although instead of the green of chlorophyll, there was the pink of blood running through tiny blood vessels.

Was this what had called to Ben? It certainly wasn't her. It was never her. Not anymore. But it wasn't possible. Was it? There had to be some other explanation. She rubbed her eyes and looked again. But the meaning became no clearer. She was tired and upset. Everything would make more sense in the morning. It had to. Tomorrow she would see that it was just an ordinary, malformed foetus. They had them all the time. But why had it interested Ben? Maybe she was looking for patterns and meanings where there weren't any. Nothing Ben did made sense anymore. Her brain tried to calm her and keep her from catastrophizing, but her body knew. In its shaking limbs and roiling stomach, it knew.

The foetus was a vine, and it was growing.

8

Tilter lay on his back, arms and legs splayed. Even in sleep his head was tilted to the side, his mouth wide open.

"Wake up." Centa patted him lightly on the cheek, and the boy snapped his mouth closed and sat up with a start.

"What? What is it?"

Centa wanted to get the foetus out of incubator as soon as possible, and she needed an extra pair of hands. She didn't have control over much. She couldn't fix Ben, couldn't make new workers grow, but this she could deal with.

"We need to get to work early today," she whispered and handed him his shoes. With every passing second Centa imagined that *thing* growing larger and stronger.

Tilter padded behind her, through the mothership and the link to the lab entrance.

"The embryo we implanted the other day needs to be purged." Centa handed him his white coat.

"Purged? But…"

"It's not developing properly," Centa snapped. "It won't survive another day." She didn't want to speak about the failure and its implications. "You get started and I'll be right behind you."

Centa hesitantly opened the cell culture incubator to check their pre-implantation embryos. She didn't have to look at them to know they were all afflicted like the embryo in the gestation lab. The slightly spicy smell in the warm, humid air was enough. This was no one off, no fluke, no isolated contamination event. Vine DNA was likely in the gametes of all the workers felled by the dust. Maybe everyone in the community carried the potential for their cells to give rise to vine. All the spores they'd breathed in or swallowed with their food over the years. All the times they'd rubbed leaves on open wounds or chewed them to open their minds for counselling. The vine could be a part of them all. Her head spun.

Centa closed the cell culture incubator and held onto the edge of the bench until she could breathe properly. Once she could trust her legs again, she rushed over to the gestation lab. She shouldn't have sent Tilter in there alone.

The first thing she noticed was the tapping. Any strange noises usually meant there was a mechanical problem with the air handlers or even one of the incubators. But this was different. It was coming from where Tilter stood, open-mouthed.

It had been less than an hour since Centa had left the small, malformed embryo, and now it filled the whole chamber. A profusion of green and flesh-coloured leaves pressed against the glass, pulsing and tapping as though looking for escape. Some of the leaves looked like hands.

Centa froze at the door trying to think through her next steps. Could it force open the birth channel valve? How had it grown so fast? Ben had always said the vine possessed an intelligence they didn't comprehend. Maybe the threat of its destruction had spurred its rapid growth.

They wouldn't be able to purge the incubator in the normal way. It was too dangerous to release this new organism. She would have to call the priests to destroy it along with the incubator. It would be a shame to lose such a precious piece of equipment. But they had seventeen others and it seemed unlikely they would ever fill them all again. The best they could do now was contain this outbreak. But what then? Fighting the vine had become as ineffective as bringing down a fever without addressing the underlying infection.

The tapping became a banging.

"I'm going to get the priests," Centa called out.

The incubator wobbled from side to side, juddering like one of the washing machines in the laundry hab. Tilter reached out to hold it steady, but it wrenched out of his grasp. With the next thud of its base against the hard floor, cracks appeared all over the glass surface like the small veins in Skyfather's bloodshot eyes.

"Don't—" Centa shouted. But it was too late. The incubator exploded, spraying amniotic fluid and glass all over the room. The stems, leaves, and leaf-hands of the vine-foetus surged forth in every direction and Tilter was instantly engulfed. The monstrosity pulsed and spread, exploring every crevice of the room, every inch of the floor and ceiling, and every incubator in its path.

Centa threw herself back through the door and slammed it behind her. It was hopeless. They were all doomed. This was how the people on Earth must have felt before they gave up on their planet. She wished she'd said yes to Ben that night in the cavern, wished she'd convinced him that they didn't need to go back at all. Then none of this would be happening.

Perpetua found her then. "What are you doing on the floor? Is that dust I smell?"

Centa wanted to tell Perpetua it was nothing more than a faulty air filter. They'd summon a technician, and it would soon be repaired. She should have been making plans for the future. Adjusting new worker numbers to fit the expansion projects of the masters. Not fighting to keep the settlement from destruction.

"Yes." Her voice shook. "Tilter's in there. One of the embryos. It was vine."

Perpetua was the calm one for once. "We need to get him out before he's overcome." She took two dust masks from the wall and handed one to Centa.

"It's too late." The vine-foetus had leapt for him as thought it would swallow him whole.

"Don't be a coward." Perpetua scolded her. "I'm going to get help. You need to at least try. He wouldn't leave you behind."

Perpetua was right. It could have been her trapped in there. Perpetua and Tilter wouldn't hesitate to come in after her.

Centa put on the mask and pushed open the door. The vine-foetus's growth had calmed, but it still inched steadily towards the door. She would have to be quick.

"517, can you hear me?"

There was no answer, just a sickening squelch from the mass of growth closest to the shattered incubator. Centa waded over, feeling her way through the foliage as thorns scratched her wrists. The vine was as turgid as a well-watered plant, warm as human skin, and sticky with sap not yet dried to dust. She pried the appendages apart and reached for strands of Tilter's brown hair. Tendrils of vine circled her fingers. A hand-leaf—rubbery and boneless, yet strong—grabbed her wrist and thorns vibrated and sought purchase in her skin. She screamed and pulled back, the taste of sap on her tongue. Her vision blurred.

She backed towards the door, fumbled it open and collapsed onto the laboratory floor. She willed the world to cease spinning and her vision to clear. There was nothing she could do for Tilter. She had tried. The room would need to be quarantined and incinerated.

Voices and footsteps surrounded her. She was dragged from the doorway and propped against a wall. She had generated something new. Something even more powerful than the vine alone. The masters would not be pleased.

First Interlude

Nothing much had changed for Rae in the thirty years since she'd been plucked from the vine, ripped from Earth and tugged back to her body by an invisible tether. Not until the day she was reunited with Ben. And then everything changed.

The first thing Rae had known, all those years ago when her nightmare had begun, was that she couldn't move. Nobody could hear her scream. Or see the tears that refused to form. Master Ophelia, the medic, shone a light into her eyes, stabbed her foot with a pin, and proclaimed her non-responsive.

Days went by in a haze of pain and terror. Fluids were taken out of her. Others were dripped into her. She tried to let them know she could feel it all. But her body wasn't really hers anymore. She didn't fit properly. Like an ugly sister wedging her foot into Cinderella's slipper.

There were arguments over whether she was alive or dead. But her heart still beat. Her lungs still moved. And something Master Ophelia couldn't explain was happening with her brain waves.

The white plastic above her head in the med hab snapped in the wind, and dark ovals of vine leaf alighted atop it, only to be blown away and replaced by others. Rae imagined the vine was sending knights in search of their lost princess.

They soon noticed Rae's body didn't require interventions to keep it whole and healthy. And, like Peter Pan, she wasn't growing.

Her father proclaimed she was a link to the spirit of the planet. For once he wasn't wrong. Over the years she came to understand the vine was an extension of Aceso. It probed her mind and created a familiar language of images and memories. The planet didn't care about the behaviour of its human intruders. It simply wanted them gone. Contrary to her father's teachings, there was no action, ritual or sacrifice that would alter its opinion. They were an itch on its surface. And now as the vine strengthened on the borders of their settlement, its voice had become thunderous.

Rae yearned to follow the workers who'd been consumed by the vine and streaked like shooting stars on their way to Earth. Those like her who were severed from the vine before it could consume them completely lived in a half-sleep, their bodies useless. Every now and then she passed through them like ghosts in the place outside her body that she'd come to call the forest of nothing. The ghosts mumbled about returning to the vine or tending failing crops or breathing in smoke from the pyres.

She recited her own stories and picked up her memories of Earth to examine them. She remembered Father scolding her as she hid in the enormous hangar where the mothership rested. She remembered tents on their lawns filled with believers. The sky, red and thick with dust. Father's lackeys kneeling or bending over to gaze into her eyes and say, *Your father is a very special man. He will save us all.* The tears of Nanna, Poppa, and her uncle Dexter when she'd hugged them goodbye. Entering her cryopod.

She preferred to remember the shine of sunlight through glass. The shimmering surface of the swimming pool. Virtual reality games and story time with Nanna and Poppa. Slices of pineapple, juicy, sweet, and cool. She held onto those like a trail of moonlit stones that led back to Earth.

On the day that Ben came, the vine called her to the forest of nothing with the promise of a gift. That was where she found him. He was faster and less dust-addled than the other ghosts, but she still approached him slowly. An unremarkable face. Brown eyes, dark ponytail, crooked grin, square jaw. He had little to distinguish him except that, where the others were mostly children, he was a grown man. No taller, but much stockier.

He spoke with the ghosts that all clustered around him, and she gleaned that he had been the one to send many of them out amongst the failing crops. They called him Disciple Ben of Earth. She remembered him. His voice had deepened over the years, become smoother and more certain, but it was him.

He met her gaze, and his face flickered in and out, but he didn't drop his eyes or wander away like the others did. There was intelligence there. An intelligence to match her own.

"Rae!" He broke free of the crowd and rushed towards her.

He remembered her.

Ben had taken over reading aloud to her when her mother had died. From the careless talk of the masters and medics, she'd learned that her mother had suffered from multiple organ failure, the result of a faulty cryopod. Her body had become a patchwork of improperly frozen pockets, and rot had formed during the centuries-long journey. She had abandoned Rae like a typical fairy tale mother.

Ben had read uncertainly at first, in his low-pitched, creaky teenage voice. It seemed he'd been unfamiliar with reading for pleasure. Over time he became more confident. He took on the voices of witches, princesses, kings, and animals. Sometimes, when no one else was around, he told her about his former life in ramshackle lodgings he called caravan parks. The friends and family he'd left behind on Earth. The constant hunger. Rae came to think of him as her best friend.

One day he'd said, "I don't even know if you're listening," and her heart broke. She had imagined he might fall in love with her. Kiss her back to life.

Not long after that her stepmother, Victoria, had closed Rae's eyelids and she hadn't been able to open them ever again. Not in the real world. She came to know people by their smells. The sterile chemical smell of Master Ophelia. Victoria's perfumes and soaps. The henna smell from the markings Victoria placed all over Father's body. And later, after his stroke, the faint toilet stench whenever Father was wheeled in. Ben had smelt increasingly of soil and decomposing plants before he stopped coming. She later overheard he had joined Master Helena in agronomy.

And now here he was. Ben, who had abandoned her when she'd needed him most.

"Rae, you're here too!" His forehead furrowed and his jaw dropped.

It had been so long since Rae had seen any kind of facial expression. The others in the forest of nothing were always so blank. But Ben really saw her. It was like being fully in her body again. Like being fully alive. She wasn't alone anymore. There was so much she wanted to say to him. But they had time. Too much time.

He told her he had control over his body, unlike the other ghosts in the forest of nothing. But he was being restrained.

"I must help them," he said of the apparitions that flocked to him.

"You must help me," Rae said. She would not let him abandon her again.

If he focused, he could interact with the physical world, but it tired and confused him, he said. Faces appeared far away and distorted, as though they were at the surface of a lake, and he was stuck in the mud on the bottom. Words faded before they drifted down to him. Nothing from his past life mattered anymore. Whole sections of his mind and personality were closed to make space for what was essential—returning to Earth.

The dust had been kinder to him than others. He had built up a resistance over the years and now he alone could bridge the gap between the forest of nothing and the waking world.

He alone could free her.

• • • ● • ● • ● • • •

Aceso delighted Rae with images of a Thumbelina child bursting from the leaves of the vine. Their two species merged, one from Earth and one from Aceso. She wanted to reach out and hold it in her arms. There was so much excitement in the vine network, those fine threads that connected every native consciousness on the planet via the soil.

The so-called masters surged into the bridge unexpectedly. There had been few meetings since Skymother had taken control. Rae smelled her father nearby. It must have been an important meeting if they'd wheeled him out. Since his demise a year or so earlier, Victoria had extended her reign with false claims that Skyfather communicated through her. Bolstering the egos of rich men was her area of expertise. Matters of running a community on a hostile alien planet were not. The masters went along with it all. Not one of them wanted the responsibility of ruling a kingdom with more failures than successes. No one wanted to be the first to proclaim that the Emperor had no clothes.

They took their places around the table and shouted and jostled to be heard over each other as Rae listened in, desperate to understand the source of their agitation. A worker spoke of creating a chimera of vine and human. This was the new beginning that Aceso had been speaking of. What Ben had seen. The Thumbelina child. The vine strengthened with every soul it gave back to Earth and adapted with its expanding knowledge of its human trespassers. Now this new lifeform would change everything.

"If I understand this correctly," Master Kara, the builder, said, "this new supervine grew from the offspring of two of the comatose workers. But if it can grow from their sperm and eggs, what about the rest of their bodies?"

"What do you mean?" Master Anton sounded agitated.

"What have you been doing with the bodies of the comatose workers once you're all done studying them?" Master Kara asked.

"Have you seen my baby?" Master Ophelia, the medic, asked in a high, pitched voice. It was a poorly kept secret that she was suffering from dementia, and the others went on as if she hadn't spoken.

"Once they reach the point where they can no longer breathe unassisted," Disciple Zenia replied, "we hand them over to Master Anton's laboratory."

A sound of shifting again as they all turned towards Anton.

"And we send them to the recyclers to extract what we can for our embryo culture media, with the rest used as—"

"Fertiliser," Master Helena interrupted, before Anton could commence one of his speeches. "They're fertiliser for all our crops."

The room was silent for a second.

"And over the years," Master Kara said in a heavy voice, "as we've grown new workers in a soup made from these contaminated corpses and ploughed what was left back into the soil for our crops, the vine has become more potent and the workers less able to resist it."

"I can't find Georgia," Master Ophelia said. "Father said I had to leave her behind."

Rae had heard enough. They would only keep going around in circles with their plans to destroy the vine—plans that had never worked and would never work. Their fear of the vine had become so tiresome over the years. She no longer yearned to tell them that they should listen to the siren's call and submit to the vine until all their bodies became one with the planet and they were finally free. They'd had their chance.

She retreated from her senses more deeply into the forest of nothing and was immediately struck by the change she found there. There was something new, a blossoming path to a body that was not her own and that had not been there before. This wasn't the first time something like this had happened. There had been a flickering from her father's unstable consciousness ever since his stroke, connecting his mind to the forest where she dwelled. She'd ventured down it only once, however, and had barely escaped the despair that it had led to.

This path, however, was stronger and brighter, and as she padded the first few, tentative steps through the forest canopy toward it, she understood why.

It led to Master Ophelia.

Rae was Ali Baba at the entrance to the treasure-filled cave. She flowed through the connection until, for the first time in years, she could see the real world, through Ophelia's eyes. But she didn't have time to marvel at her returned sight, because then she felt it. The part of her that had previously been helpless in her own body, or incorporeal in the forest of nothing, had merged with the elderly woman's muscle and bone.

A constant high-pitched whine obscured the woman's hearing, and her body ached in places, was numb in others. She inhabited Ophelia's body, but not in the same way she'd ever inhabited her own. Ophelia's body was like a building with windows to the outside world via her senses. But as well as looking through the windows, Rae could wander about inside, repairing holes in the walls and scratches on the furniture. She could heal, the way she'd never been able to heal herself. But that wasn't why she was there. What Rae needed was assistance.

Ophelia's mind was jumbled and degraded. Whole sections of her brain were empty. The rest was occupied with simple biological survival and memories of the child she'd left behind on Earth. She no longer had a grasp on reality.

"Ophelia, it's me Rae."

"Rae?"

"Yes. I need help. I'm trapped—"

"Have you seen my daughter Georgia? I can't remember where I left her."

Rae didn't know how to answer. She had no experience with delusion.

"I'm trapped, Ophelia. Look to your left. I'm right there, lying on the platform. You can—"

"You were playing with her on the lawn just this morning, weren't you?"

"That was many years ago, Ophelia. But I need your help now."

"Where's my Georgia?"

Why did it have to be Ophelia whose mind had become open enough to let Rae in? Ophelia's eyes had been red and puffy all those years ago when they'd prepared for cryostorage. Rae hadn't realized she would be the only child who wasn't a worker to make the journey to Aceso until she'd emerged from her cryopod dripping with goo.

Ophelia's grief reminded her of her own lost mother. If her mother were still here and healthy, she would have saved Rae. She wouldn't have let this happen to her.

Rae ignored Ophelia's voice and pushed herself into the woman's limbs. Finding the control centres in the brain took some trial and error. At first she could do no more than make a fingertip twitch. Soon, though, she was moving whole fingers and hands and arms. Rae felt the exhilaration that Pinocchio must have felt when he'd become a real boy.

A call pulled Rae back into the forest of nothing. It was Ben, his face red, his eyes wide. "I'm coming for you. Be ready."

"No!" Rae shouted. "Not now! The masters—" But it was too late. He was out of the forest and in command of his body.

Of all the times for him to break free of his physical and chemical restraints and make her the priority. The masters wouldn't let him anywhere near her. That was even if he made it past the priests who were no doubt stationed at the door. The vine dust and the sedation had taken away any sense of stealth or cunning he might have had.

Rae retreated to her own body, there would be time to explore Ophelia's potential later. The masters were still arguing about the strengthening vine. She strained to hear Ben's arrival at the Bridge.

"We've tried every herbicide we can synthesize," Master Helena said. "This planet contains an underground mycorrhizal mycelium network far more sophisticated than anything I'd heard of on Earth. Resistance to herbicides develops far and wide within hours of our attempts. And how many times do I have to explain that the vine is the dominant plant-like life and our main source of oxygen? I also suspect it absorbs atmospheric radiation and detoxifies the soil the way fungi do on Earth. The planet would be unliveable without it. And the vine bugs are the only pollinators we have now that all our bees are dead."

"Can I bring everyone back to a more pressing issue?" Master Anton asked, raising his voice. "All of our foetus incubators have been demolished. No workers mean no one to plant or harvest crops, no one to clear the vine, no one to collect water and algae, no one to hunt lizard-pigs, no one to wipe our asses when we get too old."

"I think it's time we let them breed the old-fashioned way," Master Kara said.

"Skyfather has never lifted that prohibition," Skymother snapped. "And he never will. It would only anger the planet further."

Master Kara scoffed. "No one really believes that. Our Father—*Earl*—didn't want the workers to have something they cared about more than their work."

"Watch yourself," Master Anton warned, and then lowered his voice. "You may now leave, Worker 9. And you as well, Disciple Zenia. Take Master Ophelia back to her room. She's overdue for a rest."

The bridge doors creaked apart, and shouts came from the corridor beyond.

Ben. Rae had known he would be caught. If her eyes could weep, tears would be streaming down her cheeks. Why had she allowed herself to hope? She'd accepted her situation for so many years, and then Ben had come along, and she'd become a weak, emotional child once again.

Through the clamour and shouting she heard him call her name.

"RAE! She needs to be returned. Leave me be. She's suffering." His voice faded as the doors to the bridge closed.

Two escapes in two days. They would restrain him more securely now. She should have known he would never be able to save her. He had abandoned her all those years ago and had never been to visit her, not even once. She couldn't rely on any of these people. None of them understood and none of them cared. The only things she could rely on were herself and the vine. No amount of sedation, no restraint, no baton-wielding priest could stop it from coming for her, for all of them. But Aceso had been promising to free her for so long. A planet couldn't understand human timescales. It could be in one hundred years, or it could be tomorrow.

She wouldn't get her hopes up again. Hope wouldn't be what freed her. She would be the one to free herself. When the vine created the opportunity, she would be ready.

9

Centa put her mouth beneath the washroom tap and gulped from the stream of water. A full bladder was the first step in her plan to save Ben.

Back in the dorm, she settled into her sleep cell just before lights out. All the possible ways her plan could go wrong dashed around in her head. But she had no other choice. He was her only priority. He'd been a pitiful sight when he'd tried to break into the bridge. Somewhere along the way he'd lost his hospital gown and had been wearing only underpants. He was thinner than ever, his face more drawn. Zenia had looked at him as though he were less than human. A problem to be solved, an irritation.

Yet he was Ben. The disciples had all travelled from Earth together. Didn't that mean something to them? Ben had contributed invaluably to the settlement. That at least should make him worth trying to save.

And Disciple Flannery had been so angry. She'd even wielded a baton. The only time Centa had ever seen a priest use one had been years earlier, when an aggressive lizard-pig had broken into the dormitory and nibbled on the ear of an infant.

They'd made it obvious Ben's time was limited.

Perpetua stood by the bank of sleep cells and stared at her, eyes glinting in the dim light.

"Can we talk?"

"I'm tired." Centa closed her eyes and clasped her frayed sheet tightly in her fist. She couldn't discuss Tilter or the lab wreckage, not again. Not without risking tears.

After the gestation lab had been torched there'd been nothing left of the child. Not a single bone recovered. The vine-deaths had always been so distant, amongst workers she'd had no interaction with. Now that it was someone she'd known so well, someone she'd invested time in, Centa began to understand the despair Ben had felt. And the masters hadn't expressed even a moment's sadness for the lost child. To them the workers were single use, as so much on Earth had been before its environmental collapse. They were all disposable. She hoped the vine came and ripped these self-appointed masters' limbs from their bodies, and for once she didn't feel bad for thinking it.

Perpetua sighed loudly and climbed into her own sleep cell.

Centa couldn't recall falling asleep, but as planned, her bladder roused her in the dead hours of the morning. Workers snored or breathed evenly nearby. Except for Perpetua. She wasn't in her cell. Of all the nights for her to be wakeful. She was likely in the washroom. Centa couldn't delay. The order to dispose of Ben could come at any time.

She slipped out of the dorm and pulled on her boots. She took deep breaths to calm herself and entered the mothership. If she encountered anyone, she would say she was checking on something in the lab. Although there was nothing to do now that their gestation room was destroyed. Which was why she was surprised when Perpetua emerged from the laboratory link.

They stared at each other across the silent hallway.

"What were you doing in the lab?" Centa finally asked.

"I just..." Perpetua's gaze rose to the ceiling, a sign she was looking for a believable lie. "Just couldn't sleep and wanted to do some cleaning up."

"Right." Centa didn't care what Perpetua was up to. Nothing mattered except helping Ben. "Good night then." She stepped aside so Perpetua could pass.

"You're going to *him*. Aren't you?" Perpetua stood her ground. "Are you leaving the settlement?"

Centa didn't answer. It was pointless to lie.

"Can I come with you?"

"What?" Centa had never expected Perpetua would want to leave. It was obvious she wasn't content, especially with Master Anton's attentions, but she was always so meek and obedient.

"I don't think that would work."

All her life Centa had done what was best for the community. Now she needed to do what was best for her, and that was to be with Ben. The two of them alone. Perpetua wouldn't understand. Centa had enough doubts and worries of her own without adding Perpetua's disapproval to the formula.

"Never mind." Perpetua walked past her and towards the dormitory. "I have things I need to do here first anyway. Maybe I'll come and find you one day."

"Maybe."

It would be strange not seeing Perpetua every day. As children they'd fretted whenever they were apart. When they'd reached shadowing age Perpetua had initially been assigned to the Materials Production and Recycling Team in the cargo hold. She'd petitioned Master Anton for a place beside Centa in the Worker Replenishment Laboratory, citing her boundless admiration for him and his work. Her insincere flattery had worked too well though. He had kept her close to him ever since.

Centa continued to the med hab. The lights were on in the clinic, everything shiny and clean and ready for a patient. If she was caught, she would say she had a pain in her stomach. The ward itself was dark, as though the comatose patients cared about the distinction between day and night.

A young medic slept, sitting up in a chair at the edge of the ward. At least it wasn't Disciple Zenia. Centa didn't know what she'd do if the medic roused and tried to stop her or called the priests. Not that she hadn't spent hours lying awake thinking through every possible scenario. She couldn't face another cleansing and counselling session. If she was made to confess her truth now, of how she knew it was all fake and Skyfather was a fraud, she would surely be sent straight to the pyre.

She could sneak back to her bed and forget about all of it. But the end of the settlement was coming no matter what she did. And she had saved Ben from the vine patch and that couldn't have been for nothing.

She unfolded one of the wheelchairs stacked against the wall and eased the ward door open. Light from the window-slit near the top of the hab fell on Ben's face.

She kissed him on the cheek and whispered in his ear, "Wake up."

He came to with a loud grunt. Centa looked at the medic, but she hadn't moved. Ben tried to sit up. Centa quietly loosened his restraints and he pulled himself free.

"It's me, Centa," she said in a low voice. "You know me, don't you? We're going to our secret place."

"To the vine?" he asked loudly.

She put a hand over his mouth and looked again at the sleeping medic. "We can speak about that later. Let's get you out of here now."

He lay down and closed his eyes.

"Come on. Let's go." She pulled him up to sitting again. "We need to get you into this wheelchair."

"Yes, to the vine," he murmured and stood.

She guided him into the seat and his head fell back as he dozed off again.

"Hey, what's going on?"

Centa spun around. The medic was on her feet, her voice tentative and fearful. Every possible response flashed through Centa's head and she grasped for the only power available to her. In a blurred second, she swooped and picked up an empty metal bed pan and strode over to the medic.

"We're leaving now and if you say or do anything, I'll... bash your head in." She held the bed pan within striking range.

She visualized the medic's head cracking as though it were a roasted beetle carapace. Her legs felt weak and shaky with adrenaline. Would the medic even believe she was capable of such violence? Did Centa herself believe it? The fear on the medic's face reflected her own horror at the situation. Centa hoped she wouldn't call her bluff.

"All right," the medic whispered. "I didn't see a thing. I slept through it."

Centa pushed the wheelchair in front of her as she ran. She didn't trust the medic to keep her word once they were gone. She rushed Ben through the mothership and down the ramp into the cargo hold, not daring to turn on the lights. She wasn't sure she could withstand another confrontation.

She guided Ben through the 3D printers, tools, broken pieces of equipment, spare parts, and workbenches that had over the years replaced the crates of supplies brought from Earth. She wedged the outside door open with her foot to provide some light and fitted dust masks to both of their faces. He stirred for a second then fell back into sleep.

The night air cooled her flushed skin. Lizard-pigs chittered in the shadows. She wheeled Ben down the ramp and roused him again when they reached the vehicle hab. He climbed into the passenger seat, seduced by Centa's whispered assurances they were going to the vine.

She slid in behind the wheel, removed her mask and took deep calming breaths of filtered air. They'd made it to the buggy. She hadn't even been sure they'd make it that far.

"All right. This is good. One step at a time."

They drove away from the sleeping community. The sky to their right had lightened several shades, foreshadowing the approach of morning. Every minute or so she checked the rear-view camera and was relieved to find no headlights in pursuit.

At Rae's Bridge the vine had cleared the root barrier trench. Tendrils stretched and unfurled towards the centre of the settlement, as though diffusing into a region of lower concentration. Could this be the end Ben had predicted? It felt inevitable. As inevitable as humans wanting more than any planet could give.

The buggy rattled and listed over clumps of vine. The father star rose—and the reassuring shape of the mountains appeared through the trees ahead, as though someone's hand had slipped while drawing the horizon—she looked behind them for clouds of dust or the glint of light off a windshield.

Their only hope was that fighting the vine incursion was deemed more important than pursuing a disciple marked for disposal and a worker whose job had become hopeless.

Ben roused and stared out of the window, seemingly mesmerized by the endless expanse of vine, changing from a grainy grey to a sharp green as the father star returned its colour.

"The vine."

"Yes."

"We need to take Rae to the vine. And the others. The ones I failed. They all need the vine."

"We can't go back. They'll recycle you, or even put you straight on the pyre."

"They need me. They need the vine." Ben pulled on the handle of the locked door.

"What are you doing?" Centa braked and took his hand. She would say anything to keep him with her for a little longer. "Fine. Listen to me. We'll go back. At night. It's nearly morning now. We'll be caught if we go now. We'll go back when it's dark. We'll take them all to the vine."

She hoped one day Ben would forgive her lies.

He let go of the handle and relaxed back into the seat. As she drove, she tried to remind him of who he was and their history together. She spoke of the cavern and his plan to run away, the times he'd questioned Skyfather and Father's Law, amusing incidents from his life on Aceso. She pointed out old scars on his limbs from tangles with lizard-pigs, gardening equipment, and juvenile clumsiness. He responded to nothing.

She needed to be patient. Eventually, with her help, he could emerge from this brain fog.

They arrived at the mountains not long after dawn. Centa parked behind a big rock, out of view of anyone coming from the direction of the settlement. Everything looked different in the morning light. The mountain was a dark, blood red. Beautiful against the bright green of the vine. Tiny plants grew on the surfaces and in grooves and crevices.

The second Centa turned off the buggy's engine and released the door lock, Ben was up and out. He stood breathing deeply, with no mask, of course. He raised his nose in the air, sniffed, and ran into the dark, away from the mountain. She hurriedly fitted her mask and made her way after him, clutching a mask for him and two headlamps.

She found him only metres away, lowering himself onto a lush patch of vine. The tendrils and leaves shifted and closed in around him like a sigh. Lizard-pigs squealed loudly in all directions. Centa forced the mask over his face and pulled him upright.

"No. Please, Ben. Not yet."

"I must return. Earth is calling. Why can't you leave me be?"

A vine bug traipsed along the folds of his ear.

Why couldn't she leave him be? If this was what he wanted, why did she keep trying to stop him? She should have left him that night outside the mothership. He didn't want her anymore. She was trying to keep him here for her own selfish reasons.

"But we need to go back and get the others. They need to return too." She couldn't give up yet.

He opened his eyes.

"I won't do it without you. If you want to return them or lay them on the vine or whatever you'll have to help me."

She clung to him and the life they could have away from the Sky Human community as though it were her umbilical cord. The settlement was close to collapse, and her faith and the sense of purpose she derived from her work was gone. She couldn't let him go too. She couldn't be completely alone on this planet that was never really her home.

He sat up. Vine adhered to his skin for only a moment before it detached with a sucking noise.

"Now?"

Had he genuinely forgotten what she'd said less than an hour earlier? Maybe his brain was more damaged than she thought.

"Not now. We need to rest. We'll go during the night, when there are no priests or medics wandering around. There's a safe place for us inside the mountain." She led him around to the tunnel and fitted both of their headlamps. "Through here."

Manipulating him as though he were a juvenile was repulsive. She needed the Ben who was older and wiser and had so much to teach her about life. Even if he did scoff at her naïveté and self-delusion sometimes.

He climbed into the tunnel first. The way he entered, confidently with no questions, reinforced her belief that he had some memories still intact.

When she reached the end of the tunnel, he wasn't waiting to help her, as he had been the first time. He stood a few steps away. The light from his headlamp reflected off the rushing water of the stream. Centa pulled herself through into the cavern. Rock tore at the knees of her trousers and grazed her palms.

The cavern wasn't wondrous or interesting to her any longer. She didn't bother letting her eyes adjust to the luminescence. She felt her way over to the stash of supplies and lit the battery-operated lantern. She lifted her mask briefly and took a small sip of air. It was still free of the scent of vine dust. She removed her mask completely. Like a child who'd grown out of sucking their thumb, it no longer gave her comfort. She'd always trusted the masks to protect them, but they hadn't been enough to ensure the safety of the community.

The cold, damp air of the cavern seeped through to her bones. Her head pounded and her leg and back muscles cramped from lack of sleep and repeated adrenaline bursts.

But she had to begin.

She sat Ben down on the blankets and spoke until her throat was dry and her jaw ached. She repeated what she'd said in the buggy. There were only a finite number of accounts and facts about Ben that she possessed and a finite number of experiences they'd shared.

The hard ground numbed her backside. She shook her legs and stretched her shoulders. Ben didn't seem to suffer the same discomforts. He sat motionless, sometimes with his eyes closed and sometimes looking straight through her. When he did respond, it had nothing to do with whatever she'd been speaking about. Just *Earth has room for you too*, or *We are still Earth's children*. Occasionally he even used her name, and she glimpsed a future where he was by her side as they faced the daunting challenges of a life outside the settlement. He even looked into her eyes when she touched his hand, embraced him, or kissed him on the temple.

Her last weapons were his memories of Earth, which she wielded with some guilt. They weren't good memories, and he had shared them with her grudgingly and with an implied trust, but she had nothing left to try.

"When you were ten, your part of Earth was hot and dusty, and when it wasn't dusty, it was flooded. There was even less food than we have here, and clean water was even more precious. You and the other children who lived in the caravan park with their families, ran wild while your parents scavenged. You spent your days playing, stealing, and taking any psychoactive drugs you could get a hold of. Kids disappeared. Some of them were conscripted into firefighting or enslaved by local militia. The air was regularly thick and smoky, the sky either red with dust or brownish-grey with pollution. There was barely anything green left on Earth."

A smile spread across Ben's face. "Yes, Earth."

"That's what you want to go back to?"

"The vine will send all of us to Earth."

"I don't think I want to go there. It sounds horrible. And the vine devours people. It doesn't put them in a ship to send them home. I don't even understand what you expect to happen if you let it have you."

Still smiling, Ben paid her no mind. She needed to get through to him. Her sharpest weapon, left in reserve in the hope of never having to use it, was his most painful memory.

"One night your parents hid you behind some metal barrels while they scaled the fence of an industrial food complex. Your mother was an expert at picking locks. They were going to break into a big garbage receptacle and collect as much discarded food as they could carry. They'd done it before. There was never any trouble. You sat behind those barrels in the orange glow of the lights from nearby factories, and you heard gunshots. Then nothing. You waited all night. Your parents never came back."

She paused for a response. Ben stared off into the distance as though he hadn't heard a word. Centa hadn't understood biological families before he had shared his grief over the loss of his parents. Skyfather had been the only parental figure in her life. Ben had said the bond wasn't the same.

"You sat there all the next day in the baking heat. Your tongue became fat with dehydration, and your skin burnt and blistered. Sweat soaked your clothes and dried to salt. You were barely conscious when your aunt found you at dusk. She took care of you until she couldn't anymore. Until her pollution-induced emphysema made her desperate for medication and she sold you to Skyfather. You never found out if your parents died that night or were taken somewhere. You never heard from them ever again."

Tears streamed down his cheeks. There was a softening in his face, the kindness she remembered.

"Ben?" It was the most reaction she'd had from him all day. It was something.

"I'll see them again, on Earth." He lay down and turned his back to her.

"They're dead now. There's no one there for you." Centa wiped her tears and snot with the hem of her shirt.

He was already snoring. He'd given in to the sedatives and vine dust damage once again.

She lay behind him and pulled a blanket over them both. She needed his comfort to remind her why she was there and what she could lose if she failed. She placed her arm over his hip and pressed the front of her body against his back. He was warm and solid. In his sleeping form she saw the possibility of the man she loved.

Spears of rock dangled above, ready to fall and impale them. She was certain they'd made progress, but she would need to keep at it once they'd both rested, or all her efforts could be in vain. She kissed the back of his neck and he sighed with what sounded like contentment. Her heart leapt. He was still Ben, and he was still hers.

· · · ● · ● · ● · ● · ·

Centa was flushed from the peaceful womb of sleep by a drip of water in her ear. She didn't know how long she'd slept. All her bones and muscles ached, and she was thirsty and hungry.

Ben was gone.

She sat up. The cavern glowed green with bioluminescence, as though they were inside the vine, being devoured by the planet. He must have set out for the settlement when night fell.

How had he left without waking her?

Centa rushed to the tunnel, snapping the thin, hollow stalactites in her way. She winced as she knocked the scabs off her knees against the rough rock. She'd failed. She'd thought she'd known him well enough to get through to him. Maybe nobody could really know another person, not unless they climbed into their skin and looked out through their eyes. Maybe not even then.

Outside the sky was cloudy and dark. Blood dripped from her knees and dried on her shins. The thought of repairing herself with vine leaves was repugnant, a capitulation to the vine's power. She called out for Ben, but there was no answer.

The buggy was still where she'd left it and the patch of vine that he'd lowered himself onto when they'd first arrived looked undisturbed. She searched the immediate area with no luck. Maybe he hadn't come out through the tunnel. The story of his parents seemed to have gotten through to him. A little. He could still be in the cavern somewhere, exploring or making preparations for their new life. He'd laugh at her for assuming the worst.

Back in the cavern she followed the stream to the tunnel that Ben had shown her on that first visit. He'd spoken of a lake with edible algae on the other side. She tightened her headlamp and after a short crawl through ice-cold, wrist-deep water, the tunnel opened into another cavern with a small lake, about the size of the mothership. The surface was covered with glowing blue algae. It was breathtaking, as though a piece of the sky had been painted on the floor. Maybe there was a Spirit of Aceso, only Skyfather had no connection to it.

Ben wasn't there. She sat and hugged her knees to her chest. She didn't know what to do next. Embedded in the rock of the cave wall in front of her was the bottom half of a fossilized, elongated jaw with pointy teeth. She'd never seen a living animal that would fit such a jaw. There were billions of years of the planet's history that they'd never know or understand. They barely knew what lay more than one hundred kilometres from the settlement.

She turned off her headlamp and let her eyes adjust. Slowly, as though she were turning the knob for the lamp on her microscope, green luminescence appeared on every surface.

Trickling water echoed around the rock walls. Maybe she could sit there in the blue and green heart of the planet, doing nothing and feeling nothing. Her gaze mapped the contours of her rock chamber. Her attention kept returning to a place on the opposite side of the lake. A darker swirl in the luminescence, etched into a boulder. It was a hole that marked another, smaller tunnel.

She stretched out her legs, walked over to it, and stuck her head inside. "Ben?"

His name echoed away, but there was no response. She switched on her headlamp again and crawled inside. Air from somewhere ahead kept her moving forward until she emerged into an even bigger cavern, three times the size of the mothership. The space was filled with stalactites and stalagmites.

Ben wasn't there.

She switched off her headlamp and waited. Several dark tunnels and alcoves dotted the walls, and the floor was littered with objects: lizard-pig skins sewn together, rusted metal bowls and tools, and small rocks arranged in concentric circles. Many of the items were fused to the floor with a material of the same texture as the stalactites and stalagmites, and they were all covered with a film of glowing green algae.

Did the masters and Skyfather know anything about this? They were too arrogant to look beyond their own settlement. They preferred to think of themselves as alone and unique in the universe, and they did nothing but sit around in the mothership trying to create some semblance of the life they thought they were entitled to. They'd kept the workers' worlds small so that their expectations and ambitions would match.

Centa wiped away algae on a smooth section of wall and discovered a set of intricately detailed paintings. The first showed a circle, maybe a planet, engulfed in flames. The second showed a ship or a comet streaking through the darkness of space. In the third, it had cracked open on the planet's surface, and long-limbed, non-human creatures were climbing out.

This was an account of the lives of the beings who'd once inhabited the cavern. This was art. Ben had told her about art. In her mind she'd equated it with the moving pictures used to teach the children. But this was something else.

Centa rushed to decipher the rest of the account. Stylized leaves and tendrils crowded the edges of the next panels, and the beings fought the vine with tools and bare hands until they were completely entangled, their ship smothered in vine. Some of them had fled to the cavern she now stood in. But the vine had found them there too. The final panel was empty, a white square painted on the rock.

Whoever or whatever they were, they were gone now.

There was no hope. The Sky Humans had been destined to fail from the moment the mothership had landed. Centa and the other workers were nothing more than antibiotics targeted at a resistant infection.

She couldn't breathe the damp, stale air any longer. He headlamp dimmed a fraction and the rock walls and ceiling seemed suddenly closer. She ran and scrambled through cavern and tunnel, without stopping for tears in her clothing or scrapes on her skin.

Outside the father star had risen and its rays warmed her cold, damp clothing. Bat-birds screeched from one treetop to another.

Not far from the entrance of the cave was a patch of vine that hadn't been there the evening before, the approximate shape and size of a human.

The approximate shape and size of Ben.

Something glistened between two leaves. She leaned closer. An eyeball, one of Ben's beautiful brown eyes, slid slowly backwards into the vine, transforming from white to gelatinous green. Another cruelty from the vine, to make her last memory of Ben to be as no more than flesh and organs. She pushed aside her mask and retched. Her bile sent a cloud of vine bugs into a frenzy, and she spat to get the taste of dust and vomit out of her mouth.

There was no one around to police her emotion, so she screamed at the sky and punched herself in the chest. She hated Ben, hated how he'd hurt her more than she'd ever thought possible. He'd made her do stupid things and make unforgiveable mistakes. But could she stand a life without him? It would be easy to lie down alongside his shape in the vine. He had made it seem peaceful and honourable. This planet didn't want them, but a planet across the universe did. She felt it too. She'd always felt it. The call of Earth.

She shook the thought from her head. She needed to escape.

She replaced her mask and began to climb the mountain, scrabbling to get away from the vine. Rays from the father star burnt into her scalp, and sweat ran between her shoulder blades and darkened the armpits of her shirt. The scabs on her knees cracked and bled freely, soil coating the open wounds on her palms.

After nearly an hour she reached a plateau near the highest peak. A strong gust of wind blew dirt into her eyes and whipped her hair around her face. She looked towards the settlement. The trees and their steadfast companion, the vine, stretched out as far as she could see. Broken here and there by small rocky mounds and splodges of water that looked like organelles inside a cell, like the whole planet was a cell and humans were only pathogens that it was trying to neutralize and expel.

There was nothing left for her. Her attempts to make things better had only made them worse.

She put her face in her hands and visualized smashing her head against the rocks until her skull split open and bone shards penetrated her brain.

. . . ● . ● ● . . .

The smoke of the pyre guided Centa back to the settlement. The vine was so much thicker on the ground than the day before. She couldn't even make out the root barrier trench. She drove slowly, on the lookout for the posts that marked Rae's Bridge.

Further along, where their fields had been, stems of kudzu reached out from amongst the vine, their leaves brown and wilted at the edges. Beyond the fields the vine rose into a dome-like shape. She halted. That was where the agronomy hab had been. She could just make out its entrance among the greenery. The scene was more unreal than a vine leaf-induced cleansing trance. It had all happened so fast.

Centa didn't dare leave the safety of the buggy. She leaned on the horn. Nobody came from the hab or the surrounding fields. If they couldn't walk to her then they were beyond any help she could give.

A trio of chickens ran around the side of the building, leaping over tufts of twisted vine in their path as something chased them. It was green and almost, but not quite, chicken shaped, and it flopped and oozed as though it had no bones. What had they been breeding at the agronomy hab? Was she hallucinating already? She watched the quartet disappear around a corner. The events of the past days had left her numb, and she didn't know what more it would take to shock her.

As she drove, everywhere she looked was green and alive. Light sparkled off trillions of particles of dust. Vine draped over the habs and mothership like bacteria on an agar plate, suffocating the community with the efficiency of Master Anton's hand over the mouth of a malformed newborn.

Workers meandered in circles through the dust and burrowed into nests of leaf, their skin ashen and their eyes empty. She hit the horn and shouted at them, but they didn't even turn their heads. There was no saving any of these Sky Humans, many of whom she'd raised from frozen clumps of cells. Her work had been worthless. All these lives, worthless.

Centa edged the buggy to the edge of the mothership and took several deep breaths of clear, filtered air before fitting her mask. She closed the door swiftly and held her breath. Her mask was as good as useless against this concentration of dust. A worker skittered past, muttering about Earth and vine, but Centa ignored her, sprinting to the cargo hold door and pulling at the handle. It was locked. She'd never known the cargo hold to be locked.

"Let me in!" she screamed, unable to hold her breath any longer, her lungs burning as she pounded on the metal door.

But no one came.

Her vision shimmered and danced as she stumbled back to the buggy and crawled inside. Dust covered her clothing and formed clumps on the oily skin of her face, and the world was spinning faster and faster all around her.

She flew from the surface of Aceso, tossed by the tilting planet through endless, empty space until she was hurtling towards a marbled sphere of green, blue, white, and brown. She would find what she needed there. She need only lie on the vine.

Centa shoved the hallucination away and took deep breaths of clean air until she was back in the buggy with the vine-choked settlement still dying around her. Even if she did make it into the mothership or a hab that hadn't been breached, what then? They would soon run out of food and water. The settlement was finished.

She could drive away, return to the mountains, where the vine was placid. But Ben had only collected a week's worth of supplies, and she would be alone with nothing but the promise that the vine would find her eventually.

And where was Perpetua in all this chaos? It was painful to think of her dead.

A worker knelt in a patch of vine a few metres from the buggy. Their eyes met Centa's, and they smiled before slipping beneath the surface, as though they were diving into a lake. Maybe it wouldn't be so bad to open the vehicle doors. But as Centa reached for the handle, a tendril snaked over the buggy bonnet. She pulled her hand away. What was she thinking? She must have inhaled too much dust.

She lifted her foot to press the accelerator but stopped herself. On the ground near the front of the buggy was a hand-leaf like the ones she'd created from worker gametes. She leaned forward and peered through the windscreen, squinting against the dust. Once she'd spotted one hand-leaf she saw more, linked together along vine tendrils and runners. They were grotesque. But hadn't the abomination she'd created been incinerated along with the incubators? Unless more embryos had been fertilized.

Perpetua.

She followed the trail of hand-leaves to the laboratory hab, whispering *die, die, die* as they crunched and popped beneath the buggy's wheels. The vine had found a weakness in the thick plastic of the link near the laboratory, and the hand-leaves held the breach open like surgical clamps. At the other end of the link, where it joined the mothership, the door was shut tight against the questing vine. Perpetua was in the lab. Centa knew it in the way she knew where her own arms and legs were. In the laboratory she would learn the truth about everything. And the vine would take her home, take her to Earth.

She fixed her mask and climbed out of the buggy. All around her, the habs were being reclaimed by a healing blanket of green. And it felt right.

There was nothing but suffering left for her on Aceso. Especially without Ben. She would have liked to have him here beside her, holding her hand while Skyfather's dream collapsed.

She shoved streamers of vine aside and stepped through the breach. The room was alive and crisscrossed with green. Hand-leaves opened and closed with the rhythm of a heartbeat. Stems, tendrils, and runners wound around the benches and over the equipment. One of the hand-leaves held a pipette aloft.

Centa heard a moan to her left. "You came back. I knew you would."

Perpetua was suspended in a web of vine, limp and pale.

Centa fought her way through. "Perpetua!"

"That's your name for me," she said, her eyes unfocussed and pupils fully dilated.

"What?"

"Perpetua. That's what you call me."

"It doesn't mean anything." Centa suddenly felt ashamed of the name she had given to the person closest to her. The person who knew her even better than anyone, even Ben.

"Yes, it does. It means we'll always be together." Perpetua shifted and the vine around her vibrated. "We were waiting for you. Now the vine can return us." The room pulsed a deeper green. The vine grew stronger, greener, lusher, while Perpetua dissolved into it like salts in water.

"Wait! Tell me what happened!"

Perpetua opened her eyes, only her face still visible from her cocoon of vine, and smiled. "I fertilised them all."

They had frozen hundreds of ova from the comatose workers. The incubator would have been overflowing with dishes.

"Why?" Dust coated the inside of Centa's mouth and nostrils. The vine glittered around her with an inner light, and Centa *knew* why, even as she raised her arms above her head and tendrils loosed from Perpetua's own bundle of vine and lifted her, ever so gently into the air, drawing her close, Centa *knew*. Outside, day was giving way to dusk as the father star set on their community for the last time.

"It was a trap," Perpetua said, head tilted at the glossy patch of vine heaped beside Master Anton's office. "But it was stronger than I expected. I didn't know it would be a gift to us all."

For years Centa had pretended not to notice or care how Master Anton had used Perpetua for his own sick and selfish desires. Centa had failed her friend like she'd failed Tilter, like she'd failed Ben. But now she could let it all go. Now she could let the vine bear it for her.

She felt a warm tingle as the vine fused with her skin, wrapping itself almost lovingly around her legs, her arms, her neck. Maybe now she would be reunited with Ben, all of them together on Earth. She conjured a vision of him — the curve of his jaw, the golden strands of hair through his brown ponytail, the frizzy grey hair at his temples, that one front tooth at an angle to the others, the dirt beneath his fingernails, the touch of his lips on the back of her neck.

Everything became green. *She* became green. And across the universe, Earth called to her. She finally understood. Humans thought their obligation was to preserve their own species. But their obligation was to Earth itself. Earth had brought them into being for reasons they'd never understand. And Earth wanted them for itself. It had a purpose for them. A long, geological, and evolutionary game they wouldn't know the outcome of for generations to come. If ever.

Part of her knew her visions and feelings were being created by vine spores as they germinated in her brain and manipulated neural pathways. But she didn't care. She'd never felt less afraid or more peaceful. She would rather this vine trick than the feeling of her body being digested by acids and enzymes.

As her body became less, her consciousness became more. Expanded by the mycelial connections the vine had established within everyone and everything on the planet. She felt connections snap as the vine digested the bodies of other Sky Humans and sent what it couldn't use back to their source. It would be all right. She would go too, and she would find Perpetua and Ben.

Her body, as she knew it, ceased to exist. Each cell was absorbed, transformed, and recycled into something new. Finally, the last of her broke loose from Aceso's grip and she was transported from one planet to another, like sugar molecules through an intergalactic mycelial network.

Second Interlude

R ae could feel the vine. Closer. Stronger. Promising escape. Yet it wasn't close enough. She needed to touch it. Be absorbed and transformed into stems, tendrils, and leaves. Sent home to her grandparents on Earth.

All the workers were joyfully departing the planet like rockets. The dark forest of nothing was empty of apparitions. Even Ben was gone. Aceso filled her head with a babbling cacophony she couldn't understand.

The mothership was besieged. She knew she would eventually be free. But the ship's hull was strong. It could take years for the vine to break through. The so-called masters might die of starvation before then. There was a chance the vine could become even shrewder, strengthened by the absorbed intelligence of those it released. Perhaps one of the masters might even see beyond the vine's beastly guise to the prince within. Or one of them could make a mistake. But Rae couldn't wait any longer to be rescued. She was no helpless princess.

Chimera hands knocked and scrabbled against the hull. Victoria cried in the corner. She said she should never have come. That he'd fooled her back on Earth. Made her think he was someone special. Told her there was a place for them across the galaxy. But he was only a man. All her beliefs had meant nothing in the end. She pretended this was a moment of personal revelation.

"He's a brain-dead old fool. A con man who took us all for everything we had so he could be king on a distant planet," she said.

They all pretended to have their own moments of personal revelation. The naked Emperor at last acknowledged. Their anger was a performance for their own consciences.

Master Kara suggested flying away in the mothership.

Master Helena scoffed. "This ship hasn't flown in twenty-five earthyears. We don't even have fuel for launch. Or a launch pad for that matter. This was always going to be a one-way trip."

"Unless we can get to the kitchen hab, we'll run out of food sooner rather than later," Kara said. "And where's Anton?"

None of them knew what had happened to Master Anton, but Rae could feel him through the vine network. He was almost on his way to Earth.

"What about...?" Rae couldn't see her but imagined her stepmother's eyes on her. To Victoria she was nice and plump, like Hansel and Gretel fattened up by the witch.

"It's barely been a day. I don't think we're quite at the stage of stooping to cannibalism," Helena said. "We need to discuss real solutions."

In the middle of it all Ophelia whimpered. She was Rae's escape.

The arguments continued as Rae dressed herself in Ophelia's skin more completely than she had before. She kept away from the woman's highly agitated mind. The panic of the other masters had infected her. Together they stood on wobbly legs and slowly shuffled forward.

None of the others noticed them reach the door of the bridge. They had ceased to acknowledge Ophelia's presence long before. Like Cinderella, Rae left behind a slipper to keep the doors wedged open a crack. Each step took all her concentration.

Ophelia muttered. Her panic rose. But Rae held control with everything she had.

The scrabbling and pounding of the chimera hands was louder in the hallway. Rae guided Ophelia to the laboratory link. Where the call of the vine was strongest. The door was secured with a wheel handle. Ophelia's hands were thin and wrinkled. Frail. Her fingers misshapen from years of work as a medic.

They pushed against the wheel. It resisted. They tried again and again. Rae disconnected from the pain in Ophelia's hands. Skin tore and bones fractured. Ophelia cried and screamed. But Rae didn't stop. The elderly woman would be free of her body soon. Rae was saving her. The wheel gave with a jerk. The vine and its chimeras did the rest.

Her first instinct was to lean into the vine. But she fled. Leaving Ophelia to be blessed with the vine's embrace first. Rae returned to her own body. Settled into her unresponsive flesh.

The vine came quickly, through the open bridge doors. Too quickly for the dust to lull Victoria and the masters. They screamed as they were devoured. The vine encircled Rae. Its tendrils gripped and held her in a way she hadn't been held since she was a child, tighter and tighter, until finally the thorns pierced do deeply that she could feel again. But just as the pain became almost unbearable, she was freed.

Her last image of that world was a stalk of vine erupting out of her chest. Then she was on her way to Grandma's house.

Part 2

EARTH

Year 2337

10

Stargazing with Wolf, the travelling sperm-purveyor, might have been romantic if it wasn't for the wafts of rot from the toxic lake and the frantic bleats of feral sheep on the far shore.

Pixie splayed her fingers against the dirt until she could feel Wolf's aura, or life-force or whatever you wanted to call it, through the tip of her little finger. Electricity crackled across the gap between them. That's how she pictured it anyway. Could be it was just one of the fading effects of the shrooms they'd shared at full sun.

Wolf pointed up at the sky beyond the granite outcrop of Fairy Park. "See that star over there? The dim one between the two bright ones."

The stars blurred and throbbed and played leapfrog across Pixie's vision. "Yeah," she lied.

"There's a planet orbiting that star. It's called Aceso. Years ago, some of the Earth Guardian founders put themselves into cryo-chambers and took a ship to colonize it. Back when it was getting real hectic down here." Wolf lowered her arm and rested her hands on her chest, a galaxy away from Pixie's.

"Wow. That's so cool." If it had been anyone but Wolf talking, she wouldn't have believed it. She'd only met the woman days before, but she already knew Wolf wouldn't lie. And she was so much more interesting than anyone Pixie had ever met, with her tales of the road and her home at a high-tech Earth Guardian compound. At Fairy Park it was all breeding schedules, and menstrual cycles, and weeks of gestation, and *why don't you ever get off your ass and contribute to the community, Pixie?*

Merlin, the brindle-coated dog who'd started following Pixie around after she'd slipped him bits of gristle under the dinner table, pounced on her and plonked his muddy paws all over her chest.

"Ah! Get off!"

He ran back to Wolf's dog, Lucy, who was chewing on something rank by the edge of the lake.

Pixie brushed clods of mud from her shirt and lay back down. "Does anyone have contact with them?" She liked the idea of stretching her fingertips across the universe to connect with humans on another planet. The stories they could tell.

"Nope. We don't even have the technology to do something like that anymore."

They silently contemplated the stars for a moment.

Wolf cleared her throat. "Although, I've heard that the planets communicate with each other and send things back and forth. The way all the plants and trees in a forest have an underground fungal network that connects them."

Pixie sat up, leant on her elbow, and giggled. "What?"

Wolf screwed up her face. "I dunno. It's just a thing I read somewhere. It said shrooms were sent from another planet to help humanity find compassion for nature."

"Nice try, planets. I don't think it worked."

Wolf chuckled, and Pixie basked in the glow of her amusement. She was beginning to get a post-trip tension headache. Above them on the outcrop, villagers bustled and clattered about by the light of night-glowing ivy, solar lamps, and barrel fires.

Wolf removed her hands from her chest and placed them on the ground once again. The tip of her little finger brushed against Pixie's.

Pixie blushed all over. Should she take her hand? Or would that be too much? She'd never been very good at getting close to anyone. She didn't want to mess up her chances with Wolf.

The dogs bounded over and muscled their way between them. Lucy's tail whipped their faces until they were forced to scoot farther apart. Pixie's romantic intentions were foiled, or more likely she was saved from making a wrong move.

What kind of move did she want anyway? Sex had never been her thing, and Wolf had made it clear that it wasn't hers either. She claimed all her semen was deposited into glass jars, even though some villages, especially those with poor infection control protocols, offered direct deposits into a willing uterus.

The cries of a newborn came from up high on the outcrop, followed by the shrieks of a toddler who wanted their share of attention too. Pixie's face hurt from all the laughing they'd done while the shrooms were kicking in.

"Do you have to leave tomorrow?"

All the other travellers who came to Fairy Park were gruff, hairy types who never cracked a smile. They treated Pixie like she was as pointless as a crashed satellite. Especially when she made it clear they wouldn't be putting their dicks in her.

Wolf was the first sperm-woman Pixie had ever met. There was a breeder at Fairy Park who was a man, and everyone was fine with that as long as he did his duty and popped out babies. But Pixie had never thought about it going the other way. If she had the right parts, she would have loved to be a sperm-woman. Having adventures on the road would be far better than spending every day of her life defending her uterus from a parasitic take-over. Plus, Mama Gretel wouldn't be there every time she turned around calling her *as lazy as a ship in the doldrums* or one of her other nonsensical, old-timey insults.

"Gretel says she has enough of my semen for now, but she's invited me to return any time."

"I bet she did." Pixie pushed up onto her side to look at Wolf over the flea-bitten backs of the dogs.

Mama Gretel had been thrilled to get sperm from a member of such an advantageously gene-edited population. According to her, Wolf was a superior specimen, with her tall, strong build, cute, upturned nose, and perfectly straight teeth. Not like Pixie needed convincing of that. They'd had to keep Wolf's lineage a secret from Mama Rosamund though. She frequently preached that all high-tech community members were possessed by the demons of technology. Pixie could almost quote her evil neoliberal descendants rant word for word.

"Where you off to next?" she asked Wolf.

"A village to the north, I think. Just following the Traveller's Guide and Map." She pulled a small book out of the inner pocket of her jacket and waved it in the air. "This is my whole life now."

"Two years," Pixie whispered to herself.

"What's that?"

"Oh nothing." She blushed. "It's just that it could be two years before I see you again." Maybe knowing Pixie was waiting for her would add speed to Wolf's stride around the sperm circuit. "Soon there'll be little Wolf babies all over the country."

"As long as I don't have to raise 'em," Wolf said. "Did Mama Gretel try to get some of my last contribution into you?"

"She tried, but I outran her."

Wolf laughed. "You're going to be outrunning them for the rest of your fertile years."

Pixie had long ago given up trying to justify her unwillingness to breed. Why should she? The mamas had never given her a good reason to donate years of her life to their baby factory. Everyone simply accepted that it was *the way things were* or *the right thing to do* because of tradition, or human nature, or the continuation of the species, or something else that could never be challenged unless you wanted to be considered a troublemaker.

"I wonder if the breeders on Aceso have to put up with this kind of shit." Pixie grabbed Merlin around the neck and nuzzled her cheek against his jaw.

"Good chance," Wolf said. "Everyone everywhere is obsessed with reproducing. I'd be out of a job otherwise."

"Ugh. Why can't the species just die out with dignity?"

Pixie flipped over and pressed her face into the dirt. She could travel all the way across the universe and still never escape the liability of being born with a uterus.

11

Pixie was daydreaming about Wolf, her head against the corrugated metal wall of the honey shed, when Mama Goldy barged in.

"Get up, you lazy cow." There was nothing golden about the woman. She was more like a skeleton clad in papery grey skin. "The honey's overflowing."

Pixie flicked away her dried eye-snot and headed over to the extractor. Sure enough, honey had dripped over the edges of the sieve, down the sides of the pail and onto the dirty floor. Just her luck.

"Can't we just scrape off the dirty bits?"

"Don't be stupid."

Pixie peered into the almost empty pail. "Why did it overflow anyway? It's not supposed to do that. Why isn't it going through the sieve?"

"Because it's full of wax," Mama Goldy said and smacked her in the back of the head. "What did I tell you about taking off as much was as possible?"

This was the first time Pixie had completed the whole process on her own, from yanking the frames of comb away from their vicious makers, to bottling the honey. It was the test to prove she was a worthy beekeeper. Even though she was pretty sure she didn't want to be a beekeeper. But she had to do something if she wanted to get fed. Everyone had to contribute in some way.

"But that takes ages," Pixie answered.

Mama Goldy smacked her again. "I don't care how long it takes. That's your bloody job."

Mama scraped wax away from the sieve, and the honey started flowing again. She lifted a finger to her lips for a taste.

"How much smoke did you use?"

"I don't know. The usual amount."

Pixie had used way more than the usual amount.

"Bullshit. The honey's tainted. I suppose that should make me less pissed-off that half of it's on the ground."

"Let me taste it." Pixie wound a sticky glob of the golden, flowing honey around a finger and stuck it into her mouth. So sweet. It was a definite benefit of the job. She licked the honey from around her teeth and grimaced. There was a weird, burnt aftertaste.

"It's not that bad. A bit different. But you're the one who said every batch of honey's unique, depending on which flowers the bees visit. See, I've been listening."

"Enough!" Mama Goldy said. "Can't you even admit when you've done something wrong, Pixie?"

"The honey's okay. The youngsters'll eat anything sweet. I'll spend more time on the wax next time."

"The honey's not okay. Tell me you'll be more careful with the smoke. That you'll use less. A lot less."

Pixie couldn't say that. It wasn't just the bee's stings that bothered her. She didn't want their little black legs and hairy bodies to touch her. She'd use however much smoke it took. "I'll be more careful."

Beekeeping had sounded like a cool way to contribute, but the protective gear was stuffy and sweaty, and it made her even more clumsy than usual. Plus, she couldn't help squealing every time she thought a bee had gotten inside her suit or veil.

"Do you really want to be a beekeeper?" Mama Goldy asked.

Pixie screwed up her face. It wasn't the worst job, but there was no point in pretending it was more than that. "Not really."

Mama Goldy scowled at her. "Then piss off, Pixie. I'm sick of your face. Find another way to contribute. I didn't want you here in the first place. Go find Mama Rosamund and ask her to find another job for you."

Pixie stomped away, past the old pit latrine that was another failure of hers. She hadn't filled it in properly, and one of the youngsters had run over the top of it and broken his ankle in an air pocket.

Beekeeping had been cool in some ways. There were only a couple of harvests a year, and after that just minor maintenance stuff. But she'd fucked it up, like every job she'd tried. She just wanted to find something easy that she was good at and that didn't involve popping out babies. The mamas, and the universe, all had it in for her.

Merlin ran down the steep path that led up to the village, his tail wagging. He stopped to bark at the field of milk-beasts and weave through their legs. Pixie had briefly been responsible for collecting and drying milk-beast dung, until she'd found playing hide and seek with youngsters more fun, and the piles of dung had become too wet and fermented to burn for fuel. Everyone, even the youngsters, had given Pixie dirty looks after that. Mostly because no one liked the taste of uncooked food or the worms that hatched in their innards. She hadn't minded being kicked out of that smelly, boring job.

"Were you waiting for me all morning, Merlin?" The dog usually followed her everywhere, but his kind weren't allowed close to the hives.

He fell into a trot next to her. Fairy Park was quiet. Most folk had retreated to their shelters to escape full sun. A group of scavengers on the path ahead dumped their finds by the kitchen for the mamas to go through at dusk. Pixie had tried working with them too. She'd been optimistic about that one. A bit of travelling, seeing new places. But she'd always brought back smooth pieces of glass and bits of bright plastic that she found interesting instead of useful items like tools or metal. They'd told her she didn't have *the eye* when they pushed her out of their crew.

She stopped to refill her water bottle at the desalinator shed next to the kitchen. Her crime there had been leaving the shed to get some cooler air. When the unattended condenser had gotten too hot, all the sea water had been lost as steam.

She'd been shooed away from just about every job at Fairy Park. She put a lot of it down to bad luck. Now she'd fucked up beekeeping and she didn't know what to try next. It was like picking all the weevils out of your flour, only to find yourself left with no flour at all.

The mamas liked to say everyone had a purpose in life and a way to contribute, not just to the village, but to the rebuilding of humanity. They were the chosen ones who kept the flame of humanity alive through these dark times, or so Mama Rosamund said. Pixie had no idea what her purpose was. She was pretty sure it wasn't breeding. One thing she did enjoy was giving people stick and poke tattoos. But the mamas didn't consider that a contribution. Without a mama-approved purpose, Pixie was as good as useless.

The sun was fierce and the gravel under her feet burned through the worn patches on the bottom of her shoes. She paused at the side path that led to Mama Goldy's fungal grow house. The last time she'd had shrooms had been with Wolf, two months earlier. A spasm of grief tugged at her guts. She detoured off the main path and headed for the small, red-roofed cottage with a huge, chugging climate-controller, which used up most of their generated electricity, on its faded red roof. Merlin peered up at her, panting.

"You keep lookout for me." He found a sliver of shade and lay down on the hot ground, snapping at flies.

She eased the creaky door open. Inside was freezing, dark and damp, with a musty odour. The walls were lined with wooden shelves full of buckets covered by tarps. She lifted the tarps one by one, revealing a variety of medicinal fungi, until she found a flush of thin-stalked, brown-capped mushrooms ready to pick. She bent them gently to the side and snapped their bases from the soil.

She had the touch for harvesting. She'd even suggested that could be her role, but the mamas didn't trust her. As always, they knew best. She wouldn't trust herself around shrooms all the time either. She shoved her harvest into her pockets, replaced the tarp, and ran with Merlin at her heels all the way up to her shelter at the hot, dusty summit of Fairy Park.

Mama Gretel always said you needed to get out of bed to straighten the sheets, and Pixie only knew one way to get out of the messy bed that was her mind.

· · · · ● · ● · ● · · ·

Puff the dragon shimmered in the flickering light of solar lamps. Pixie tried to see the fractals. She knew she'd had a good dose of psilocybin when the geometry behind everything appeared. Wolf had called it glimpsing the code of the simulation, whatever that meant. She leaned forward on her knees and stared at the chipped paint on Puff's long, sharp teeth. The repeating triangles and hexagons weren't there. Not this time. She wasn't high enough for the dragon to speak to her and deliver the final fragments that she needed to figure out her purpose.

The youngsters giggled and whacked on the skin drum, hooting and hollering. Hansel tripped over his own feet and barrelled into her. Mab, the youngest of the shroom crew, rolled across the ground and came to rest against Pixie's side.

"Shut up, you lot," she shouted, pushing Hansel onto his ass and rolling Mab gently away. The girl was a fragile little thing and sweeter than the others, at least some of the time.

"*Shut up, shut up,*" The youngsters mocked her with their shit-eating grins.

If only Pixie didn't hate tripping alone. Then she never would have shared her shrooms with these assholes. It had been fun at first. She and Aladdin had made each other scream with laughter, though they were probably laughing at their own jokes and not even hearing each other.

She was already coming down from her mediocre high. By the time she'd weeded out the youngsters who'd laughed at her for losing her beekeeping job and divided the shrooms amongst the worthy, there had been just enough for five each. Too few for Pixie to enter what she called the fairy world, where her mind joined with Puff's. She should have scoffed some before divvying them up. Live and learn, as Mama Gretel always said.

"Puff, Puff, Puff," the youngsters chanted, their limbs snakelike and swaying.

Mab, lay on her back, breathing funny. She whispered to herself as tears streamed down her face and snot bubbled out of her cute, button nose. Always wanting to keep up with the big kids, she'd sworn she could handle five, and Pixie was kicking herself for not cutting her off sooner. But she never was much of an authority figure, even though at twenty-one, there were almost four years between her and the older youngsters.

Aladdin, the oldest, plonked down next to her, his round white face beaming. He rubbed her leg through the rough cloth of her trousers.

"Mama Gretel doesn't need to know," he whispered.

Like all the older youngsters, he was eager to get started on his breeding duties. She elbowed him in the chest. Mama Gretel had her charts and plans. And Pixie wasn't interested in being part of any of them.

Plus, she didn't like to be touched that way. Everyone supposed it was just because she didn't want to be a birthmother, but it was more than that. She never could understand the obsession all the youngsters had with sex. Sometimes she even suspected the whole *everybody loves sex* thing was all a joke or a myth. Like how the mamas told the youngest youngsters that they'd turn into rabbits and be roasted for dinner if they wandered outside the borders of Fairy Park. Could be they all pretended it was normal to be sex mad so that she'd feel different and wrong. That seemed far-fetched though. As Mama Gretel always told her, she wasn't important enough for folk to think about for too long, let alone keep up such a fancy hoax.

Merlin sniffed at Mab and whined. Pixie pulled him to her before he started licking the snot off the kid's face. She was peaceful now with her eyes closed, smiling up at the sky.

Mama Rosamund appeared out of the darkness below, all hips and thick legs. She brought the aroma of mutton fat with her. "Suppertime," she yelled and glowered at Puff and his worshippers. "You're all idolaters." She whacked Hansel—the last of her birth-sons, conceived accidentally during what the mamas called *the change of life*—in the ear. "You know what happens to idolaters? The greedy and the tech lovers were all idolaters and look what happened to 'em. Look at the mess they left behind. You should all be doing your contributions or your lessons." Soon she'd be talking in tongues again.

"Okay then. Time to go." Pixie struggled to her feet and headed up the outcrop with Merlin sniffing at her ankles.

"You just leaving this mess behind?" Mama Rosamund yelled at her back. "It's always you, Pixie, making the mess and never cleaning up."

Blah, blah, blah.

Babies cried relentlessly inside the breeders' shelter. That sound, all day and night, would do her head in.

"You skipping supper, Pix?" one of the breeders called as she passed. "That's not like you."

She wasn't hungry. Shrooms did that to her. She ignored the voice and climbed to her shelter at the summit. Beyond the reach of the torches and solar lamps, where the only light was the weak luminescence of a smear of moss on the rock.

"Let's look out," she said to Merlin and put her rounded hands to her eyes like they were binoculars.

She was supposed to keep an eye on things from up there and report on any strange folk, storms, fires, or floods heading their way. She didn't usually bother because there was always some other do-gooder who noticed something before she did anyway.

Moonlight glinted on the water of the drowned city in the distance. Merlin sniffed the air and gave a single bark. Someone was coming. Pixie focussed her hand-noculars. A small light, like a fallen star, moved between the night-glowing shrubs that lined the roadway below. Likely a jizz man or some other trader. Lucky bastard, able to travel and see the world.

She yanked down her pants and squatted. Her piss pooled on the rock and a hot gust of wind blew across her baby hole. She sighed. Merlin sniffed at her ass, and she yelped at his cold nose.

"Sniff it up, Merlin."

She yanked up her pants, moved a few steps away from the puddle and lay on her back. The stars pulsated above. The shrooms had given her super eyesight. She stretched out her arms and legs. Now she was a star too. Merlin nestled into her side, soft and whining.

"Your fleas are gonna have to battle my lice for the top spots," she told him as a mosquito alighted on her arm to feed. She didn't begrudge the bloodsuckers of the world. After all, that's what folk often called her too.

12

Centa was moving at high speed, propelled between the stars and planets.

Other travellers crossed her path or ran in parallel, some of them human and others not. She was consciousness without perception, not unlike a dream.

Then, suddenly, she was tiny, unable to think. Wings beat the air around her—her wings?—as a thousand new sensations inundated her. Wind currents ruffled past her, chemical signals flowed through hairs all over her body. Gripping claws and suction pads on her six tiny feet bathed in something red and sticky. Liquid came from deep within her and through her mouthparts, all over the red sticky, then she mopped it up and drank it down. A second of satisfaction before doing it all over again.

Her consciousness strained at the extremities of her container. She found eyes, but the colourless, fragmented visuals meant nothing to her. Every thought fled before she could grasp it. Sensation overwhelmed her. She wanted to think, wanted to recall who she was and how she'd come to be there. Without the narrative of her life, there was no real consciousness.

Motion in her peripheral vision sent her into the air, tiny wings beating impossibly fast. Others like her swarmed and navigated expertly around each other as they found places to settle on the red sticky once again. She experienced these actions with no will or control.

Then she felt a pull and a path opened towards something bigger. Without comprehension of how or even what was happening, she flowed out of the small organism until she was a collection of mass-less particles travelling with purpose, momentarily disembodied once again, but now with some control over her direction. She filled the warm flanks of something bigger, much bigger than where she had been, though still cramped, still smaller than her extremities.

This organism scurried, twitching, fast and alert. She found her way to the eyes and adjusted to the rapid saccades. Shadows invaded by slices and specks of light danced around her, everything blurry and tinged green. The sense of smell was strong and urgent. FOOD—the concept, if not the word, dominated all thought as the organism moved through the dark on the lookout for a meal. Feelers on its face brushed against surfaces and lit the brain with data.

This brain was more complex, and she was able to recall her name.

Centa.

She had been human. Was human. The large creatures around her were human. Noisy young humans, shouting and playing percussion instruments.

The organism hid in the shadows, the concepts of FOOD and DANGER competing for dominance in its head.

There were paths to these humans, but they faded when she tried to travel down them. Then a pull and a brighter, irresistible path opened, and she was again disembodied.

She shifted into a bigger space, something akin to the body she'd known. The brain was as complex as her own. She felt through the synapses, and the resident consciousness scrambled to get a hold on reality. Sensations warped. There was hard ground beneath them, scratchy and loose, and a cacophony of pounding, screeching, laughing. Voices with no discipline. The eyes were closed, yet nonsensical colours and patterns danced along the optic nerve.

Centa retreated to deeper parts to think. She felt tentatively through the body. This was a child. A girl.

The child opened her eyes, and Centa pushed forward to look at the world. Above her loomed a green monster, red eyes, pointy teeth, and cavernous nostrils. But the girl wasn't afraid. The monster wasn't alive. It was metal and paint, animated by shifting light.

The girl looked beyond the monster to a sky filled with stars. Not the stars Centa knew. Not the stars of Aceso.

A thought filled the girl. WHO ARE YOU? MY NAME'S MAB.

Centa's consciousness linked hands with Mab's. They folded and twisted around each other like complementary strands of DNA. She inhabited the child's senses and co-opted her brain to access her own memories. The vine, Aceso, Perpetua and Ben. Loss, destruction, bliss and then escape. What had the vine done to her? Was this the afterlife? Or maybe it was a trick of her brain. How far back had reality ended and this, whatever this was, begun? Master Anton used to say that after centuries of scientific endeavour, there was still no robust mathematical model of consciousness. This had to be some sort of death-dream or vine-induced hallucination.

"No, stupid," the girl told her. "You're with me at Fairy Park and we're high on shrooms, that's all."

"You can hear me? I need help. I don't know how I got here." Now that she'd been acknowledged, Centa wrestled to get control of her panic. This was real. It was happening in some plane of existence. She tried to focus on the facts. "I don't understand anything you're saying. Fairy Park?"

"Yeah, my village. You need me to talk slowly or something? You an inbred baby?" The child snorted and laughed.

Had the vine sent her, and maybe all the others, to Earth as it had promised? Were there any other planets humans had colonized?

"What is the name of your planet?"

Mab guffawed. "You're a tripper. It's Earth. What planet are you from? Planet of bum-head trippers?"

"I've come from Aceso."

"Huh? Are you one of the worms in my shit? They have no eyes, but they wave their little white heads at me like they can see into my soul."

"What? No."

"Are you a guardian angel or a fairy godmother?"

"I'm not familiar with either of those terms. I'm a Sky Human. I've come from Aceso." She suspected Mab would continue asking ridiculous questions if she didn't take control of the conversation. "What year is it?"

"I dunno. The mamas would know, but I don't pay much attention in lessons."

The conversation was going nowhere. The psychoactive properties of a molecule coursing through Mab's body bled into Centa. Their memories became one. Their life on Earth was hedonistic, careless, and joyful—running and hiding when Mama Belle called them to lessons with her low, husky voice, chasing chickens, pushing other kids into the shit pit, drinking a pungent, throat-burning liquid that left them intoxicated and giggling, catching crickets for the fryer. There was also pain and hunger—denied meals when they hadn't contributed, burns from the sun while collecting dung for the kitchen, cuts on their leg from scavenging the edges of the drowned city, days of fever while infections raged. Getting whacked on the bottom by Mama Rosamund when they whispered during prayers.

Centa pulled away and her thoughts and consciousness disentangled from and lay parallel to Mab's. She considered the child's experience of Earth. All Centa had known of the cradle of humanity was what Skyfather and Ben had told her. Mab's memories confirmed that there were numerous dangers. It was as hot and dusty as Ben had described, yet there were days when the sky was clear and the air fresh, and vegetation had overtaken places that used to be concrete and metal. The people were nowhere near as frightening as Skyfather had portrayed them. Mostly they lived in peace, busily occupied with the requirements for survival. Either things had changed in the centuries since Ben and Skyfather had been on Earth, or they had exaggerated the dangers. Maybe both.

Mab's perceptions overwhelmed her again. Sound was an organism made of numerous parts all working together. Rhythmic banging expanded and contracted the air as though everything breathed. The sounds separated and presented themselves individually. Skin drum, recorder, triangle, banjo, xylophone, harmonica, Mab said. The sounds merged again and twirled on, accompanied by chants. Not like the chants Centa knew from Aceso. These were more joyous and free form. Mab said it was music and hadn't Centa ever heard music before? Centa was entranced. If she had a body of her own, she would have danced until she was one with the sound.

Reality, this reality, became more and more dream-like. Light and bodies streaked through her vision. Centa was certain she had achieved some higher purpose. It was all so clear. The vine wasn't the evil agent they had been pitted against since the founding of the settlement. It was a force for good. A protector and repairer of planets. All along, the vine had been trying to restore Aceso's natural state and dismantle Skyfather's lies.

The planets and stars across the galaxy were all in communication. She had sensed it when she was being transported. There was a network like the mycelial network Ben had told her of between the roots of plants. Centa could see it in the sky—repeating geometric patterns made up of lines that connected all the stars and the planets between them. At that moment, she wouldn't have been surprised if someone told her that fungi had created the universe. The threads that Disciple Zenia had seen in the brains of workers overcome by vine dust finally made sense. Vines spores had germinated to become the link between their consciousness and this intergalactic mycelial network that carried them to their true home.

Every single living thing on Earth was descended from a single strand of DNA, the one original lifeform. They were all part of a nearly infinite and intricately complicated global family. Centa became a thread in the web that held the Earth together. Her love for Ben was a part of the fabric of this planet's reality. They were threads woven together. They would find each other.

· · · ● · ● · · ·

As the psychoactive fungal compounds were metabolized and cleared, wonder drained from the world, colours lost saturation, and music became less beguiling. Mab fell asleep with a pile of other youths in a dirty, brick dormitory. Her consciousness became soft and nonsensical.

The stench of unwashed humans was thick until Centa found that she was able to dial the senses up or down. The reduction in stimulation and the waning effects of the shrooms gave her the opportunity to think clearly and assemble what she knew.

Everything had made sense under the influence. Now doubt filled her again. There was still so much she didn't understand. She supposed she would learn. She could experiment, compile facts. But was there any point? As far as she knew, whatever this was could end at any moment. How was she here in another human's body and brain? She imagined the shape of her own body and brain like a ghost overlaid on Mab's. A wave of claustrophobia heightened her awareness, and she felt a pull from without, as though she'd been prodded with electricity.

A path opened where before there'd been a barrier she couldn't stretch beyond. She ventured a down it and the world, and her perception of it, fell away. A small part of her stayed with Mab as though she had jammed a foot inside an open door to stop it slamming.

The part of her that travelled spilled out of Mab and into a kind of void with no end. It wasn't exactly dark, but so empty it may as well have been. The place felt separate from the world, neither part of Earth nor part of Mab or even Centa's own consciousness. It felt as though it belonged to millions of others, just beyond her reach.

Without the push and pull of the planets dictating how she interacted with the world, her thoughts, memories, and identity became smoke that diffused to fill this endless container. She pulled all her molecules together to follow the glittering trail of the signal that had called her to the void. A second, weaker signal tried to tug her off course, but she ignored it.

A fuzzy blob in the shape of a person became larger and closer as the original signal strengthened. She considered fleeing, but her curiosity was stronger than her fear. Maybe they, whoever they were, had answers.

A face and body resolved. A smiling face. That was good. Better than an angry one. Their sandy curls and broad, crooked-toothed smile were familiar, but it wasn't anyone Centa knew from the small community on Aceso. Until coming to Earth, the only unfamiliar faces she ever saw were those of newborns.

"Hello!" The person was translucent and flickering.

Centa looked down. She was embodied but also insubstantial and translucent. Tears sprang to her eyes. Were they actually her own eyes? Were they tears at all? She knew her corporeal body had been taken by the vine. Was this the closest she would ever come to inhabiting it once again?

"I thought I sensed other Sky Humans about," the stranger said. "My name's Quinn."

Centa knew where she'd seen the face—in the mothership, on the photo wall dedicated to workers lost to the vine over the many years of the settlement.

"What's going on here? Is this real? I don't understand."

"I don't really understand either. All I know is that bastard alien vine got me, and I'm guessing it got you too."

"It got everyone. The settlement has fallen."

"Completely fallen? Christ! It's been twenty-five years since I got here. That old charlatan did better than I reckoned he would. You know when he recruited—"

"Where are you? The rest of you, I mean. Do you have a body?" Centa felt lost without accurate, scientific words to describe and quantify what was happening. She didn't want to hear old accounts of Aceso and Skyfather, not right then. She needed answers.

"I've set up shop in this old bloke. Isaac, they call him. Well, he wasn't that old when I first found him. Now he's too old to travel and he's kicking back here until he dies."

"This has to be a hallucination or a dream…"

"Well, if it is I've been waiting for years to wake up or sober up. It really does seem to be Earth, although two-hundred-and-something years after I was last here."

"It can't be. It doesn't make any sense. There's no scientific explanation."

Quinn nodded, as though she'd heard it all before. "You'll get used to it."

"Get used to it?" How could she get used to something she didn't understand? How could she get used to not having a body of her own?

"I don't have any answers for you. Old Isaac reckons we're all the dissociated personalities of the universal consciousness."

Centa blinked and tried to parse the words and the concept.

"He's a bit of a philosopher," Quinn added." And you know what they say about them being full of shit. Here give me your hands." She reached out to Centa and it was more like holding water than flesh. The void dissolved around them. Centa flinched.

"It's a memory," Quinn whispered. "There's no danger."

The longing for something absent overwhelmed Centa. Homesickness. Even though she'd never had a place she'd called home. She missed Earth. Then came the fear. Would they be eaten by great beasts or killed by the sting of a strange insect? Or would the vine strangle them in their sleep?

Centa retreated from the overwhelming emotion and found she was able to watch the memory from a distance.

The mothership was dull and dented by its journey. Vine curled around its base and covered the ground all the way to the horizon. She stood with two others. Aster and Henry. No older than teenagers. Fear on all their faces. Dressed in clunky space suits. Earl, he wanted to be called Skyfather now, was there. He kissed them all on the forehead before they fitted their helmets. Did he linger a moment longer with her? Probably not. She had thought she was special to him. Why was he sending her away? She begged silently with her eyes. He turned and left. They exited through the cargo bay doors and boarded a buggy.

They drove past the vine-draped wooden frame of the temple they'd tried to build for Skyfather, and through the dead trunks of the trees that had promptly withered when their companions had been felled. After they'd put several kilometres behind them, the dying trees thinned and were replaced with healthy specimens with bark like reptile skin and leaves that twirled like streamers. Small mammal-like creatures hissed down at them from the branches. And all the while they flattened vine beneath their tires.

On the second day they came upon a stand of dead trees surrounding a circle of stone houses. There were no warm coals, rotting food, downed tools, or remnants of bedding. Henry said that meant no one had been there for a long time. They didn't know what else to look for. They were kids. She sat in the buggy in the middle of the ruins and sucked a tasteless paste out of her ration pouch.

Two days later the vine thinned until it disappeared completely. The vegetation was composed of a variety of grasses, trees, shrubs, and colourful flowers. Hordes of flying creatures sloshed through the sky like water in a tub. They drove further and found air free of dust.

After being confined to the buggy for days they peeled off their suits and ran and jumped. They lay on the grass and stared up at the stars. The night was filled with the sounds of living things.

Henry said they should stay and not return to the mothership. Aster said Skyfather was a creep and a paedophile. Quinn wasn't decided. They had enough ration pouches to stay for a few more days. They would decide then. What would they eat? Would they be able to build shelters and find fresh water? The nights were mild at that time, but what if there were cold and wet seasons? Aster said they needed to use all the survival training they'd been given on Earth.

Nothing seemed right. It wasn't like it had been at the Earth Guardian compound, where people had surrounded her and patted her on the back and told her she was special and had great potential. She'd felt happy and loved and safe for the first time in a long time when she was there. Skyfather was different on Aceso. She could tell he had doubts.

Aster and Henry started sleeping together and Quinn was jealous. Not that she wanted a romance with either of them, but she felt lonely. They didn't notice the vine creep day by day across the ground towards them, hiding its tendrils in the long grass and bushy shrubs.

Quinn resolved to return on her own in the buggy. She would leave early in the morning while Henry and Aster slept in each other's arms. The moons moved across the sky above her head. The whispers and fumbling nearby gave way to snores. Quinn couldn't sleep. As soon as it was light enough, she would be on her way.

She awoke entangled. "Henry! Aster!" Dust rose from the surface of vine leaves and filled the air around her.

They didn't answer. She took big gulps of dust. Calm descended as her brain clouded with dreams of Earth.

The memory faded and Quinn let go of Centa's hands. "How did you do that?" Centa asked. "It was like I was there."

"You can do it too." Quinn took her hands again. "Think about the final hours of the settlement. Imagine you're there."

The vine was everywhere. Hand leaves and fallen bodies.

Centa showed it all to Quinn.

When it was over, Centa asked, "Do you think all the Sky Humans returned to Earth? Can you sense any others?"

"I can sense one, but they've landed in a mozzie or something equally brainless. Any others who made it here must all be too far away."

"Have you seen any pattern to where people are sent?" When she had been influenced by the shrooms Centa had identified patterns in everything. Now she wasn't so certain.

"Honestly, I dunno for sure. I suspect the vine looks for some connection, however thin. I remember visiting this place, Fairy Park, when I was very young. I think my grandparents lived somewhere nearby."

"If there was someone in particular that I wanted to find, how would I do that?" Ben had to be on Earth too. He had left before her. Although time didn't seem to be as rigid and important on Earth as it had been on Aceso.

"Jeez. They could be anywhere. Earth's pretty bloody big."

She would never find him.

"What about the masters?"

"What about them?"

"They could be here too."

"Screw them. Those bastards have no power here."

A life free of the masters. It was what Ben had always wanted.

They spoke throughout the night and Quinn told of her experiences since returning to Earth, including her symbiotic relationship with Isaac. He provided a vessel with which to experience the world and she provided healing powers.

The path back to Mab began to fade and dissipate.

"You need to return to the girl in the physical plane," Quinn said. "We have to spend most of our time anchored in a physical body. Too much outside of one and we fall to pieces."

"What happens?"

Quinn shrugged. "That's like asking what happens when you die. Only those who've died know, and they're not talking."

Now that Centa had become comfortable in the void, she could see dozens of other slim, faint paths snaking through like illuminated thread. "What if I take one of these paths instead of the one back to Mab?"

"You'll end up in an insect or a bird if you're lucky. A mammal if you're even luckier. Paths into humans don't open too often. They need to be in an altered state of consciousness as far as I've been able to figure out. There's no rule book here."

Quinn obviously wasn't a scientist. Reality always had rules.

Centa remembered the disorientation and lack of brain power she'd experienced in the fly, like putting the accelerator to the floor on a buggy and going nowhere. She remembered eating and regurgitating blood. She remembered the rat's fear. Mab was more familiar, comfortable, and they had begun to develop a rapport. It wasn't ideal, but she wouldn't be a terrible person to share an existence with.

Returning from the void to Mab was like being water sucked back up through a hose. The child was still sleeping, so Centa searched for sites of damage throughout her body—ruptured capillaries, infiltration by bacteria and viruses, damaged DNA—and found she too had the power to heal, just as Quinn had described. Having control over something on this plane was reassuring.

She watched Mab's dreams of jumping higher and higher until she flew up into the air in one long, leg-flailing leap over Fairy Park and its strange multi-coloured wooden and stone habs, over forests of green and brown, over the debris of fallen cities, over water where dark shapes glided beneath the surface, to a figure wearing a dirty, white robe in a forest clearing. As the trajectory of her leap returned her to Earth Mab thrashed and tried to halt her fall. The figure smiled up at her with sharp, rotten teeth. Their eyes glowed red as hot coals, and there were grey, ashy swirls on their cheeks. *Mother Feeder!* Dream-Mab screamed, and she roused with a start.

"Bloody nightmares," she mumbled and rolled over in her blankets.

"Good morning," Centa said.

Mab squealed and whipped her head around as though trying to fling Centa loose. "No, you're not real."

"It's me. Centa."

"Shrooms don't last all night. You're supposed to be gone." Around her, the other youths slept in piles on the floor.

"I'm real. I explained all this last night." She'd thought they'd made a connection. Centa would have to go through the whole account again when the child calmed. It was tedious.

"GET OUT."

"Calm now." She had no experience in soothing others and she'd never seen this intensity of emotion in another person. She'd only ever felt it herself. "Breathe in and out slowly." She recalled all the strategies the priests had taught her for handling strong emotion.

"FUCK OFF!" Mab rocked and slapped at her head. Her cries built to screams.

Centa retreated. She didn't know what else to do.

"You're still there. GO! LEAVE!"

Others emerged from their blankets and crowded around Mab.

"What's wrong, Mab?"

"Did you have a bad dream?"

"Wake up now. You're having a nightmare."

"Too many shrooms. Pixie was right, she shouldn't have had that many."

The youths embraced Mab and brought her water and dried fruits. Outwardly she continued to whimper while inwardly she chased Centa through her mind and yelled at her to leave. Centa flitted from place to place and tried to be small and to keep her thoughts quiet. There was no escape.

Except to the void.

Centa hadn't been there on her own. She'd only reached it by following Quinn's signal, but she brought to mind the way the signal had glittered and electrified the air, and a path appeared. She retreated to the void and called out to Quinn. Quinn had no useful advice except to be patient and that the child would get used to her eventually. Isaac had taken some time to come around too. The clincher had been when she'd healed a suppurating ulcer on his leg.

Soon the path began to dissipate again, and, with no other option, she returned to Mab. The child shrieked and wailed.

Centa scolded her. "You're being ridiculous. Stop this behaviour at once."

"GET. THE. FUCK. OUT!"

Centa hadn't been so irritated since Tilter had dropped a whole stack of tissue culture plates on the laboratory floor during his first week as her shadow. If any worker had displayed such uncontrolled emotions, the priests wouldn't have even bothered with a cleansing ritual. The offender would be sent straight to the vine pyre.

After some time, Mab focussed her senses outward to a big woman, the Mama Rosamund of her memories.

The woman pushed her face up near Mab's, her skin red and her pores big and oily, and peered into her eyes as though she saw Centa hidden there.

"I warned you, with all your idolatry and taking medicines that aren't meant for you. You opened yourself up and let in a demon."

13

"**W**addaya know about this?" an enraged Mama Rosamund shouted, spraying spittle all over Pixie's face.

Mama Gretel, Pixie's birthmother, had dragged her from bed and down the outcrop before she'd even had her morning piss. Half the village had been standing outside the youngsters' shelter. Breeders and sperm-sacks murmured and shuffled their feet by the door, and youngsters giggled, jumping and playing tag. Fairy Park's resident dogs darted around the outskirts, wagging their tails at all the carry-on. Merlin stared up at Pixie with an "Oh shit, you're rooted now" expression on his doggy features.

A statue of a witch bearing an apple in her open palm marked the path to the doorway. There was a story, passed down in whispers through generations of youngsters, that the witch lurched to life while everyone slept and put slices of poison apple in the mouths of anyone who snored.

Shards of sunlight speared the mattresses, blankets and clothes strewn all over the floor of the shelter. In the middle of it all sat Mab, her dark-blonde curls matted at the back. A school sore wept down one of her cheeks. Kind of funny considering Mab hated lessons so much.

"Smells like youngster farts in here," Pixie said to lighten the tension.

"I know you gave her shrooms last night," Mama Rosamund said to Pixie with a shake of her fist.

Pixie wound her fingers around the edges of the holes in her pockets.

"Go away," Mab wailed. "Please, go away."

"I think she wants us to leave," Pixie said.

The two mamas glared at her. "Shut your trap," Mama Gretel said. "She's not talking to us. Poor darling says someone's in her head." She turned to Pixie. "Rosamund says she spied you with some youngsters last night, singing to Puff."

"Why are you here?" Mab whimpered like a kicked dog, peering into the space in front of her like she could see something the rest of them couldn't.

"She says they're in her head talking to her." Mama Gretel rubbed Mab's arm with a tender expression that squeezed something in Pixie's innards.

Mab's eyes darted from face to face, suddenly lucid. "It's a person like us, sorta. They say they were made by humans who left Earth in a spaceship years ago and flew to another planet. They've got no body of their own anymore and they want mine."

Pixie laughed and the mamas glared at her again. A couple of months before, just after the traveller Wolf had left, she'd told the youngsters all about the Earth Guardians who'd fled to another planet generations ago. It must have stuck in Mab's head and returned during her shroom hangover. That was all.

"Give her some food and she'll be okay," she said.

Gretel scowled. "I'm at the end of my tether with you, Pixie. I really am."

"It's a tech demon. I know it," Rosamund said. "Those greedy capitalists put their spirits in pieces of plastic, but they became trapped in their tech nightmares and become demons. Then their own creation—the plastic-eating fungus—freed them.

Now they're all around us, yearning for the natural bodies they once had. We can't see or hear them, but they're always waiting for an opportunity to possess the unwary."

Pixie rolled her eyes and Gretel pinched her on the upper arm. She was a hypocrite. She didn't believe in Rosamund's tech demon rantings either.

Mama Goldy barged through the crowd at the door, brushing soil off her hands. "Just as I thought. A flush of psilocybes has been stolen. I hope you had your fun, Pixie."

"Why is having fun always such a bad thing?"

The mamas started on her all at once.

In Pixie's experience these carry-ons didn't last long. The mamas had all given up on any real efforts to change her. She was unfixable. Plus, they needed her fuckups to make them feel better about themselves. She twisted her fingers even tighter into the holes in her pockets and blocked out their voices with a memory of the time, as a feral youngster, snoozing in there with all the other youngsters, they'd shoved rat turds up the nose of a sleeping girl who was about to leave them to join the breeders.

Mama Gretel got right into Pixie's face and held her by the shoulders, blah-blah-blahing about the old dying traveller who needed shrooms to accept his death. All the while spouting her nonsense old-timey insults.

Pixie stared at the puckered red scar across Gretel's cheek where she'd removed her own melanoma, until it blurred and doubled in her vision. Gretel went on and on and changed the topic to how Mama Ariel needed the shrooms for her headaches.

It was all bullshit. Especially in a village where everyone, in the words of Mama Rosamund, strived to share everything and renounce the greedy, consumerist concept of ownership.

Then someone, Pixie wasn't really paying enough attention to say who, said the word banishment.

She broke her silence. "What?"

"If you don't start behaving like you're part of community instead of being so selfish maybe you should go out and try living on your own," Mama Rosamund said.

The other mamas didn't argue against this idea. Even Gretel stayed tight-lipped. Pixie's mind scrambled back through their jabbering to figure out how they'd gotten to banishment. The last thing she'd remembered was Gretel saying Mama Ariel needed shrooms for her headaches.

"There's lots of dried shrooms. Just use them."

"They're for barter. For flour and antibiotics and fabrics. You know that. I just don't know what we're gonna do now. And I didn't even have a chance to save any spores from the ones you took. You better hope a new batch grows." Mama Goldy huffed. "That reminds me. Mama Alice says someone, a traveller she suspects, has lit the fire in Ticket Booth House."

"Oh, yeah. I saw a lantern coming from the east last night." Pixie was glad of the change of topic, until her neck jerked with a slap across her cheek from Mama Rosamund.

"You didn't think to mention that a stranger was approaching? Watching out from the outcrop is your only contribution. Could have been a raider," Mama Rosamund sputtered, gleeful for another reason to be cross with Pixie.

Pixie shrugged. There hadn't been raiders for years. "I was high." There was no point in denying it anymore.

"You're about as useful as tits on a bull," Gretel said.

Mab cried out from her fetal position on her mattress, and they all turned their attention back to her. It was like tending one of the breeders while they gave birth. There was nothing anyone could do. Mab just had to find her way through it.

·　·　·　●　·　●　·　●　·　·　·

Pixie's womb sister Snow sat in the front room of the shelter that served as Gretel's clinic and study.

"Hey, Pix." She looked up from where she'd been writing by the light of the night-glowing ivy all over the walls. "What's happening?" She pushed her short brown hair behind her ears and gave one of her sweet grins.

"Could be a jizz man." Pixie pointed over her shoulder in the vague direction of the bottom of the outcrop. She was always the one sent to meet the travellers, just in case they were actually raiders or they'd brought some illness with them. The benefits of being the most expendable adult.

"A traveller, you mean." Mama Gretel handed her some dried prickly pear slices.

Pixie poked her tongue out. "Yeah, yeah. A travelling jizz man."

Snow snickered. As youngsters they'd been inseparable. They'd grown apart when Pixie had refused to move with her from the youngster's shelter to the breeder's shelter and become a walking baby incubator. Snow, less than a year younger than Pixie, was now Mama Gretel's assistant in all matters medical and reproductive, while Pixie was still a pain in everyone's ass.

"Remember when we thought we could be jizz men?" Snow said.

Pixie tutted. Finding out they needed testicles to deliver semen had wasted that bright idea.

"Don't you call him that to his face," Mama Gretel said. "You mind your Ps and Qs."

Pixie rolled her eyes. "Whatever that means."

"Only you could eat so many shrooms and still not develop any empathy or insight."

Snow crossed her eyes and stuck out her tongue behind Gretel's back.

"We'll come good on that banishment threat if you don't get your ass into gear."

"I've already got pants on. Just gimme the disease screener."

Mama Gretel sighed and stretched up to reach a metal box on the shelf above all her decaying science and medical textbooks. She took out a plastic rectangle, a little larger than Pixie's hand, and gave it to her.

"Keep it clean and bring it straight back." Mama Gretel was always frightened of losing or breaking the last of the tech she'd hoarded. "I charged it after the last traveller was here so it should be good for a couple of screenings."

Pixie tucked the solar-charged screener into her pocket and winked at Snow as she headed out.

"Don't forget to find out his name and community of origin," Mama Gretel shouted. "And guard the screener with your life! There are fungal spores everywhere."

"It's fine," Pixie said from the doorway. "You can trust me."

Mama Gretel guffawed and Pixie wasn't even offended. The more you bombarded folk with bullshit, the less they trusted you, she supposed. Poor Mama Gretel. If she wasn't so desperate to prove her most disappointing birth-child wasn't completely useless, she could've sent someone more reliable. Or gone herself. Oh well.

Merlin jogged behind her all the way to the bottom of the outcrop, where the smell of bread baking in the kitchen mingled with the smell of soap from the laundry. Most of the villagers were well into their contributions for the morning. Babies crawled or toddled in the rocky dirt, never straying too far from their personal milk-factories. A group of men and women carried snared rabbits and armfuls of foraged weeds to the kitchen. Others headed out, with tools slung over their shoulders, to tend the gen-enged crops.

Pixie climbed onto a low stone wall and yanked herself up to join Mama Alice keeping watch on the laundry roof. Merlin put his front paws on the wall and panted, tongue out the side of his mouth like a slice of raw meat. A thin column of smoke rose straight up from the chimney of Ticket Booth House.

"One person. One canine," Mama Alice said. "Seems like a traveller."

Heat swept up Mama Alice's face and reddened her ears. The previous autumn she'd ascended from breeder to mama in a dual ceremony that mourned the death of her reproductive potential and celebrated the birth of her wisdom and freedom from child-bearing. She was the only mama who could make hot flashes look tough. She ran a hand over her shaved head.

Pixie adopted Alice's wide-legged stance and touched her own shaved head. Mama Alice likely shaved hers for an advantage in skirmishes, not to deter lice.

"You know the drill. I'll wait here until you give the all clear." Alice shifted her rusty axe from one hand to the other.

Snow and Pixie used to joke that Mama Alice defended Fairy Park by putting the fear of tetanus into any raiders who came by.

Merlin scampered ahead, through the dandelion field and down the path to Ticket Booth House. A black, barrel-bodied dog ran out to meet him, their tails both wagging as they sniffed each other's asses and yipped. Dandelion puffballs exploded around them, and Pixie waved the seeds away from her face. Pixie recognized the dog.

"Lucy?" It couldn't be. Not so soon. It had only been three months.

A person came to the door, hands raised. "Ahoy. I'm a traveller and sperm purveyor. Wolf of the Earth Guardians."

Pixie stopped a few metres from the brown brick building. It was Wolf. Lovely Wolf. The memories of her time spent with Wolf had become her top obsession since the traveller had left around two months earlier.

"It *is* you!" Pixie waved her arm in the air for Alice to see. Two long arcs for *all okay*.

"Pixie! It's good to see a friendly face. Still keeping those legs closed?"

"Ha!" That was one of the things that had impressed her about Wolf. She always said exactly what she was thinking. Pixie preferred that. It meant she couldn't disappoint her with her inability to read minds.

"What are you doing back here already?"

"Are you not happy to see me?"

Pixie blushed. Time had not dampened her feelings for Wolf. She took a step forward.

"Best if you don't get too close." Wolf gripped the door frame and leaned back. "There's some sort of disease about." All the humour had gone out of Wolf. Pixie had never seen her so serious. "Three villages ago. Reminded me of all the stories of the ROSE outbreak. I haven't shown any symptoms, but I can't be sure." Wolf's voice cracked as she spoke.

"ROSE? Nah. It couldn't be," Pixie said. According to Mama Gretel, there hadn't been any ROSE around since over a decade before Pixie was born, back when they'd slaughtered all the prion-infected deer and feral livestock and buried them in a marked pit.

"The symptoms were just like all the old reports."

Pixie held up the disease screener and waited until a pulsing white circle appeared. She curbed the impulse to be loud and jolly and clever. Being with Wolf felt like the moment before leaping from a high branch while holding a tree swing.

Wolf's gaze went everywhere, but Pixie's face. "You're one of the last places to have a functioning screener."

"You're thinner than last time you were here."

"It's been a while since I've eaten properly. I skipped past the last two villages just in case I'm infectious." She yanked up a sleeve to show a green panel of skin. "I've been supplementing with photosynthesis and whatever edible plants and fungi I could identify."

Pixie raised the screener for Wolf to see. "This might take a while." The boot up time seemed to be getting longer and longer, and one day it likely wouldn't start at all.

They stood in silence as the dogs nipped at the heels of lowing milk-beasts in the field beyond. Wolf didn't appear unwell. Pixie couldn't remember the symptoms of ROSE, but she didn't want to show her ignorance.

"Don't your folk have super genes to defend you from everything?"

"Some," Wolf said. "But it's not foolproof. How've things been here? Any illnesses?"

"Same shit really. We lost a couple of youngsters to lung infections after the last dust storm, and there's an elderly traveller who's in bed dying, but I think that's just old age. Could be cancer." She hadn't really been interested enough to ask questions.

A blue box appeared on the screener. She couldn't read the words, but she knew the box was for the sample. She stretched forward and held the screen out to Wolf by the tips of her fingers. The sperm-woman took the screener in shaking hands. She closed her eyes for a moment, then pricked her finger on the testing panel.

Pixie moved from one foot to another. It wouldn't be the first time she'd had to send someone away because they had some sort of illness. The sexually transmitted diseases were the ones they were most worried about, but there were lots of other diseases that could wreck a village like theirs.

The screen flashed green.

Wolf let out a long breath. "I should do a saliva test too. It's more accurate for prions."

When the saliva test also came back negative, tears rolled down Wolf's cheeks. Pixie stepped forward and patted her on the shoulder.

Neither of them were huggers, but Wolf grabbed Pixie and then reared back. "I hope you don't mind. It's just been rough lately."

Pixie yanked Wolf towards her. Wolf smelt of sweat and dirt, like life on the road. There weren't a lot of folk in the world she'd expect to enjoy a hug from, but Wolf was one of them.

· · · ● · ● ● · ● · · ·

Snow and Mama Gretel pored over the breeding records. "Hm, yes," Mama Gretel said. "We can definitely use some more sperm from Wolf. We only achieved one continuing conception from his last visit."

"Her."

Mama Gretel raised an eyebrow. "Her last visit."

"Could be poor quality sperm," Snow said.

Pixie tutted to herself. Not a chance.

"No, I don't think so." Mama Gretel pointed to the ledger. "There was also one early, spontaneous abortion. So, two conceptions out of five insemination attempts. Higher than our usual rate. The sperm seems hunky-dory."

"Hunky-what now? What the hell does that mean?" Pixie mouthed at Snow.

Snow chuckled and picked up a piece of charcoal and a sheet of paper. "Who do you suggest for the next attempt at conception?"

Mama Gretel consulted her book again and looked up at Snow. "How's your discharge? You should be just about to ovulate. Little Arthur is fully weaned now, correct?"

Snow lowered her head and nodded.

Pixie couldn't help herself, even though she knew it was pointless. "You could just say no."

As expected, Snow and Gretel ignored her. Before Pixie, none of the youngsters with a uterus had ever said no to becoming a baby incubator. It was just what they did. There were incentives for sure. Breeders got the respect and reverence of the rest of the village. They were served the best grub. Their shelter had comfy beds, natural light, and fresh air. Those were the carrots, as Mama Rosamund put it. The sharp end of the stick was the scorn and disapproval aimed at those who refused.

Pixie had known from the age of six, when she'd first understood her destiny as a breeder, that it wasn't for her. She'd seen them green in the face and vomiting in the early days of pregnancy, seen them grotesquely swollen and struggling to walk towards the end. She'd heard the screams as their bodies were torn open, smelled the blood and shit. She'd seen them die in childbirth or from infections not long after. And sometimes the baby died *in utero* and the breeder had to give birth to it anyway. If mom and baby both survived, the babies cried all night, and the breeder's bodies were never the same. The older ones even had to shove stone pessaries up themselves to keep their uterus from falling out of their baby holes.

When Pixie came of age, Mama Gretel had appealed to her sense of duty. She said they were responsible for repopulating the world during this time of genetic bottleneck. Mama Rosamund had bullied her and called her evil any time she came within shouting distance. Mama Alice had threatened to exile her. Mama Goldy and Mama Belle had talked up the benefits and glories of being a giver of life. Mama Wendy had ignored her when it came to divvying up the scavenger's spoils. Mama Ariel, in charge of the kitchen, had come the closest to breaking her. She still gave Pixie the stingiest servings and worst cuts of meat, and often refused to serve her until, in her words, *she came to her senses.*

"I thought now that I was giving you a hand, I could give up childbearing," Snow said, smoothing the sheet of paper against the table surface over and over.

"Now that you're giving me a hand, you should know better than anyone just how desperate we are for fertile women. You've brought a life into this world before. It was difficult, but not terribly life threatening for you. We stopped the bleeding and got all of the placenta out and we can do it again. We're all here to support you."

Snow nodded. She'd had a lot of the same misgivings as Pixie, but unlike Pixie, she cared what folk thought of her. Pixie found that if she ignored the cross words and dirty looks, it was almost as if they didn't exist. Snow, however, withered under Mama Gretel's disapproval. Her surrender was more a disappointment to Pixie than a betrayal, like biting into a fallen fig that was full of ants.

"For fuck's sake," Pixie said. "Just say no."

After Snow's first long, painful childbirth, she'd been stitched from baby hole to asshole and had lost a flood of blood. And then she'd needed leaf compress after leaf compress for her mastitis.

Worst of all, for months afterwards, tears would roll down her cheeks for no apparent reason. Pixie had worried she would never get out of bed again.

"Shut your trap, Pix," Mama Gretel growled and hit her across the shoulder with the ledger. "Not everyone wishes to be a good-for-nothing like you. Having a child is a blessing and a miracle."

"It's a blessing and a miracle to go through all the pain and shit and nearly die?" Pixie asked.

Mama Gretel shut her pregnancy ledger with a solid thud. "When you get the reward of the baby at the end, then yes, it is."

"Sure. If you consider a having a totally helpless human completely dependent on you a reward. And then, once you're nice and fond of them, they're weaned and taken by the mamas and aunties to be raised. Meanwhile, you're expected to get knocked up again and go through it all again."

Gretel tried to hustle her towards the door. "Enough. You're living in a fantasy world while the rest of us have to deal with reality and its obligations."

Pixie slipped out of Gretel's grasp and sat at the table.

Tears splashed onto the paper in front of Snow. Pixie didn't know what to do for tears, but she knew she'd pushed it too far with Gretel. She changed the subject.

"Wolf said something about an illness in one of the villages she passed through."

Mama Gretel whispered something to Snow too quiet to hear, then turned to Pixie and raised her eyebrows. "Another one? What kind of virus is it this time?" Travellers were always spreading rumours of outbreaks, and they were usually false alarms. "I hope you didn't forget the disease screener."

Pixie poked out her tongue and put her hands on her hips. "No, I didn't forget the disease screen. And Wolf didn't know for sure, but she thought the symptoms were a bit like ROSE."

Mama Gretel stood up straight. "ROSE? That's a load of old tripe. There haven't been any cases of ROSE since I was a young woman. Where would it have come from?"

"She said something about there being pigs around, attacking folk, before the outbreak."

Gretel frowned. "She must be mistaken. The disease was never carried by feral pigs."

"I did a prion screen anyway. Just to be sure."

Mama Gretel stared off into the distance, her gaze unfocused. "Folk were sick as dogs before they died. Some of them got the rage. That's where the Mother Feeders came from, you know."

"We know," Pixie and Snow said in unison.

"And the Earth Guardians kept their treatments for themselves in the end." She shook her head. "But the disease died off eventually." She slapped her hands on the table decisively. "It can't be ROSE. Wolf just got her knickers in a twist over nothing. We'll be fine as long as we stick to our quarantine procedures. You two keep this to yourselves, and I'll discuss it with the other mamas."

Mama Gretel flicked a sour look at Pixie. "And cheer up, Snow. The first babe's always the hardest."

· · · • · • · • · ·

Pixie stood in the shadow of Ticket Booth House, waiting for Wolf's jizz. She yawned and rubbed at the grit in her eyes. After this it would be time for the full sun snooze. Heat shimmered between Pixie and the dozy milk beasts under their shelter on the other side of the path. An aunty—one of the retired breeders not special enough to be promoted to a mama—moved around the outside of the cluster of the hardy hybrids of cow, camel, and goat and filled a pail with vitamin rich milk.

From the outcrop above came the sounds of Mab screaming and Mama Rosamund yelling. The girl's bad trip hadn't subsided like Pixie had expected, and Rosamund's constant proclamations of evil doing didn't seem to help.

Pixie leaned her head closer to the door and pictured what Wolf was up to inside. Heat kindled in her pelvis. A heat she didn't often feel. She'd never understood the youngsters, breeders, and sperm-sacks being so keen to jump from one bed to another. Pixie liked orgasms well enough, but having them with other folk was just messy and emotionally fraught. You had to consider the other person's needs, and then there was the worry about pregnancy or disease. But every now and then something unexpected made her think it might be cool to share sex with someone else.

The retired breeder headed up the path with her full pail, just ahead of a hunting party. Merlin caught the scent of the feral cow strung up on a pole. Experience had taught him that a closer sniff wasn't worth the inevitable kick from a heavy boot.

The door opened, and Wolf handed her a small glass jar clouded with warm semen. Wolf's cheeks were flushed and her hair was tousled.

Pixie held the jar between her palms. "You wanna hang out later?"

"For sure." Wolf smiled and Pixie wanted to kiss her. "Hey. What did the mamas say about ROSE?"

"I'm not sure they believe it."

Wolf clenched her fists. "Be careful. This disease is no joke. Once I recover some strength, I'm heading home."

"Home? To Earth Guardians?"

When they'd first met, Wolf had told her that she had felt stifled at the Earth Guardian compound and had wanted to travel and have adventures. Pixie imagined the life of a traveller to be full of excitement and adventure, wandering the country, seeing new places, going whole days without having to talk to anyone. She'd pictured taking off by herself lots of times. But no one would feed her if she didn't contribute something of value, and she couldn't think of a thing she could do that wasn't worthless.

"They have fences and medicines. Guns too. It'll be safer there if there is an epidemic."

"Makes sense." Pixie held up the jar. "I should..."

Wolf's smile returned. "Yeah. I'll see you later."

"It's a date." Pixie winked and jogged back up the outcrop. Merlin ran next to her, ears flapping.

Outside Mama Rosamund's shelter, a dusty, sweaty crowd had formed. Mab could be heard sobbing and pleading within.

Pixie stopped running. "What's going on now?" she asked Aladdin.

"Mama Ros is trying to catch Mab so she can beat the demon out of her, but she's slippery." He blushed. "Hey, wanna hang out later, just me and you?"

He had that gooey look in his eyes again. Pixie recoiled. "Nah. I have plans."

One of the breeders, a woman just a couple of years older than Pixie, though the bags under her eyes made her seem almost a decade older, tapped her on the shoulder and pointed to the jar of semen. "Don't you need to get that to Mama Gretel before the swimmers die?"

The breeder was annoying, but she was right. Pixie skirted around a group of toddlers throwing rocks at a feral cat and jogged the rest of the way up to Mama Gretel's shelter.

Snow was already on the table with her knees up. Her gaze was fixed on the ceiling, teeth grinding. There was a slight tremor in her hands, but only Pixie knew her well enough to notice.

"You don't believe in this demon thing, do you?" Pixie asked Mama Gretel. She was always the rational, scientific one, the one who had hoarded teachings from the golden years of science to ward against superstition.

"You don't wanna know what I think about Mab's situation." Mama Gretel loaded her baster with semen. "I think that poor youngster's condition is all your fault."

"Harsh."

They were still blaming her? Sure, she'd given Mab the shrooms. But she hadn't forced them on her. Mab had come to her, hand out. If anyone was to blame, it was the mamas for being stupid enough to believe in demonic possession. She swore the mamas had a secret meeting every day where they decided what new problems they could blame on Pixie.

If Mab had any sense, she would pretend the bad trip was over so Mama Rosamund would fuck off. And it should have been over by now. Could be Mab liked the attention. Unless there really was something wrong with her. Mama Gretel was always warning Pixie about the consequences of shoving whatever drugs she came across straight into her body.

"Why aren't you giving her a hand, Gretel?" Pixie asked. "Could be that drug-induced psychosis you're always warning me about."

"That's Mama Gretel to you. And I'm trying, but Ros is a force to be reckoned with when she has a bee in her bonnet regarding the spiritual health of the village."

Pixie had no idea what a bonnet was—could be an old-fashioned term for ass?—but she got the idea. "Bloody politics."

"Ros'll wear herself out soon enough. I've got other fish to fry." Gretel waved her hand over the now empty jar of jizz and Snow lying on the table. "Lift your knees to your belly, Snow. You know the drill."

Pixie copied Gretel's hand waving. "Why do we even bother with all this?"

Mama Gretel tutted. "What do you mean?"

"Folk are dying off everywhere and still we're pretending we can preserve the human race."

"We have to try. What else is there to do?" She leaned over Snow with the baster.

"But why do we have to try?" Pixie crumbled some dried rosemary leaves from a bunch hanging from the ceiling, and held her fragrant fingers to her nose. "What's so special about humans that we're fighting so hard to avoid extinction?"

They were like those stray ants who carried around gains of dirt after their whole nest had been wrecked by boiling water.

"I'm sick of your stupid questions, Pixie. Piss off."

"We've gotta have a greater purpose I guess," Snow said as Pixie shut the door behind her.

• • • • ● • ● • ● • • •

The sun was setting when Pixie ran past Mama Rosamund's shelter on her way to Ticket Booth House. Things had quietened down and folks were drifting away. Mab's performance had ended abruptly after a few slaps from Rosamund, and she was sleeping off her exhaustion.

Merlin peeled himself away from his gang of dog buddies and staggered towards her. He rubbed his muzzle in the dirt and pawed at his nose.

"You okay, mate?" Pixie asked, scratching behind his ears. He leaned against her legs. "Come on. Let's go see Lucy and Wolf."

Wolf answered the door of Ticket Booth House brandishing a machete. "Let's go around to the lake."

"Yikes! Are you taking me out there to gut me?" Being around Wolf made her bouncy and giddy.

Wolf waggled her eyebrows. "Does that not sound like fun?"

If you kiss me, I'll let you do anything you want, Pixie stopped herself from saying the words aloud and poked her tongue out instead.

The lake, at the back of the outcrop and below the sharp drop-off behind Pixie's shelter, was a cool choice. Folk steered clear because it stank like rotting green things, a bit like Mama Rosamund's breath. Also, the water was toxic and useless for anything other than firefighting. Mama Goldy, their fungi specialist, had tried a mycofiltration system for a while, but the water still gave everyone the squirts.

Wolf smirked. "I thought that if I caught one of the feral sheep who hang out there, I could trade the carcass for some meat from the smokehouse to keep me going for the rest of the journey home."

"Sounds fair." Pixie hated hunting. She hated anything that could be considered a contribution, but if it meant hanging out with Wolf, she didn't mind.

Merlin tossed his head around as though snapping at invisible bugs. Lucy sniffed him cautiously and backed away, growling.

"What's wrong with your dog?" Wolf asked.

Pixie shook her head. "Dunno. He's not really mine." She pointed up the outcrop. "FUCK OFF, Merlin." She wouldn't let him ruin her time with Wolf.

The dog hung his head and staggered away. He'd probably eaten something bad. He'd get over it.

At the lake, Wolf crouched by a saltbush and scanned the far shore. The sky shone pink as the sun sank into the horizon.

Pixie stood atop the remains of a post that had once formed part of a jetty when the lake was massive. Lucy darkened her paws in the green scum at the edge.

Nobody at Fairy Park was old enough to remember a time when the water wasn't toxic. When Pixie was a youngster, they used to tell a story about a Mother Feeder who fell into the lake and turned into a monster who scoffed anyone who ventured too close.

"Is it this fucked up everywhere?" Pixie tilted her head to the porridge-like sludge of blue-green algae and oily mud.

"Not everywhere," Wolf whispered. "Nature has taken back lots of places. Around the edges of the old nuclear power plant is actually one of the nicer spots. The animals and plants are thriving there without humans to bother them."

Pixie took Wolf's lead and lowered her voice too. "It's weird how they can handle the radiation." She stepped down from her post and crouched shoulder to shoulder with Wolf.

"Bloody weird. I only went to the edge to check it out and now I'm paranoid I'll get cancer."

"You shouldn't be so nosy then."

"I couldn't help it." Pixie could feel Wolf's breath on her neck. Their eyes met and they both beamed. Pixie's heart sped up. If she leaned forward just a bit, their lips would touch.

"Baa."

A shaggy white head, followed by a puffed-up body covered in matted wool, appeared from behind some rushes on the other side of the lake. According to Mama Gretel, the feral livestock were direct descendants of those abandoned when free market farmers couldn't make a living off the land anymore. Widespread culling during the ROSE outbreak, even though sheep were never proven to carry ROSE, had nearly made them extinct, but their numbers had increased again in recent years.

Wolf brandished her machete and held a finger to her lips. "This is going to get bloody. Do you want to give me a hand?"

"Nah." Pixie liked her meat already skinned and cooked. That's why she hadn't lasted more than a day dressing the kills the hunters brought in. "I might head back up the outcrop for a bit."

"Fair enough. I'll be back." Wolf crept away with her machete held aloft.

Pixie headed back through Fairy Park thinking about the moment she'd supposed she could kiss Wolf. If she wasn't so squeamish and had given Wolf a hand with the sheep, they might have kissed after all. She could even have gotten more. Did she want more? She'd never had more. Everyone else seemed to think it was pretty special. She wouldn't even know what to do. When it came to sex, she was like a toddler still learning to walk and falling on her ass every few metres.

Half-way up the outcrop, the youngsters were huddled together beside Puff. Mab sat in the centre of them with a solar light under her chin, sending up spooky shadows across her face.

"And then the woman in my head said: I've had enough of this. I'm sorry for all the fuss. You're an awesome kid. The best kid at Fairy Park." She drew out her words in as deep a voice as she could manage, no doubt imitating the papas when they told ghost stories.

"She did not say that," another youngster called out. "She never even met any other kids."

"Did so." Mab shifted her weight on the pile of blankets beneath her and grimaced. Mama Rosamund must have gotten the paddle to her backside at least once.

"Where'd she go?" Someone else asked.

"She said she had to hop off. Had to find an animal or something to jump to. Then she was gone. Maybe she's in one of you now." Mab waved her finger around the circle.

The youngsters' eyes were wide as they looked at each other for signs of who now hosted the demon. All except for Aladdin, who rose from his place at the edge of the circle and flounced up to Pixie like a puppy.

"I see Mab's enjoying her fifteen minutes," Pixie said, and then recoiled. That was one of those nonsense things Mama Gretel would say. Snow would laugh at her. They'd sworn they wouldn't become like the mamas, especially not their birthmother.

"At least no one's talking about the shrooms anymore. Maybe you're in the clear now." Aladdin smiled down at her. When had he gotten so tall?

"I'm not worried." Everyone could think what they wanted. She hadn't forced Mab to scoff those shrooms. It was a relief to see her back to her old self though.

Aladdin blinked at her coyly. "So, maybe we can hang out now."

"Hm." She looked him up and down and then grabbed him by the collar. She might as well see what the massive deal was about sex and get some experience she could draw on if anything went down with Wolf.

She dragged him off the lit path and into the shelter where they'd stored all the crumbling animatronic fairy tale characters of the old park. "You pull out before you deliver, or I'll tell Mama Gretel you've been spreading around your seed without permission."

Aladdin grinned and nodded vigorously. "Yeah, yeah. Of course. Thanks, Pix."

"For fuck's sake, don't thank me. It's not like I baked you a bloody cake or something."

"Okay, sorry." He yanked down his pants.

She couldn't see well in the darkness, but his little white dick was pointed right at her. Could be this wasn't her best idea. She should just get it over with so she could say she'd tried when folk bugged her. It had to be done sooner or later, like finding a job to contribute to the village or digging out that ingrown hair on her inner thigh.

She took off her own pants and hopped onto the edge of a bench with her knees spread. The unwelcome picture of Snow with her own legs wide open to receive Wolf's semen popped into her head. She closed her eyes to picture Wolf while Aladdin prodded her with his dick.

"Ow, jeez. You have no idea what you're doing do you?" Pixie tilted her pelvis to show him the way. She was tempted to reach down and guide him to the right spot, but she didn't want to touch his dick with her hands.

At last, he found the baby hole and pushed forward.

Pixie felt like a knife was being thrust into her. "Ah, stop, stop." She lifted her hands to Aladdin's shoulders to push him away, but not before he spasmed inside her.

She'd been leaning hard against one of the fibreglass fairy tale characters, and it splintered behind her, sending shards into her back. Aladdin fell back onto the floor.

"You knobhead!" Pixie shouted. "I told you not to deliver in me." Her baby hole felt torn. She pressed her legs together tightly.

"Sorry, Pixie. I couldn't help it."

"Just fuck off." Pixie pulled up her pants.

Could she be pregnant now? She'd never had jizz in her before. She didn't even know if she could get pregnant. She was untested but thought that she was unlikely to be pregnant after one time. Plus, Aladdin wasn't even all the way in properly. She would just try to forget this had ever happened and never bother with this shit again.

Third Interlude

Rae was on the edge of sleep, warm and loved, with Nanna and Poppa nearby. Outside her bedroom, the forest of nothing whooshed past as though her room was running on chicken legs like Baba Yaga's house.

The roof was torn away as if by a giant hand and then the walls crumbled until it was just Rae on her bed, flying through the forest of nothing.

"Nanna! Poppa!" she screeched but they didn't answer. Her bed dissolved beneath her.

Then she stopped moving and the forest stilled. She was no longer on Aceso. The ghosts that had been a permanent presence in the forest there were all gone. Except for one. A pale, blurry figure too far away to recognize.

Sunlight broke through the tree canopy behind her, and she was pulled backwards, out of the forest and into an unfamiliar body, older than her but younger than Ophelia. Nourishment came in via a vein in her arm, and Rae was terrified that she had traded imprisonment in one tower for another.

She sampled her surroundings through the body's senses. She was no longer on Aceso. The gravity was slightly stronger. It had to be Earth. That was what she had been promised. But where were her grandparents? The thought that she would one day see them again, that she would be held and loved, was all she had clung to during her isolation on Aceso.

There were muffled voices nearby and the rush of air in and out of tubes and valves. They called the unfamiliar body Vanessa and Professor Mann. The same surname as Rae's. The name of her father and her grandparents. They had to be nearby.

"Nobody infected has recovered once they've reached this stage. Eventually Vanessa's vital functions will be compromised. No one will oppose my decision to let her go then."

"You think we should incinerate her along with the ROSE samples?"

"I didn't say that. But we have a duty to protect the rest of the community."

A door opened and closed with a noisy whoosh, and the conversation ceased.

Rae searched inside the body for the source of the woman's curse. The poisoned vine thorns had prevented her own body from awakening on Aceso, but she could heal this one. Part of the vine's gift.

The woman's brain was full of sticky gunk and holes. Memories were disappearing like stories being deleted from a reader. Rae grasped one:

Walking down a gravel path at night. Stars above in a clear sky. Distant voices laughing and talking. A warm breeze rustling the glowing hedge lining the path.

Rae recognized the constellations from her childhood, and she understood the source of the hedge light. It was bioluminescence. Her grandparents had been working on creating bioluminescent plants when she was a child. Their initial offerings were paler and patchier than these specimens though. Did that mean the vine had returned her to a different time? Perhaps they'd perfected the technology a few years after she'd left.

The hedge ahead and to the left of the path shuddered. The professor smiled to herself and walked on. A small child jumped out of the foliage. "Rah!" The professor clapped her hands to her mouth. "Bella! You frightened me!" The girl grabbed the professor around the waist and hugged tightly. The professor squeezed back, kissed the long dark hair on the top of the child's head and took a deep breath of its soapy, floral scent.

Beyond the child's head, Rae caught a glimpse of a building with long glass windows and plants growing all over the roof. Just like her home on Earth. Her mother's flower bed was gone though. Staked tomato plants had taken its place. She was certain now. She was home. Just in a different time.

Other fragments of memories like shards of broken mirror reflected a life that had little meaning to Rae. She searched them for her grandparents' smiling faces but found only strangers.

The woman's final memory before falling into endless sleep flared before her eyes:

A laboratory. People in white coats. Jerking, slurring, unable to walk. Falling. A view from the floor. Light in and out of focus on the ceiling. A large animal grunting and sniffing at her face. A pig. Like illustrations of the three little pigs. Only the illustrated pigs were pinker. Friendlier. Not as terrifying. Then gunshots and the pig's squeals faded into the distance.

The memory evaporated, gone forever.

The body would soon die. But Rae found that she was able to recognise the agent of the curse, a tiny particle that recruited others to its evil work, dispersed throughout the organs and tissues of her new vessel. The deeper parts of the professor's brain had endured less destruction and was almost pristine. These parts kept the body alive. Rae halted the curse in the brain first, then searched the whole body for more of these particles. Once they were all destroyed, she repaired the pathways to the body's senses and those that controlled muscle and bone. But the woman's memories and sense of self were already gone.

The professor's body was hers. She felt into the limbs and along the surface of the skin. Rae came to life. Opened the eyes. *Her* eyes. Bright lights hung above beside a whispering air vent set into the ceiling. A blue blanket covered her. She sat up in a small room with white walls. There was a metal toilet and sink in the corner, a window set into a white door, and a chest of drawers beside the bed. Someone in a kind of space suit was there fiddling with a computing tablet. They didn't see her immediately.

"Ahem."

The suited figure stumbled back and fell into the wall. "Professor Mann!" He surged towards her with his nose pressed against the plastic face shield covering his face and his eyes wide. "You're awake!"

"Am I?" The professor's voice was high and warbling. A thrill ran through Rae. They were the first words she'd spoken in decades. She was overjoyed to have control of a body again.

"Do you remember what happened?"

Instinct told her to keep her real identity secret. She didn't know if anybody would understand or if it would be safe. She waited for the man to rush into the silence with details. The professor's memories had left her with more of an incomplete puzzle than a detailed picture. She worked to get saliva into her pasty mouth and dry throat.

"My head's still a little foggy," she said. Her breath was foul. In fairy tales, the princesses always awoke from their long sleeps as fresh and sweet as flowers.

"I'm Jon," the man said, biting his lip. "Do you remember me?" She sensed the answer was important to him.

"Of course. Yes. Jon. You were..." She rubbed at her temples.

"Your postdoc." His voice was high-pitched and excited.

"Yes. Jon. My...postdoc." Rae stretched out her stiff, aching limbs. She had no concept of what a postdoc was.

He beamed, then composed himself again. "You've been sick for over a month now. Do you remember anything about that?"

She shook her head.

"I'll fill you in as much as I can. I'll message Arabella. She's been in charge since... Um, anyway she'll probably want to come tell you some of the details herself. I don't want to wear you out either, since you've just regained consciousness."

She took a risk and asked after her grandparents. "Where are Sam and Breeana?"

"Who?" Jon said absently as he tapped at his tablet screen.

"You don't know them?" He would if they were present on the compound. They would have been akin to royalty. "Sorry. I'm a little confused."

She was certain of where she was, just not when. She waited for the topic to come up naturally. Her years on Aceso had taught her patience.

"First, let's give you a disease screening." He took samples of the professor's blood and saliva and applied them to the screen of a small device. "This will take a minute or so. We have reason to believe it became airborne." He raised his eyebrows as though expecting a response.

"Really?" She mirrored his expression. At least she tried to. She was still getting used to creating facial expressions in her false skin.

Green symbols flashed on the device, and Jon whooped. "You're clear! That's excellent."

"Great. Can I please get out of this room now?" She was certain the answers to all her questions were beyond this windowless, chemical-smelling enclosure. As was the sky, the air, and the soil of her childhood.

He winced. "I'm waiting to hear from Arabella. She should get back here soon. In the meantime, we'll perform all the standard tests."

Jon assessed her reflexes, muscle tone, sight, and hearing. The professor's body had suffered some wasting but was in generally good condition. He then had her recite the alphabet forwards and backwards, count down from a thousand by tens, repeat phrases and sentences that he told her, and finally remember items he'd placed under a blanket.

Midway through returning the items to their places around the room, he froze mid stride. His face through the visor of the suit went suddenly slack.

"Sorry," he said after a few moments. "Arabella just contacted me. She's had a look at the results I sent through."

"She's, um, quite busy. She won't be able to see you today." He avoided eye contact. Rae wasn't sure if his embarrassment was for the professor, this Arabella, or for himself.

"She wants you to stay in quarantine for another three days." Rae sagged against the bedhead. The walls of the room were so close. Three more days until she could see the sky and feel the breeze. She wanted to meander and explore and wear out shoes like the twelve dancing princesses. The despair she felt was out of proportion to the situation. She had spent years imprisoned in her body on Aceso. Why should three days upset her so much? She considered pushing Jon aside and running for the door. But attracting attention with outrageous behaviour could only harm her chances of suspicion-free survival. All the tears she'd been unable to shed over the years spilled from her eyes.

"We'll give you a daily disease screening," Jon said gently, looking at anything but her face. "When you've had three clear days, we can get you out of here. In the meantime, I'll bring your tablet to help pass the time and prompt your memories. She'll interface with you tomorrow when she's not so busy."

He grinned. "You know what she's like. Probably best if you're not in the same room together. A microcentrifuge got broken last time!"

Rae frowned at Jon, unsure whether the professor would have tolerated such overfamiliarity. What kind of drama had the vine dumped her into? She'd had years of listening to other people's troubles on Aceso, and they were always tedious.

Jon's grin faltered and he cleared his throat. "Anyway, I bet you're eager to get back to your work."

Rae was neither interested, nor suitably experienced, in the professor's work, whatever it had been. She didn't know how she was going to successfully assume the identity of someone she'd never even met. Her only defence against suspicion would be to claim anything unexpected or unusual about her behaviour was a long-term effect of the disease.

Jon paused at the door. "Arabella has requested we give you a brain scan to assess the damage you've sustained."

"NO!" Rae said more forcefully than she'd intended. She didn't understand much about brains or imaging technology, but she suspected the result wouldn't be consistent with the recovery she'd displayed.

"Are you sure? It could tell us—"

"I said NO."

"Okay then. You're the boss."

Interesting. It seemed the professor had some power in this place and time. Yet she still didn't know the year.

Her heart, the *professor's* heart raced. It was a sensation Rae hadn't felt in many years, but she remembered that it was the body's response to strong emotion. "Um, Jon?" she asked. "What year is it?"

Jon tilted his head curiously. "It's 2337."

The expression on the professor's face must have given away Rae's shock and dismay because Jon patted her shoulder with his clumsy, suited hands and said "Don't worry. It'll all come back to you."

"Of course it will." It had been over two centuries since she'd left Earth. Her grandparents would be long dead. People didn't live forever outside of cold-sleep. But the vine had lured her with images of them. It had lied. She'd felt a bond to Earth, but her strongest bond had been to her grandparents. Earth meant nothing without them.

· • • ● • ● • • · ·

If Rae couldn't have her grandparents, at least she would have her freedom. She couldn't wait to climb down from her tower of isolation and see what had become of the world.

Rae stretched and bent and reaccustomed herself to having a body. Eating was another activity to relearn. She lingered over her first meal, grinding bread between her teeth and letting it rest on her tongue until it became sweet. She crunched slices of apple and burnt her mouth on her first spoonful of soup.

Jon brought her the professor's tablet, as promised. She remembered being quite proficient with something similar as a child. She accessed the professor's files with her palm print and iris pattern. An imposter.

She made the tablet's surface into a mirror and smoothed down her shoulder length hair. Strands of white, grey, and black gave it a silvery appearance. The professor's skin was darker than her own had been and covered in freckles and age spots. The professor's eyebrows were thick and black, though she had few eyelashes around her brown, deep-set eyes. Rae stuck out the tongue and pulled back her lips. Good teeth. Only a little crooked.

This was her body now. She promised herself she would stop calling it the professor's. That person was gone. Mostly. Every now and then Rae felt another presence inside her skin, but if something of the professor remained, it was only emotion and muscle memory.

For long hours Rae's only companion was the tablet. Every now and then she was tugged back into the forest of nothing. She reached for the hazy figure she found there. And they reached for her. But they were too far apart to connect.

From files on the tablet, she soon confirmed she was indeed back in her old home. It was still known as an Earth Guardian compound. The group her grandparents had been establishing when she'd been dragged away from them and from Earth. They had endured for over two hundred years, and it seemed other compounds had sprung up around the world. The movement was her grandparents' legacy. She was happy for them. And proud.

The professor's scientific notes filled numerous folders on the tablet, but they were incomprehensible, full of jargon and numbers. There was no story. No heroes, villains, or quests. The woman's journal was more interesting. The few entries Rae skimmed, detailed the kinds of concerns she'd heard daily from the masters on Aceso—water purity, crop failures, population control. It seemed Earth had its challenges too.

On her second day in isolation, the tablet flashed with a call from Arabella. Rae's finger hovered over the button to ignore it. She had no interest in this woman or her violent and combative relationship with the professor. But her name was mentioned frequently in the journal and scientific notes. The professor would likely have answered this call. Or perhaps she wouldn't have. Rae had no idea.

She huffed and pressed Accept.

A woman's scowling face filled the screen. With her dark hair and deep-set eyes, she look remarkably like the professor, only younger. Perhaps they were related. It would make sense in a small, isolated community and would explain the intensity of emotion between them.

"Give me a moment." Arabella dismissed her and turned away to bark something to someone off screen.

Rae hadn't spent a lifetime eavesdropping on narcissists to not recognize the power play. This meeting was political. Rae didn't care about all that. She didn't want influence over the community or the laboratory. All she wanted was a life.

While she waited, she assessed Arabella. Her voice was familiar, which was strange considering Rae had been back on Earth for less than two days. Then it dawned on her. This was the first voice she'd heard when she'd arrived in the professor's body. Arabella had been in the room with Jon. She was the one who had wanted to dispose of Vanessa's body, even though it still clung to life. She'd been so matter of fact about it.

"Forty-seven infected. Seven in quarantine as we speak." Arabella's attention was back with her. "Thirty-nine people have died."

Rae lowered her head as though getting control of great emotion. "Yes," she said in a tone she hoped expressed sorrow. "What a pity."

"A pity, Mom? Everyone lost at least one loved one."

Mom. So, she was the professor's daughter. How sad. Rae would have given anything to save her own mother when she was sick on Aceso. She couldn't imagine any child feeling any differently. But Arabella had been ready to recycle her.

Rae vowed that if she ever had a child, she would cherish and protect them. Her own childhood had been destroyed by her father's delusions and ambitions, but she knew, if given the chance, she could do it differently. Better. She absent-mindedly reached for her Cindy doll and then remembered she had been disposed of years before.

"Everyone blames you," Arabella said into the silence. "They might not say it, but they do. Everyone here is so damn polite and too scared they'll be kicked out if they speak up. You created a culture of fear and unquestioning loyalty, and it ended in tragedy. Well done."

Arabella's lower lip wobbled. Rae suspected she'd been practising her speech for this very moment. She lifted her chin defiantly. "Your ROSE research is over."

"I agree." Rae had no idea where to even begin with the Professor's research, and Arabella had just provided a way out.

Arabella's face brightened for an instant, and then her anger returned. "It only took you nearly dying and killing dozens of others in the process to change your mind. Your disease had over a 90% fatality rate! What will you put me through next?" Arabella thumped her fist on her chest and blinked back tears.

"90%? What happened to the other 10%?" Rae asked. If there were survivors besides her, it could mean that others from Aceso were here too, healing the way she'd healed this stolen body. That could account for the faint signal she'd detected in the forest of nothing.

Arabella shook her head, her chin wobbling.

"I've put you through enough," she said, wishing she could give Arabella some words of solace. "I'm giving up the research. You can be completely in charge."

It never hurt to give people what they desired, especially if it didn't cost you anything you couldn't afford to lose. Another lesson in diplomacy from her years on Aceso.

Arabella's jaw dropped. "Who are you and what have you done with my mother?"

Rae froze in fear, but Arabella's expression softened. "I'll believe it when I see it." She became stern once again. "I've already destroyed all the frozen ROSE samples."

"I understand. You did what you had to."

Arabella huffed and closed the interface without another word, and Rae stared into the distance thinking over the exchange. If Professor Mann was Arabella's mother, then what exactly was her own connection to these women? They had the same surname and lived in the same place, only centuries apart. Could they possibly have branched from the same family tree?

A living relative. That softening of Arabella's face, just for a moment, gave Rae hope that she might come to know the comfort of family after all. But for that to happen, she needed to understand what had happened here. She looked back to the tablet to search for ROSE and found an old article.

Earth Guardians Urge Patience During Search for ROSE Cure
Truth News
September 2305
Earlier today Professor Mann of the Eastern Earth Guardian community released a statement regarding the outbreak of Rapid Onset Spongiform Encephalopathy known to most as ROSE.

ROSE is a prion disease transmitted by an infectious protein in bodily fluids and tissues. Symptoms include stiffness and difficulty walking, jerking movements, hallucinations, confusion, and fatigue. Occasionally infection sparks a murderous violence in victims, but this symptom is claimed to be rare. Medics, scientists, and historians alike claim ROSE is more terrifying than any previously identified prion disease due to its extremely rapid onset and high rate of transmission.

In her statement, Professor Mann explained that antibiotics and vaccinations don't work against prion diseases, and ROSE is no exception. Earth Guardian scientists are working on a gene therapy that will enable proteins inside the brain to resist being converted to diseased versions by the ROSE prion.

The professor has called for an end to the picketing and blockading of their compounds to allow free and safe movement of goods and personnel while they develop this treatment. She claims that once they have perfected a treatment, it will be distributed amongst needy communities. In her statement, the professor asked for the public to remember that Earth Guardian scientists released their hardy and nutrient-dense gen-enged crops and livestock for free public use as soon as corporate security and government agencies were no longer able to enforce restrictions.

Anti-tekker protestors outside the Earth Guardian compounds claim ROSE is a form of biological warfare created to eradicate them and that the devastation of the Earth Guardian communities is a false flag.

In the meantime, culls of feral deer, identified as the reservoir of this disease, as well as warnings about consumption of venison, continue. If you suspect you or a relative may be infected, be aware there is currently no effective treatment. Quarantine of infected individuals has proven to be the only method sufficient to limit transmission.

But this article was from years ago. What relevance did ROSE have now, and what kind of research had the professor been doing?

Searching through the data proved too confusing, so she re-opened a string of recent messages between Arabella and the professor that hadn't interested her on first look. They were mostly bickering, but she scanned them now for mentions of ROSE and quickly found what she was looking for.

16th September 2337 Professor Mann to Arabella

I've been going back through my notes on people who survived the violent form of ROSE infection and experienced personality changes. Their loved ones described them as having their "brains wiped and reloaded with a stranger."

This may be a clue for consciousness transfer. I'm not sure how exactly. I'll need to think on it some more. Still, I'm excited. I think I'm close to a breakthrough.

In other news, I've found the code to override the security on the old android stored in the shed, and I've recoded it to my own biometrics. I've also found details of a whole factory of androids that was abandoned decades ago. Might be worth sending someone out to explore! Those could be another piece in the consciousness transfer puzzle.

I don't have all the answers yet, but I feel like these are good places to start. My first step might be to thaw some ROSE and infect one of your pigs as a pilot experiment. I'm sure you can spare your mother a single pig!

17th September 2337 Arabella to Professor Mann

Let the record show that, although I had many concerns, I indulged your anti-ageing research. I'll admit I was optimistic there might be something of value for our community and for trade with other EG communities. But after several years and tons of resources down the drain, you could demonstrate next to no increase in human lifespan or healthspan from your work. Also let the record show that I invited you to come on board with my microbiome work for tolerance of E. coli contaminated water. And you ignored me.

But now consciousness transfer!!! And, even worse, ROSE!!!! I don't know how you expected me to respond. I asked you not to go down this track. Research on consciousness transfer is a pointless waste. We're going to be even more of a laughingstock. You know that, right? We're part of a wider community. We're expected to do our part for the preservation and advancement of humanity, not play around with anti-ageing and consciousness transfer like spoilt 21ˢᵗ century billionaires.

I didn't even know we had ROSE samples in storage. We must dispose of them immediately. This is so incredibly dangerous. You're not in your right mind. We need to talk about this. Please stop avoiding me. And don't touch my pigs—they're for the micro-biome work.

Rae put the screen down on the bed. She'd remembered Earth as far superior to Aceso. But she'd been a sheltered child. Things were just as rotten here as they'd been in Skyfather's cult. Her grandparent's intentions had been noble though. She was sure of that. How would they feel if they knew the group they'd established for the benefit of Earth and humanity had gone so wrong?

The relationship with Arabella seemed beyond repair. Maybe that was fortunate. Rae wasn't ready to pretend to be someone's mother. She remembered her own and the despair that came with her vague, childlike knowledge that the most important person in her world was dying. That intensity was not something she could fake.

The professor and Arabella might have been related to her, but any emotional link had been broken by time and the vast expanses of space. Family seemed further away than ever. But freedom was growing closer.

. . • . ● . ● ● . ● . . .

On the third day, Jon pricked Rae's finger and smeared a drop of her blood on the disease screener. She knew what the results would be. She had eliminated every single prion from her body. It was time for her to embark upon this new chapter of her life.

"What happened to the pigs?" she asked as he worked. The messages between the professor and Arabella had ended before the outbreak of ROSE, but it clear the infected pigs were involved.

"Ah, good. You've remembered." Jon transferred a swab of her saliva to the screener. "Are you sure you're ready to hear all this? Everything's under control now. You could take a couple more days to rest."

"I'm back to myself. I need to know what happened."

"Right." Jon stood up straighter and glanced towards the door as though searching for an escape route. "Well, three of the infected sows became aggressive and escaped. They infected a lot of people. It seems the infection became airborne. We found you on the floor in the lab."

She remembered the Professor's memory of the pig standing over her. She made the expected shocked and dismayed face.

The disease screener dinged.

"You're clear." Jon grinned and removed his visor.

The curse had been broken. He emerged from his suit like a hero from a bearskin. It was as though his dull features had been coloured in. Pink cheeks. Brown eyes. His head was tiny on top of his oversized suit. He ruffled his damp, brown hair.

"Time to rejoin the world. It's good to have you back, Professor. What would you like to do first?"

So many things. She didn't know where she wanted to begin, but she knew where she needed to.

"Take me to the quarantine station. I want to see these others who have recovered as miraculously as I did."

Rae was certain there was an Acesoan there, healing ROSE sufferers. She intended to find out exactly who they were.

Outside, the sky was huge and blue. Bluer than Rae remembered. The wind was alive and boisterous. Green life sprouted between buildings. Herbs, foods, and medicines, she later found out. In broad-brimmed hats, the young and the elderly tended these plants. Some of the smaller buildings had been moved or replaced and others had sprung up, but on the whole the compound was recognisable from her childhood. She took it in and tried to assemble her thoughts and memories.

"Professor!" People clustered around her, breathed on her, stared and reached for her. She clutched Jon's arm.

"Please," he shouted. "The professor is still recovering. Give her some space."

The people drifted away, some of them with wounded expressions.

Rae would offend people in the coming days. People who had meant something to the professor, but not to her. Some people never spoke to her, avoided her gaze—the ones who blamed the professor for the ROSE deaths, she assumed.

Jon led her to a small open-sided buggy and drove her out of the gates and down the hill. Insects buzzed. Birds chirped and squawked. Vibrations from the corrugations in the packed dirt road jolted her bones and shook her brain in its skull. She had forgotten the range of pains experienced by the human body.

The surrounding forest was a messy tangle of leaves, branches, and strips of bark. Nothing like the orderly dark green fairy tale forests of her imagination. She felt a tug back to the forest of nothing. The hazy figure was more solid. Almost familiar. But still too far away.

Rae returned to the physical world. Doors of splintered wood, set into mounds of dirt covered in grasses and flowers, appeared on the sides of the road. Four mismatched dogs, as unkempt as the houses, chased the buggy. A man in a stained singlet and shorts stepped out from a shadowed entrance. Jon waved to him. His expression hardened.

She had many questions but didn't know how long she would be able to deny a brain scan if they imagined the professor had completely lost her memory. She simply said, "What happened?"

Jon swerved around a large hole in the road. The back tire clipped the edge, and she bit her tongue as the buggy jolted.

"The pigs escaped the compound and attacked out here. Most of the villagers died. A couple of them are down in quarantine. That man was the only one to escape unharmed.

"How terrible." Rae wondered if the professor would have felt guilt for the tragedy she'd caused.

"Yeah. Terrible for them and for us too, with no one to tend the crops or the seaweed beds."

"Oh."

"Don't you worry about it. We'll get it all sorted out." Jon gazed at her with concern. "I believe you were onto something with that research. If we'd been able to continue, I think the risks would have been worth it in the end."

"Perhaps."

"You weren't to know the prion would become airborne."

A voice, not Jon's, spoke to her. "Hello...Who's there?" She followed the voice back to the nothing.

"Rae?"

"Ben?"

14

Mama Goldy stood at the end of the first of three long tables, lit from behind by the yellow light of a solar lamp. She ladled scoops of afterbirth stew into bowls and handed them around.

Pixie passed the bowls along, taking deep sniffs. She usually enjoyed afterbirth stew ceremonies. Well, not the ceremony itself—she didn't care about celebrating the birth of another shrieking mouth to feed—but the bowl of hot, rich stew that went along with it.

This time though, she couldn't stop worrying about a future when she'd be sitting in front of a meal made from the placenta she'd shared with her own baby. It had only been a couple of days, and there was no way Pixie could tell yet if Aladdin had knocked her up. Her period wasn't due for at least a week. Or maybe two. She hadn't really been keeping track. Mama Gretel would be disgusted both at her being pregnant and at not monitoring her cycle—at Fairy Park, time was a loose concept, dictated by the sun and seasons, but when it came to menstrual cycles, folk were precise.

The open-sided dining shelter was stuffy with trapped heat from the adjoining kitchen. Pixie was in a silent elbow-space war with the breeders on either side at the cramped wooden table. The youngsters just outside the bounds of the roof looked cooler and more comfortable, with their legs spread out in the dirt. Mab was right in the middle of the pack, still a Fairy Park celebrity after her brush with alien mind invasion.

Pixie stirred her stew absently. Pregnancy wasn't her only worry. After the ceremony, she would take Wolf a bowl, and it would be the first time she'd seen her since the unfortunate encounter with Aladdin. Maybe Wolf thought of her as only a friend and wouldn't even care. They hadn't promised anything to each other. They hadn't even held hands or kissed.

Once everyone had a steaming bowl in front of them, Mama Goldy raised her hands and the villagers quieted.

"Our ancestors prevailed through storms and floods, plagues and hungers, the poisoning of the air and soil and the crumbling of the cities, and every other great catastrophe that brought humankind to the edge of extinction. They faced death in all its forms." Mama Gretel lifted her bowl and made eye contact with each of them. "Yet we endured. And now with every new life we bring into this world, we rebuild. This child may not have grown in all our wombs or from all our seed, but they belong to all of us."

"Hear, hear!" Mama Rosamund said.

Mama Goldy started going through the matrilineage of the child, and Pixie hung her head. Her mouth watered and her stomach grumbled as the tasty stew cooled. Folk were always so fidgety whenever *she* took up their time by uttering more than three sentences in a row.

Outside, Mab made a fart noise with her mouth and the rest of the youngsters burst into cackles.

"Keep it down to a dull roar out there!" Mama Goldy yelled and took a moment to compose herself.

The youngsters froze. Their faces tight with withheld hilarity. Aladdin burped loudly and the rest giggled.

Mama Goldy's face reddened and raised her bowl again. "Let us eat of this mother and child so that they will forever be one with us." She sat down heavily into her chair, shaking her head as the assembled villagers repeated the words.

"Finally," Pixie said and grabbed her bowl.

The stew was as tasty as it smelled. Merlin pressed his cold nose against her leg, but he wasn't getting any. She crossed her fingers that he was back to normal. He'd been weird for a day or so. Not drag-his-ass-on-the-ground weird or growl-at-toddlers-who'd-stepped-on-his-tail weird, but more like shaking-his-head-and-walking-in-crooked-circles weird. Mama Alice had been ready to put him down. They'd all worried it was a brain tumour. Then he'd suddenly come good.

Once the ceremony was over, Mama Gretel brought another bowl of stew over to Pixie. "Take this to the traveller," she said, "and tell him we'll get his last contribution at dawn."

"Tell *her* we'll get *her* last contribution."

Mama Gretel glared. "Just shut your trap and take the stew."

Pixie carried the bowl carefully down the path so as not to spill any. Merlin padded along behind with his nose glued to the trail of warm steam. She couldn't decide whether to tell Wolf about Aladdin. Wolf had never said anything to make her think they were more than just friends. It wasn't a big deal. Pixie didn't know why she was so bothered.

Wolf watched Pixie approach from the door of Ticket Booth House. "You've had your afterbirth ceremony?" She took the bowl from Pixie's hands. "What are the words you say?"

"Let us eat of this mother and child so that they will forever be one with us." Wolf repeated the words and tilted the bowl to her lips.

They sat silently by the light of a solar lamp, the dogs salivating at their feet. If Wolf was the person Pixie thought she was, then she wouldn't hate her for having fooled around with Aladdin. And monogamy was such a twentieth century concept. The mamas actively discouraged the formation of couples. Once breeders shacked up with sperm sacks, they resisted popping out more babies, especially with different partners.

Pixie's thoughts went round and round. She didn't know where to begin or how to raise the topic naturally. What conversation could possibly lead to her saying: *Ha ha. I know what you mean. I actually just the other day lost my baby hole virginity to someone I've known since we were kids and have no sexual interest in whatsoever.*

She cleared her throat. "So, tomorrow will be your last contribution."

Wolf nodded and wiped a dribble of gravy from her chin.

"Will you leave after that?"

"As soon as the sun sets."

"And you suppose you'll be safe there, with the Earth Guardians?"

"I hope so. It's the safest place I can think of." Wolf frowned. "If those pigs are real... if they come, will Fairy Park be ready?"

Pixie shrugged. She'd told the mamas everything she knew about the pigs. They'd all seemed sceptical. Pixie was sceptical too. Wolf herself hadn't even seen them. There was still grub to be collected and prepared, babies with bums to be wiped, clothes to be washed, wounds to be tended, and paths to be swept. Nobody had any extra time or energy to prepare for something that might not even happen.

Wolf produced a bottle from her pack. "Road wine?"

"Go on then." Pixie had been banned from grog rations from the village until she was contributing. Maybe it would give her the courage to talk about what had happened.

Wolf handed her a cup of the milky-looking, foul-smelling wine. Pixie held her nose and downed it. The sour, fermented liquid coated her mouth and tongue.

"Ugh, that's rotten."

Wolf laughed. "You get used to it. I need something to keep me entertained on the road."

"Couldn't you trade for grog from village stills?"

"Costs too much. Easier to grab something sweet and ferment as I go." Wolf put down the empty bowl and wiped her mouth on her sleeve.

"Do you want me to finish that spider web tattoo I started? Tonight's our last chance."

It was also the last time they would spend together until Wolf came to Fairy Park again. Pixie would miss her like a pillow or a pair of shoes or some other thing she could live without but would never want to. They could never have something serious with all the time they spent apart.

"Sure." Wolf took off her shirt and sat backwards on her chair.

Pixie took her black ink and needle wrapped in thread from her pocket. A warm buzz from the alcohol radiated out from her lower back. She ran her fingers over the shoulder Wolf had chosen for her tattoo. Goosebumps rose over Wolf's skin. In the past Wolf had made it clear she didn't like being touched. Did the goosebumps mean that regardless of all that, she liked it when Pixie touched her? She was glad Wolf couldn't see her blush.

"So where exactly is this amazing community of yours?"

"A couple of days to the west of here. On a big hill near the coast."

"Will they welcome you back? I mean you were sent out to be a traveller so they mustn't want any more of your sperm." Pixie placed a steadying hand firmly on Wolf's back and added tiny black marks to the web with her needle.

"They don't care so much about inbreeding there. They actually encourage it to keep the gen-enged traits from breeding out. Then they just inject gene silencers for any undesirable genes. It's quite eugenic really... another reason I'm not completely thrilled to be heading back."

Pixie dabbed the excess ink on Wolf's shoulder with a cloth and on impulse said, "Could I come with you?"

"Why?"

"I'm sick of it here." *And maybe then we'd be able to spend enough time together to work out if what we have is more than a friendship*, she thought but didn't say.

"I don't know if you'd be welcome. They don't often let outsiders in."

"Fair enough."

It made sense, and she'd expected as much. But the rejection still hurt. Pixie knew in her mind it was the Earth Guardians rejecting her, but to her innards it felt like a rejection from Wolf.

Pixie cleared her throat. "I think I'll miss you." Her heart thumped, unsure how Wolf would respond.

"I think I'll miss you too."

Those words were enough to let Pixie believe the feelings weren't one sided. She was even less certain about telling Wolf what had happened with Aladdin. It was the kind of thing they should be able to laugh about together. But it felt more like a betrayal now that she knew for certain Wolf had some feelings for her. Plus, it might hurt her more if Wolf did laugh, or if Wolf didn't care at all. Pixie wanted Wolf to care. She wanted Wolf to be jealous.

"So why a spider web?" Pixie steered the conversation somewhere safer.

"I don't know. It's the first thing I thought of when you offered."

Pixie was always offering to give folk tattoos. She had supposed it could be her contribution. But the only ones who were ever interested were the youngsters, and they had no say over what was considered a valuable contribution. Some of the littlest youngsters asked for silly things, like boobs and dicks, or for impossibly difficult compositions, like portraits of their birth-mothers. Often, they couldn't even sit still for long enough, or shouted about how it hurt like childbirth. Older subjects put more thought into their tattoos. Wolf was the first to ask for a spider web.

"So, no deeper meaning?"

"Nah. Well, I don't know." Wolf shifted in her seat. "Near the radiation exclusion zone there are a lot of spider webs. But they're all screwed up. Like the spiders are off their heads and can't remember how to spin. I guess it got me thinking about how we've fucked up everything on Earth."

"Well, it wasn't really us." Pixie imitated Mama Rosamund's voice. "It was The Greedy and The Tech Lovers who lived through the eras of decadence."

Wolf laughed, even though she'd never properly met Mama Rosamund or heard her dramatic ramblings. "I suppose. Still, would we have done the same if we'd lived then?"

Pixie shrugged, then remembered Wolf couldn't see her, so she said, "Shrug. It would have been more fun than atoning for their sins and excesses like Rosamund reckons we're doing now."

"True. I guess I thought if I could have one perfect thing, this spider web, the way nature intended it to be, it could serve as a reminder or a talisman of what could be."

"If it weren't for bloody humans."

"Exactly. Also, I thought it might look cool."

"Sure."

"It does look cool, doesn't it?"

"Yep. Don't you worry."

Wolf turned and tried to make out the tattoo on her shoulder. "Maybe I shouldn't have got it on my shoulder. You could be doing some fucked up radiation web for all I know."

Pixie stretched her arms over her head and beamed. "Nah, just dicks and boobs."

Wolf threw her bunched-up shirt back into Pixie's face.

"Kidding, kidding. It's beautiful."

Wolf turned back and Pixie leaned forward with her needle and resisted the impulse to kiss Wolf on the back of her neck.

They joked around and chatted about safe topics until it was time for Pixie to leave so Wolf could get some rest for her upcoming journey.

Pixie paused at the door and plucked a white, wriggly termite from the crumbling wood frame and popped it into her mouth to chew on.

"Um. There's something I wanted to tell you." Shit. She'd made it sound too big and important. It was too late now. She'd already started talking. "The other night I had sex with Aladdin. I think I told you about him and how he was always pestering me. And I wanted to see what it was like. So I did it. Finally."

She'd screwed Aladdin because she was curious. It was the kind of impulse she'd followed every day of her life without caring about the consequences. Stupid decisions were how she learnt. The mamas could tell cautionary tales until their words painted the whole world with danger signs, but Pixie never really learnt anything until she'd made a mistake for herself.

Wolf furrowed her brow. "Okay... Cool. How was it?"

Her calm response made Pixie step back into the darkness outside. She'd wanted Wolf to ask her never to do it again. It would be the sweetest, most amazing thing anyone had ever asked of her. Maybe she had been wrong to think Wolf had any interest in her in that way.

"Not that great actually," she muttered, unable to meet Wolf's eye. "He's just not the right person for me, I think."

Wolf nodded slowly. "Right."

"Well anyway. Good luck on your journey back, and hopefully I'll see you again soon." Pixie ran from Ticket Booth House and back up the outcrop before Wolf could even reply.

It would be okay. They would still be friends. It would be easier. More Pixie's style. Her heart wasn't breaking one single little bit.

•‌ •‌ •‌ •‌ •‌ •‌ •‌ •‌ •‌ •‌ •

Pixie stood at the top of the outcrop and peered down the path that Wolf had taken out of town only days before. That last evening had been so confusing. First, Wolf had said she'd miss Pixie and then she'd been untroubled about the Aladdin thing.

The next morning Pixie had gone down to see her off. But Pixie was never an early riser, and Wolf was long gone and had left no message of goodbye. Maybe that meant she was angry. And you didn't get angry unless someone had hurt you. The only way Pixie could have hurt Wolf was by breaking her heart. She had to know for sure. Not knowing Wolf's feelings would be like never hearing the end of a great story or abandoning a delicious meal before seeing the bottom of the bowl.

All she'd need were some sturdy shoes and a pack full of food, and she could set off to find her. So what if they didn't let her into the Earth Guardians compound? She could camp outside until Wolf came out again.

She squeezed her biceps against the sides of her slightly tender boobs. There was a chance this was just a natural hormonal variation. Sometimes she got sore boobs along with her period, especially if she'd been eating a lot of salted meat. If there was one thing all the potential breeders at Fairy Park knew, it was the particulars of their cycle.

Pixie felt no connection to a bundle of cells that may or may not even exist, but she would take the herbs to be sure. She should have done it straight after Aladdin had unloaded in her. In a life considered stupid by most, that had to be the stupidest thing she'd ever done. She'd never before wished she could go back to fix a mistake. It was all because of Wolf. She cared what Wolf thought of her. Soppy.

She shook the soppy away and made her way down to Mama Gretel's clinic. Yells were coming from inside. She'd intended to sneak down while everyone slept but, as usual, she'd woken too late. Now they were all up, getting as much done as they could before the dragon's breath heat of the day. And by the sound of it, Mama Gretel was well into a procedure.

Pixie opened the door a crack. A sperm-sack was on the table, thrashing and yelling, while two older sperm-sacks held him down. Could be a bladder stone. Snow stood by Mama Gretel and handed her instruments. The ruckus might be enough of a distraction for Pixie to get to the herb jars unnoticed. Or she could come back another time.

Patience wasn't one of her strongest qualities. She slipped inside and flattened herself against the wall. Snow raised her eyebrows, but Pixie put a finger to her lips and tilted her chin towards the herb jars. Snow frowned and placed herself in Mama Gretel's line of vision. The sperm-sacks were too busy trying not to faint to pay any attention to her.

She moved sideways along the wall and grabbed the whole jar, scared she'd make too much noise opening the squeaky lid. Mama Gretel's head was still between the poor man's legs. Pixie slid back towards the door with the jar clutched to her chest. The screams stopped as the patient passed out.

Just as she slipped outside, Mama Gretel yelled, "Don't think I didn't see you, Pix. And don't think I didn't see what you took. We'll be having a conversation about how you've worn out your welcome in this village. You've got more front than a row of shops."

"What the hell's a shop?" She yelled over her shoulder, mostly for Snow's benefit, as she jogged down the outcrop with Merlin following.

Pixie collected hot water from the kitchen to brew the purging tea. The words *worn out your welcome* played over in her head. Surely the mamas wouldn't come good on their endless threat to banish her just because she'd taken some herbs from the clinic. She took her tea to the bottom of the outcrop to what the mamas called the playground. They couldn't have a conversation if Mama Gretel couldn't find her. It would give her some time to concoct a convincing lie for why she'd wanted the herbs. There was no way she was telling Gretel about what she'd done with Aladdin. She'd never hear the end of it. But her biggest fear was that Mama Gretel would decide she and Aladdin were a desirable genetic match and the mamas would force her to have the baby.

The playground was a desolate place, mostly concrete, with faded and flaking paint amongst tetanus-laden metal, splintering rotted wood, and tiger snakes. The mamas said youngsters in the past centuries weren't allowed to play anywhere else, just in these playgrounds, and adults had to watch them carefully because they were incredibly fragile. The past was messed up.

She crawled into a concrete tunnel lined with round holes like windows and brushed away gravel to make a smooth-ish spot to sit. Merlin curled up next to her. The tea smelled foul. She blew on the surface and sipped it slowly. She was tempted to down it quickly, but she'd seen Mama Gretel dispensing the cure to enough breeders to remember the specific instructions to sip slowly over fifteen to twenty minutes. She wasn't the first to screw someone she wasn't supposed to. They never threatened to banish the other breeders who made that mistake. They just had it in for her.

Once the cup was drained, she heard the chatter of villagers coming back from the fields. It would soon be full sun. She had to stay away until her period came and there was no way to save her could-be baby. She curled up in the tunnel, her head on Merlin's belly for a pillow.

Before she drifted off, she thought she heard the grunting of a pig in the bush behind the playground. It was probably just some youngsters fooling around. At worst it was someone else's problem and not a good enough reason to keep her from her nap.

15

Merlin's human, Pixie, tossed and turned in the narrow concrete shaft and settled her head on his belly. Centa had come to know Pixie well by her scent and voice. The dog felt most safe while sleeping back-to-back with her.

The dog licked his genitals, and if Centa had a body of her own, she would have shuddered. Mab's tantrums and Mama Rosamund's bullying had forced Centa to jump into the nearest receptive creature. Merlin had been just outside the door, drawn to the yelling and commotion.

It was a choice she soon came to regret. The dog sampled everything with his nose and tongue. He ate rotten morsels whenever he could sniff them out. Worst of all, her intelligence had morphed instantly. She no longer knew her story or her purpose. Colours were muted, her eyesight a little less sharp, but the world came alive in sounds and smells and pure, unanalysed emotion. She felt as though she were looking through a microscope without any awareness of the world outside that tiny field of light.

It hadn't taken Merlin long to tolerate and accept her presence. He couldn't think further than a few minutes ahead or fathom human language. Certain words held meaning for him though. Words like *fuck off*, *get out*, *come on*, *something to eat*, and *good boy* and his name.

The air was stagnant in the enclosed space, and the Earth star at midday was fierce. Merlin was confused. The human's usual bed was a soft mattress at the top of the outcrop, rich with comforting scents. Not this sharp, hard concrete in the playground. Centa was also confused by the habit of the humans in the community to sleep during the day. Midday had been a productive time on Aceso.

Merlin panted, open-mouthed, and drifted into a fitful doze. Centa slipped completely into the void where she could think like a human again, though her thoughts were stuck on a loop of the same unanswerable questions: Where was Ben? And who was she, now that she had been separated from her corporeal form? How much of who she was came from her physical experience? On Aceso, the masters and Skyfather had owned her body. Did they own her consciousness too? Or was Disciple Quinn correct when she said they had no power here on Earth?

She had to find a human that would accept her the way Isaac had accepted Quinn. Then she might have more ability to think these problems through. Quinn, during one of their conversations in the void, had told Centa that she could hop into the next person who altered and opened their consciousness with too many shrooms or alcohol. The only other option was to stop struggling and give in to the pull of disintegration. If she stayed long enough in the void, she would break up into tinier and tinier pieces until she no longer existed, the way a dead organ disintegrated into cells, and then molecules, and then atoms, and then subatomic particles. A kind of death by transformation.

Quinn believed the transformation would make them one with the Earth. She was nearly ready to let go. But Centa wasn't ready for that ending. She still thought she might make something of this existence.

As though Centa's thoughts had conjured her, Quinn appeared in the void, her form dishevelled and flickering.

"There's a sick pig running amok all over the outcrop. I think there are more of them down near the playground. Get your dog to wake Pixie. She could be in danger." And then she was gone, back to help Isaac.

An unfamiliar scent brought Merlin to full alertness before Centa could act. Two animals coming closer. They stank of dirt and faeces and blood. Then he heard them—soft grunts and a clopping sort of sound.

He rose to his feet and growled, the hairs on his back stood on end. A snorting face covered in flaked mud stared down from one of the holes in the walls. Centa screamed silently. She'd never seen anything so monstrous. Corticotropin and adrenaline flooded through the dog and blood rushed to his limbs and organs. He barked and scrabbled across the inside of the concrete shaft, backing away from the beady eyes.

Pixie roused from sleep with a sudden screech and kicked at the face in the hole until it retreated and light flooded in. Distorted yells came from somewhere further up the outcrop.

The light darkened at the end of the tunnel, and one of the animals trotted towards them. Merlin growled as it advanced and, against both Centa and Pixie's pleas that he calm himself, lunged and buried his teeth in the dirt-caked shoulder. Centa retreated to escape the taste and smell of excrement and blood. She watched the scene as though it were happening far away. The animal shook its head from side to side and thrashed Merlin against the concrete walls. The dog's bladder released.

Life on Aceso, even with all its problems, had never been so physically violent. The violence had instead been slow and psychological, or had happened when she wasn't present. She coped in the only way she knew how. She concentrated on her work. She mended cracks in bone, tears in skin, and spilling capillaries.

A strangely folded protein entered Merlin, and she pulled her attention away from the injuries and dismantled every one as soon as they formed. When the injuries ceased, she followed the trail of proteins to a set of tears in the skin of his back leg. Teeth marks. Centa repaired them and returned to Merlin's senses.

He yipped and circled a cadaver. The animal had an axe through its skull, and blood leaked in a pool around its head. Centa glimpsed Pixie on a bridge above the shaft. She screamed and kicked at one of the monstrous animals and whacked it with a chunk of concrete.

Another human, Mama Alice they called her, strode up and pulled the axe out of the dead pig's skull and threw it at the surviving monster. Rust scattered when the axe met the steps. The animal squealed and ran into the bushes, and Mama Alice scooped up her axe and thundered after it.

Merlin licked the cadaver's hide and more misfolded proteins rushed into his lungs. Centa quickly dismantled them. A kick and harsh words from Pixie sent him skittering away. His impulsiveness and attraction to chaos had made it easy for her transfer to him, but now those traits had become a threat. He could have died during the fight. And it had all happened so quickly that he could have taken her with him. Quinn had said that without an anchor, she would disintegrate in the void before she could find another path out.

Blood from a semi-circle of punctures on Pixie's palm wet the dusty ground, and Merlin sprang forward to take a deep, disgusting sniff. The novelty and potential edibility of the blood calmed him, but not Centa. She imagined the misfolded proteins travelling from the bite through the woman's body and morphing other proteins in their path. She could heal her if only she could find a way in.

Then she could leave this simple, unsanitary creature behind and be almost human again.

16

Pixie leaned against the crumbling remains of a concrete horse and took several heaving breaths. Her hand stung where she'd been bitten.

"Well, that was weird," she said to Merlin once her breathing was under control. He whined and nuzzled at her hip. She kneed him away. "The feral pigs we get around here aren't usually so cranky."

She poked at the carcass on the ground with the toe of her shoe. Patches of mud flaked off to reveal pinkish skin. Just like the pigs in fairy tales, or more likely the cruel factory farms from the evil old days. They had to be the pigs Wolf had warned them about.

The shrubs at the end of the playground rustled and Mama Alice emerged.

"Bastard got away. At least we got the other two."

"Other two? There was a third?"

Mama Alice rested the head of her axe against the ground. "Yeah. One came right up the outcrop. Papa Isaac was up having a tinkle and sounded the alarm. Thank the mother for enlarged prostates."

She frowned at Pixie's bloodied hand. "You were bitten."

Pixie picked at the torn skin of her palm. Terrorizing the youngsters with the wound would be cool and might even earn her some new respect.

A strong cramp squeezed Pixie's lower abdomen and liquid gushed into her underpants. She grimaced. She definitely wasn't pregnant, if she ever had been. Thank whatever divine power was responsible for that small mercy. She couldn't say if it was the herbs or the fright she'd just had.

"You should stay here," Alice said, wiping sweat from her brow. "Just in case."

Pixie laughed nervously. "Just in case of what?"

"They might be the diseased pigs that traveller told you about."

"I'm sure I'll be okay."

"We should screen you anyway to be on the safe side." Alice turned her axe around in her hands. It was covered in flecks of pig blood, hair, and brains. She dropped it next to the carcass. "Stay here and I'll bring some stuff to clean and dress your wound."

"Can you bring me some rags or moss? I've just got my period."

"Sure. Sit tight. I'll be back soon."

Blood crusted on Pixie's hand while not-baby blood oozed down her legs as she and Merlin sat in the shifting shade while they waited for Mama Alice to return. Both Pixie's hand and her pelvis throbbed. She was the only one who'd been bitten. That should get her some special treatment. It might even excuse her from contributing for a while. She twisted the fingers of her good hand into the bottom seam of her shirt.

It was over an hour before Alice came back, along with the six other mamas. And they always accused *her* of dawdling and procrastinating. The magic seven all together was either extremely good news or extremely bad. Pixie had never historically been on the receiving end of extremely good news. Could be her luck had changed.

Mama Alice drew a line in the dirt with a rusty shovel. "You'll need to stay behind there. We don't want any trouble."

It hadn't.

"What do you mean trouble?" She'd been attacked by a man-eating pig, and they were calling her trouble? Where was her sympathy?

"Here, love." Mama Gretel threw a jar, some bandages, and menstrual rags over. "Clean your wound with that green decoction and it should heal up nicely."

"And clean yourself up." Mama Rosamund pointed to Pixie's bloody crotch. "Then we'll have a talk."

Mama Wendy threw over some clean clothes. "These are straight from the laundry."

"Where's the disease screener?" Pixie asked, pulling the supplies they'd tossed her together. Once she'd been cleared of infection, they could give her the sympathy she deserved.

"The disease screener won't boot up," Mama Gretel said. "There's fungal hyphae all through it. A spore must have gotten in last time it was used."

"Shit. Don't look at me like that's my fault just because I was the last one to use it. There are spores everywhere. Besides, it's been playing up for a while now. There could have been spores in there for ages." Pixie pictured her crusty, yellow toenails, but that was a different type of fungus. She swore this time it hadn't been her fault.

Mama Goldy shook her head in disapproval. "We're not here to argue with you."

"Why are you all here then?" This wasn't going the way she'd expected. Things never did.

"You have to leave," Mama Rosamund said, putting her hands on her hips. "There's no way to tell if you're infected or not. It's best if you just go. We've had a vote."

They were just going to kick her out? Send her away like some sperm-sack who'd fathered too many children? That wasn't fair. They didn't give a shit about what she was going through. They never had. All they cared about was the productivity of her body. If they saw her as a person at all, they'd see her distress. She'd been attacked by pigs, likely induced an abortion, and been told she might have a deadly disease, and now she was being exiled from the only home she'd ever known. All in one day. She wasn't even infected. Mama Gretel always said she was as fit as a fiddle or strong as a Mallee bull, whatever those were.

"If anyone's infected it'd be one of you oldies with your aging immune systems." Pixie smudged the line they'd marked in the dirt with her toe.

"You know it's not just that." Gretel shook her head. "Don't forget I saw you take those herbs without permission. I don't even want to know why you needed them. We gave you so many chances, Pix, but you never learn."

Pixie's mouth fell open. "But Mama..." They couldn't be doing this to her. While they were annoying, Pixie had always trusted that the mamas cared for everyone and made the best decisions for all of them. Now she could see that they could be as selfish as she was.

Mama Ariel placed a frayed and faded backpack within arm's reach of the line and stepped back. "We've packed enough in here to keep you going for a week or two if you're careful. After that it's up to you."

"Don't even think of coming back here," Mama Rosamund said.

Mama Gretel lowered her head. Were those tears in her eyes?

Pixie sat in the sun and cleaned her wound with the smelly decoction. She wasn't going to make this easy for them. Let them see her wound and all the blood. Could be one of them would have a change of heart if she waited long enough and made herself pathetic enough.

"Where will I go?"

The mamas were silent.

"Well?" Mama Gretel said at last. "We've all voted to boot her out. Has anyone given any thought to what she'll do now or where she'll go?"

"Not our problem," Mama Rosamund said.

"You've all been waiting for an excuse to get rid of me since I refused to be a breeder." Pixie wrapped her wounded hand in a bandage.

"And don't forget how useless you've been for anything else too." Mama Rosamund pointed a finger at Pixie and spittle flew from her lips. "And you're an idolater and a thief, and you corrupt the youngsters and—"

Mama Belle put a hand on Rosamund's outstretched arm. "Enough, Ros."

Pixie took her time going through the contents of the pack while the mamas fanned themselves with handkerchiefs and squinted against the harsh sun. The pack had once belonged to an elderly papa who used to be a travelling jizz man. It had been patched so many times she could part the threads with her fingertips. Inside she found a thin blanket, a fire starter, a compass, a water condensation tube, a knife, a spork, a bowl, slices of dried rabbit, sunflower seeds, dried prickly pear, dried figs, a loaf of bread, a small wheel of cheese and, strangely, twelve dried shrooms in a tin.

She held up the tin. "What are these for?"

The mamas all glanced at each other.

"To ease your passing," Mama Goldy said. "If the worst were to happen."

Pixie scoffed. "I'm not about to die! What's wrong with all of you?"

She wanted to throw the tin back at them, but that would be a waste of good shrooms. What if they were right, though? What if they were sending her out to die? If the disease didn't get her exposure, starvation, bad water, or a Mother Feeder might. Pixie slid the pack onto her back. It didn't seem like they were going to change their minds. Merlin thumped his tail against the dirt.

"You're not going to care for me in my final days like you do for every other member of the village?" Not that she was admitting she was going to die. She just wanted to make them feel guilty. "After everything I've done for this village?" That was likely stretching it a bit.

Mama Rosamund guffawed.

"Take that dog with you. He could be infected too," Mama Alice said.

That wasn't up to her. Merlin would follow if he wanted to.

"Good luck cleaning this mess up." She picked Alice's bloody axe off the ground and stepped towards them, over the line drawn in the dirt. "WHOO. I'm refusing to leave. I'm gonna fight you all. What are you gonna do about it?"

Mama Alice held up her shovel. "Don't test me, Pixie."

Pixie dropped her arms. She had to leave before they saw her cry. She headed into the bush, the way the pig had gone, with Merlin at her heels.

"Don't you come back here," Mama Rosamund yelled. "This isn't like all those other times when you weaselled your way back in."

Mama Rosamund was right for once. Pixie had been threatened with banishment before, but it never took. Each time they'd gotten serious, she'd hidden out in the playground until they'd calmed down. This felt different.

Pixie swung the axe with her good hand. She didn't know how she'd find food or where she'd sleep. How could she feel safe without the insulation of a village around her? Wolf and all the other travellers did it all the time. It had sounded adventurous and free, but now it was just scary. She would miss folk too. Snow especially, and some of the youngsters. The less annoying ones. Aladdin too, if she was honest. This was all the fault of those pigs.

She was disappointed not to pass anyone on the outskirts of their territory. She would have liked to provoke a bit of pity and sorrow. She might have gotten some better shoes or even a piece of cake out of that. Could be they were all up at Fairy Park talking about how great it was without her.

She held onto her anger to keep away her fears.

Once she'd killed the last pig, she could go back to Fairy Park triumphant. She squatted to rub a blade of grass between her fingers and tried to make out trampled foliage. She pictured herself as a tracker, on the trail of a man-eater. But the breaks in the trees and flattened patches of grass all looked random. She listened for clues to the animal's whereabouts instead. Something rustled in the shrubs ahead. She froze, axe raised.

Merlin growled low in his throat and sprang around a copse of tea-trees.

"No, Merlin. Come back!"

The dog ignored her, of course. She didn't know her ass from her elbow, as Mama Gretel often put it, when it came to fighting a pig. Plus, if Merlin were killed, she'd be completely alone. He was all she had in the world. Sounds of a scuffle came from up ahead. She gripped the axe. She should defend Merlin.

Not a chance.

Taking on the pig had been a fantasy. She should bolt while the bloodthirsty beast was occupied with savaging the dog.

Before she could jog away, the leaves in front of her parted and Merlin trotted through, tail and head high, a dead rabbit in his jaws. Mama Gretel said rabbits hadn't always been so easy to catch. They'd been bred this way by Earth Guardians to be a plentiful source of protein. Merlin lay with his prize between his outstretched paws.

A wave of dizziness overcame Pixie. She plonked down, cross-legged on the ground, and held her face in her hands.

"I don't feel so good."

The dog tore skin and crunched bone. Wasn't dizziness one of the early symptoms of ROSE? She hadn't paid enough attention to the descriptions of the disease. She'd supposed it was a problem for other folk. They weren't even sure that it *was* ROSE that had swept through those other villages.

Plus, Mama Gretel and Snow had said it wasn't possible. Dizziness could be anything. It could be all the blood loss, walking in the heat, all the upset she'd experienced, or another side effect of her shedding uterus. She never got sick. If the pigs were spreading disease, she'd be the last to catch it. Everyone else at Fairy Park would need a hand when they fell ill. They'd be sorry they'd sent her away.

She pictured them—the babies, the breeders, the sperm-sacks, the mamas, the elderly papas and the youngsters, Snow—all dead in their beds, their faces white and waxy, bugs crawling from their noses and flies buzzing over them. The thought made her even dizzier.

It was all so unreal. Like when she was a youngster and had seen a wall of dust on the horizon for the first time. She hadn't understood the panic of the adults, couldn't picture the devastation to come.

"We need to find somewhere to rest, old dog."

The Earth Guardian compound was the obvious choice, but she didn't know for sure how to get there, and with the way she was feeling, she couldn't afford to wander around lost for too long. The only other village she'd ever been to was by the drowned city. According to Mama Rosamund, the family of divers who lived there were part fish, part demon because they could swim deep in the ocean and hold their breath for an unnaturally long time.

They'd remember her. She'd been there with the scavengers, trading bags of cassava and pails of milk for shoes. Pixie hadn't been offered a pair of those fancy shoes, which had made it all the more hilarious when plastic-eating mushrooms had sprouted from their cushioned soles.

"How do you feel about joining the divers, Merlin?"

She couldn't swim and she was afraid of all the stinging jellyfish and the one time she'd been on a boat she'd thrown up everywhere, but she could keep their camp for them. Cook and clean. She'd seen other folk do it. It didn't look that hard. The older son had been eager to breed with her last time she was there. That could be awkward.

Maybe she could stay with them for just a couple of days until she had the strength to search for the Earth Guardian compound. A voice in her head reminded her that she might be sick and contagious, but she pushed the voice aside. It wasn't like she was going to jog up and lick them or anything.

When the dizziness passed, she started walking again. Merlin bounded ahead, barking at shadows and chasing crickets through the scrub. There was no one around to stop her, so she made a detour through the grove of fruit trees and munched on one of the sacred nectarines reserved for nursing mothers.

Fields gave way to dense bush as the sun set completely. She could barely see where she was going. Moonlight penetrated the canopy in slashes and slits. She checked her compass and confirmed she was travelling south towards the ocean. She ducked under branches and skirted around shrubs.

Every sound and shadow was a pig with blood-stained teeth. She vaguely remembered hearing somewhere that pigs had a superior sense of smell. Could be she was confusing them with dogs.

She slapped at mosquitoes on her skin and yanked spider webs out of her eyelashes. After a while she came to the main road and travelled by the light of night-glowing shrubs until the sky turned from navy blue to pale grey.

"Let's have a snack," she called to the dog and plonked down on a pile of bricks, yanking all the food out of the pack. Once they'd eaten a good chunk of almost everything, she turned off the road and headed in the direction of the beach.

Closer to the shore, the ground was littered with pieces of concrete, rusted metal, broken glass, and the occasional flayed or mummified industrial structure, all intertwined with the plants and fungi that toiled tirelessly to take the land back.

As the sun rose, the air changed from the smell of rotten green things to the smell of rotten fishy things. Woman and dog crested a small hill and the ocean stretched out before them.

A multi-coloured dune of sea-smoothed plastic and glass pebbles sloped down from the edge of the bush to the shore. Further to the west, over a kilometre down the beach and out into the ocean, were the submerged buildings of the drowned city.

History told that the city had been one of the smaller coastal towns. The divers had made their home on the top floors of the tallest building, about one-hundred metres from shore. The mamas, harsh as ever, said folk who lived in the multi-storied constructions of the greedy generations were asking for their homes to collapse on top of them.

During Pixie's previous visit, there'd been a storm surge. Water had covered the beach and lapped at weeds and trees. The shore moved further and further inland every year. Ice still melting somewhere on the globe, the oldies said. The only ice she'd ever seen were the chunks of hail that fell from the sky.

Sand clattered beneath Pixie's feet. Every now and then she stopped to pick up something that had stayed whole through time. Some had obvious functions: bottles, bowls, and cups. Most were random shapes whose use she couldn't fathom. That was why she'd been shit as a scavenger. She couldn't see the potential in pieces of junk. She followed a trail of what seemed to be plastic cutlery. The ocean salt defended plastic from the fungus. If Mama Gretel had been as clever as she supposed she was, she would have stored the disease screener in a tub of sea salt.

Merlin kept his nose down and was rewarded with a dead jellyfish. Way out beyond the buildings the remains of a sea wall breached the surface of the water for a moment before disappearing again. Birds screeched and circled a spire topped with an elaborate cross.

"Where are those divers, hey?" she asked the dog.

Last time, the divers had been sorting piles of goods across the sand. There were whispers they kept all the best stuff in their building. Access was via one of their warily guarded boats. Pixie was convinced the building was stacked with comfortable clothes and exotic, calorie-dense grub, as well as other shiny treasures her mind hadn't assigned any purpose to, but wanted anyway.

Something on the beach shimmered in the morning heat, a trio of reddish-black splodges, like spokes on a wheel. She squinted to make out the details. The arrangement was striking, even pretty. Could be it was an art project the way Mama Goldy said Fairy Park was an old art project. The sun rose higher and lit the splodges a brighter red.

Pixie's legs weakened beneath her. They were bodies. Three dead bodies.

Long, sun-bleached hair, unique to the divers, streamed over the sand from each of their scalps. They were naked, with dark patches at their crotches and beneath in the armpits of their outstretched arms. The splodges were their insides, now on the outside.

Pixie stepped back into the cover of a grassy shrub, dragging Merlin by the neck behind her.

"Could be better if we stayed here for now," she whispered.

It wasn't the first time she'd seen dead bodies. It wasn't even the first time she'd seen insides. She'd never seen them arranged in such an elaborate way though. Could be it was part of the funeral rites of the divers. Every village had their own particular beliefs and rituals. The divers might have died from some sickness, even the one the pigs spread.

She should leave. Follow the coast until she stumbled upon the Earth Guardian compound. She felt unnaturally calm. Could be she was just too beat to feel any more fear. Could be she was in shock. Could be the disease was chewing her brain and dulling her reactions.

Merlin whined and strained to escape her grip.

"No! No, Merlin. Stay with me."

Movement out on the water drew her eye. Someone was rowing a boat towards the shore. She looked more carefully at the three dead folk on the sand. They were the mother and the two teenage twins. The scavengers had reported that the father had died from an unexpected allergic reaction to a jellyfish sting almost a year before. The person in the boat could only be Tadpole, the older son.

Had he killed his remaining family? He hadn't seemed bloodthirsty. He'd been sweet and funny and had given Merlin scritches and dried jellyfish to chew on when they'd last visited. There hadn't been any aggression or tension in the family either. Not like there was at Fairy Park, where Pixie wouldn't be at all surprised if one of the villagers took a knife and slit the mamas' throats in their beds one night. The only tense moment had been when Pixie had refused a request to stay and breed with Tadpole and the younger brothers when they came of age. Pixie always knew how to bring the tension.

Tadpole dragged the small, metal boat up onto the beach. He was shirtless, his tanned body muscular and compact. He laid the corpse of his mother in the boat and headed out to sea again. Merlin wriggled out of Pixie's grip and snuffled around in the bushes behind her, the bodies on the sand seemingly forgotten.

"What do we do, Merlin?"

There was a small chance Tadpole was a killer. Was it worth the risk for access to the mythical divers' stash or even just a safe place to snooze? Her thoughts were slower and more jumbled than usual.

Tadpole rowed his mother out past their building and then returned with the empty boat. Pixie still hadn't decided what to do. Merlin shot past her shoulder. She grabbed for him too late. He slipped out of her reach and barked and skittered along the sand.

"Hey! Get back here!"

The dog trotted all the way up to Tadpole. Could be he was thinking about those tasty, dried jellyfish treats. Tadpole lifted a bat from the bottom of the boat. Then he spotted her at the edge of the bush. There was no hiding now. She would have to take her chances with the unlikely multiple murderer. Pixie walked down to the beach. Tadpole dropped the bat and squatted to hug Merlin.

Pixie held the axe at her side. "What the hell went down here?"

Tadpole shook his head. He raised his baseball cap and smoothed down his salt-crusted hair. Merlin licked tears and snot from his leathery face.

"Mother Feeders."

"Oh no." That had been her least likely guess.

"I'd had too much tequila. Mom let me lie in. I should have been there. I might've been able to protect them."

It made sense, even if she didn't know what tequila was. The arrangement of the bodies and the opening of the innards to the elements were just like the stories Mama Rosamund had told and Pixie had pretended not to listen to. Mother Feeders were convinced that the only thing of value humans could give back to the Earth was their rotting corpses. Mama Alice joked that they were the descendants of debt collectors from the greedy times who had found that money was useless and instead made folk pay with flesh and lives.

Fairy Park had been attacked by Feeders just twice in Pixie's lifetime. In the last attack, years before, they'd killed a shelter full of oldies before Mama Alice—still a breeder and not yet a mama—had skewered their heads and placed them at the borders of Fairy Park as a warning to other raiders.

In recent years there'd been talk they'd all died out. That obviously wasn't true. Now she had Mother Feeders as well as a homicidal pig to watch out for.

"I'm burying them at sea." Tadpole gently pushed Merlin away and wiped his face with the bottom of his shorts. "The sea creatures can have them. That's what they would have wanted.

They can feed the Earth in their own way. Not the way of those bastard Feeders."

Merlin sniffed at the remaining bodies and licked a pool of clotted blood.

"And that pig won't have them either." Tadpole dragged his boat back into the ocean.

"Pig?"

"Yeah. I scared it off with my bat. Ugly thing. Had rabies or something."

The pig had been there. The thought of it scared her more than the Mother Feeders. Could be because she'd been face to face with the beast while she'd never encountered an actual Feeder herself.

No movement came from the bushes at the edge of the beach. No grunts or glint of beady eyes. If the beast was around, it watched them stealthily.

· · · ● · ● · ● · · ·

She didn't even have to ask. Tadpole had been keen to lug her back to his building, once he'd disposed of his brothers. He rowed Pixie and Merlin over the concrete reef, expertly navigating the currents and breaking waves.

Under them lay a whole city, where thousands of folk had spent their days. Each of them had supposed they were important. They'd all been the centre of their own stories. Did they know the collapse of their civilization was coming? She could almost see them, fighting and getting up again after every successive blow, until one of Mama Rosamund's five horsemen got them: natural disaster, pestilence, violence, hunger, or demonic possession.

The cool winds over the water pierced Pixie's thin shirt, and goosebumps covered her arms. She grabbed Merlin and pulled his warmth to her.

Tears dripped from Tadpole's dark eyes the whole way over, but Pixie couldn't hide her excitement at seeing the divers' treasures at last.

"You must have so much stu... stu... stu." Merlin licked her cheek and whined. Her mouth wasn't working properly.

"Huh?" Tadpole spat a throat full of tears and snot into the water.

She didn't try to talk again. She was beat and she was hungry. That was all. Even though she'd scoffed almost everything in her pack just a couple of hours earlier. She'd walked a long way and hadn't slept. She needed extra calories. She would soon eat from the divers' legendary stash of goodies.

Tadpole tied up the boat and climbed a rope ladder to the top floor. He sent a bucket down for Merlin and then Pixie made her way up. Her wounded hand ached against the rope and her hips felt like they were on hinges, like she was some sort of puppet.

"Leave your shoes here."

Tadpole held aside a blue plastic sheet and she climbed into the dark building. He lit a solar lantern and led her through a central hallway with six rooms on either side.

"A long time ago this building was a place where folk who were far from home could rest in safety."

Pixie supposed that was appropriate given her current lack of a home. She nodded, not trusting her unruly tongue to obey. Tadpole didn't seem to notice the one-sided conversation. He blah, blah, blahed as he showed her around.

"We each have...had...our own rooms."

His room was filled with bats, balls, frisbees, rackets, bicycles, scooters, and helmets. The youngsters at Fairy Park would have killed for equipment like that. The stuff the scavengers brought back never lasted long. They always sprouted fungus like acne all over.

"You can stay in Kaz's room if you want." Tadpole yanked aside a piece of fabric decorated with red and blue flowers and showed Pixie inside. "We used to have doors when I was a toddler, I think. But they rusted and swelled with damp, so Mom took them all off."

The room was stacked with bright, garish plastic figurines. They were likenesses of humans, animals, and creatures who were either fantastical or whose stories hadn't made it through the harshness of history. Lots of them had ridiculously huge heads on small bodies. The smell of cold, chemical emptiness tickled Pixie's nose. Merlin headed straight for the nest of human-smelling bedding in the middle of the room.

"Unless you'd rather stay in my room..." He raised his eyebrows and his pecs twitched.

Pixie dropped her bag and pretended she hadn't heard him. She wished he'd put a shirt on.

He pointed to the left. "Down that end is a stairwell. It's dangerous though. You'll want to keep the dog out of there. The water can rise quickly. At its highest, it floods the floor below."

The other rooms were filled with the goods the divers had dredged up from the city. Shoes, clothing, bedding, fabrics, tools, plates, bowls, cups, and cooking utensils.

"We only bring up useful stuff. You wouldn't believe all the crap that's down there. A lot of it is wrecked, but even more is just useless."

The treasures weren't as cool and wondrous as Pixie had pictured. Sure, they were useful, but nothing she hadn't seen before and nothing magical or mind blowing.

"Are you hungry?"

They came to a room stocked with metal cans and bags of something Tadpole called rice. This was more like it. Most of the cans had no labels, or the pictures on the sides were scratched and faded beyond sense. Pixie had never been lucky enough to try canned food. Now and then the scavengers brought some back, but the mamas scoffed them.

She nodded and her head twitched to one side. "Yeah. I'm hungry." Mercifully her voice obeyed her. Her stutters must have been a freak occurrence. It wasn't a massive deal anyway. A lot of the youngsters stuttered and some of the breeders and sperm-sacks too. It was just a thing that happened to healthy folk now and then. It didn't mean she was sick.

"All right then. I'm not supposed to share our food with anyone outside the family." He blinked away tears and slid his hand from her shoulder down to her elbow. "I suppose you're my family now."

Like hell she was. She was just there to see the treasures and get her strength back. Staying with Tadpole long-term wasn't going to work as a plan. She'd come up with a new plan after she'd rested.

"Mom only lets us have one can each per day. They have to last. But it's just us now. Do you think that means we can have four cans between us?" His bottom lip quivered, and tears filled his eyes.

Pixie looked away. Sure, he'd lost his whole family suddenly and violently, but he didn't have to make her feel so uncomfortable.

"Lee usually cooks the rice. I don't even know how. Mom used to say it wasn't a meal without rice." He grabbed three cans. "No need to be too greedy, I s'pose."

Speak for yourself, she thought and yanked a can out of his hand.

"How do you open it?"

"I'll show you. This way."

At the end of the building was a massive room. Cushions, musical instruments, and other things Pixie couldn't identify lined a rectangular pit in the floor. In the far corner was a fire drum, a table with five chairs, and cooking equipment.

"Mom reckons this was once a swimming pool." He pointed to the pit. "She said it was kind of like having a little of the ocean inside."

Pixie tutted.

"I know. Why would anyone want that?"

They sprawled on cushions inside the oceanless swimming pool. Sheets of plastic on the windows flapped in the wind. Tadpole showed her how to cut away the metal lid on one of the cans. Inside was a gloopy, pale orange liquid that smelled a bit like overripe stone fruits. It tasted much sweeter than anything Pixie had ever had and left a weird aftertaste. The liquid felt like slime going down her throat.

The next can had a greenish paste inside that made them both wrinkle their noses. They gave that one to Merlin, who wasn't fussy at all. The third had a vaguely meaty core surrounded by solidified fat. The meal churned uneasily in her stomach. It was a novelty to eat something different, but she wouldn't want canned foods all the time. She would have preferred some fresh bread and roasted rabbit with dandelion greens to the unpleasantly textured and overpoweringly flavoured grub.

Disappointing. Everything about her current situation was disappointing.

They washed the taste out of their mouths with tea, and Tadpole bounced a ball against the wall of the pool. Merlin jogged back and forth in ecstasy. The ball bounced towards Pixie. She held her good hand to catch it and the ball whacked her in the face.

Tadpole stopped his incessant crying to laugh at her. "Wow, you're unco-ordinated." He produced a bottle of amber-coloured alcohol from behind a cushion. "You want to share this?"

Now this was the kind of treasure she'd hoped to find. Capitalist alcohol. It was rumoured to be smoother and sweeter than anything they could make these days from excess grain and rotting fruit.

She couldn't believe what she was about to say. "Later. I should have a snooze. I'm just b... b... beat."

· · • • · • · • · ·

Pixie's sleep was shallow, with tensed muscles and grinding teeth. Hundreds of plastic eyes gawked at her from the edges of the room. Merlin roused her with his growling.

She couldn't remember where she was. There was a relentless sound as loud as a storm all around her. The blanket and pillow weren't scratchy enough to be from her bed at Fairy Park. Plus, it was dark. Darker than she was used to it being at the top of the outcrop during the full sun snooze.

In the doorway was a silhouette. She grabbed Merlin across the neck. Could she get him to attack? What would she even say? *Merlin, attack* wasn't likely to work.

"Good, you're awake."

It was Tadpole. She was in the divers' building. That sound was the ocean. And there was something wrong with her body and brain.

"It's nearly dusk. There's something I want to show you on the roof."

Pixie's muscles twitched and spasmed as they climbed another rope ladder. She was glad Tadpole headed up first, so he couldn't see her squirming like a tickled youngster.

The roof was mostly bare concrete, covered in drying seaweed and jellyfish. The setting sun threw golden, shifting shapes like fish scales on the surface of the water. The dog—she couldn't remember its name—licked the jellyfish before gulping down three in a row. Tadpole didn't seem to mind so Pixie said nothing. She was worried she couldn't talk anymore anyway. The man—she could have sworn she knew his name a moment ago—stood by the waist-high wall at the edge of the roof.

"Don't lean on it. It's crumbling."

Pixie held herself tightly to contain her twitches.

"Hear that?"

Over the relentless roar of the wind and waves was the squawk of seabirds. Big deal. She shrugged.

"Coming from the land." He pointed towards the shore and cupped a hand behind one of his ears.

His name was Tadpole and his whole family had been killed by Mother Feeders, and now he was mad with grief. It hadn't been a good idea to come over to the building alone with him. What if he didn't let her leave? She could sneak away on a boat, but she had no idea how to operate one or if she'd even have the strength.

Then the wind changed direction and she heard it. Drums coming from somewhere inland.

"Mother Feeders. They're celebrating their kill." He spat over the edge of the building and the wind whipped his slag away. "The land is too dangerous for folk like us now. You're lucky I brought you over here. I'll keep you safe."

Pixie's legs were floppy. Bloody hell. She really was sick. She couldn't deny it any longer. Poor Tadpole had no idea. He hadn't asked her a single question about why she'd left Fairy Park and turned up on his beach. He hadn't even asked about the bandage on her hand and the blood soaking through it. She shouldn't have come. She should've stayed somewhere she wouldn't infect anyone else.

She was stuck in a nightmare even worse than the recurring one where she was impregnated against her will and her belly swelled so fast and so large that she burst open and became one massive fistula. A violent tremor rocked her body.

"Hey!" Tadpole stood over her, panicked. "What's wrong? Are you sick? You're sick!" He reached out to touch her then reared back and frowned. "Is it contagious?"

"Aw. Shit, Tadpole. I'm so sorry.

17

As Merlin and Pixie travelled through the detritus of civilisation, Centa felt as powerless as one of the fleas on Merlin's back. She was a parasite with no other purpose than to exist, on an animal that would scratch and shake her away if it could.

In a way, it meant she was free from the responsibility of making decisions, like a child or even a worker on Aceso. Every aspect of her life had been decided for her then, as it was now. But at least on Aceso she'd known her role and had been part of a common purpose to build and maintain the community.

When Tadpole had expelled them from his hab on the water and rowed them over to the beach, Centa had been glad. Merlin had been disturbed by the slight sway of the building and the constant roar of the ocean. And she wasn't going to find Ben there anyway.

But now, even her connection to Quinn had faded and disappeared. She was truly alone. The void was completely empty. All her life she'd been smothered by her community, and now she was smothered by isolation. She'd hated Aceso. She'd wanted Skyfather's dream to fail. But there'd been comfort in sharing her suffering with others.

Pixie staggered and slurred her speech. Merlin sniffed her repeatedly, fretful about the sickness that oozed from her pores. Every now and then a path into the human's consciousness flared, likely from the infectious protein's work within her brain, but whenever Centa attempted to enter so that she could repair the woman and have a more suitable host for herself, the paths shattered or were blocked by a psychic force.

Quinn had said that Pixie was stubborn and contrary.

The sun was fierce and when the shore and its slight breeze was far behind them, Pixie took shelter beneath the shade of a tree. Merlin climbed up next to her on a rotting wooden couch frame covered with dirt-caked shreds of fabric. He licked the side of Pixie's face as she fetched dried seaweed from her pack and shared it with him.

Centa felt a pull towards the void. She shifted her consciousness and saw two faint paths that pulsed more brightly than the threadlike ones that led to small animals and insects. But it wasn't just that. There was an attraction or familiarity to them, as though their polarities were aligned with hers. She knew, just as Quinn had known when she'd first sensed Centa, that there were other Sky Humans nearby.

The full force of her loneliness nearly shattered her form in the void, but she pulled herself together and studied the signals with as much scientific detachment as she could muster. There was nothing to distinguish them. No mystical sign or scientific evidence to suggest who they might be. Centa couldn't control or influence Merlin's direction anyway. The dog would go wherever he wanted. He didn't have the brain complexity to fathom her communications. Her early attempts had provoked a panic response that had attenuated over time until he simply ignored her. She held to the end of the unidentified paths as she returned to him.

Pixie was standing, her face green and her body swaying. She murmured something about the pig and began walking again. After two steps, she vomited dried seaweed and gloopy tinned food onto the ground at her feet. Merlin immediately licked it up.

Occasionally, Centa thought it was fortunate that she had no control over Merlin. This wasn't one of those times. But given the ability to roam, she'd be paralysed by the endless choices before her. Earth was big, and she may never find Ben. That didn't bother her as much as it once had. Her need for him was still there, but it wasn't as pure. Distance from the Sky Human settlement and the control of the masters had diluted her need for the escapism of their trysts.

Life with Merlin freed her from emotional pain. He only ever experienced fleeting seconds of anxiety or adrenaline. There was no overthinking or worrying and none of the violent and disturbing thoughts that had once plagued her. But the more time she spent with him, the more effort it took to preserve her own intelligence. According to Anton, scientists had drilled down to all the biological processes involved in the workings of the brain but couldn't explain the biology behind consciousness. He'd said that, back on Earth, some had theorised that consciousness could be altered within a brain, but not created. The same way a radio signal was created elsewhere but could be adjusted, altered, and reinterpreted by the radio controls. In the dog and even less complex animals, the hardware for playing the signal, the radio itself, wasn't as powerful as Centa was used to.

Merlin caught a friendly, familiar scent, and he followed its trail, nose to the ground. Centa let his excitement lift her as Pixie staggered on behind him, through the thick brush and shimmering heat. Except for when he circled back to nip the human on the backside when she slowed, his path tracked along with one of the paths in the void. When the signal became strong enough, Centa returned to the void and a human shape resolved out of the darkness, smoke-like and transparent. They stretched towards her as though they too were desperate to connect with a familiar soul, their form sharpening into a face and body that Centa knew too well.

Perpetua.

Of all the people to find. Looking upon her sister-worker wasn't what she'd expected, but it was almost enough. Like the times she'd wanted Ben to kiss her, and he'd given her a smile and a hug instead.

Perpetua's shoulders were lower and her forehead less furrowed than Centa remembered. The tension that had held her together on Aceso was gone, but she hadn't fallen to pieces. What kind of vessel was she in? If she were in a fly or a rat, as Centa had once been, then she could be gone at any moment, carried on the whims of these Earth animals.

Centa flitted back to Merlin for a moment to see if she could catch sight of Perpetua's vessel. A black, barrel-bodied dog ran towards Pixie and Merlin, and Merlin vibrated with excitement, every part of his body wagged as though he were all tail.

"Lucy?" Pixie said. "There's two of you. There's two of everything. Fuck."

The woman was deteriorating fast now, but there was nothing Centa could do if she wouldn't let her in.

She returned to Perpetua in the void. In this strange world, she finally had something familiar, even if it was someone she'd been trying to escape all her life. Even if her presence reminded her of all the mistakes she'd made. Maybe this existence was drawing her towards those she had a connection with. Maybe all the threads of connection that the hallucinogenic fungus had shown her were real after all.

"Worker 9! I'm so glad you're... alive," Perpetua said, twisting her hands." I'm so sorry about what I did, to everyone."

Of course her first thoughts would be of her transgressions. She never changed. But Centa had. She wouldn't let Perpetua lull her back into who she'd been on Aceso.

"It wasn't your fault. The vine was coming anyway. And don't call me that. We're not workers anymore. Call me Centa. It's what I call myself."

"Centa?"

"Short for placenta."

"You always did take too much pride in your work."

"Someone in that laboratory had to."

Perpetua's nose crinkled. "You can call me Perpetua now if you want. I know you do anyway."

Despite it all, her presence gave Centa comfort. Perpetua was someone she could trust. Someone who would share her perspective and bewilderment.

She kept a small part of her attention on the corporeal world to track the dogs' movements. They tugged at Pixie's sleeves with their teeth and led her through thick shrubs to a decrepit two-storey building entwined with grasses, trees, and weeds. A fallen chain-link fence clanged under their feet. The trio weaved through rough-edged chunks of rebar-spiked concrete and the husks of abandoned vehicles.

"How funny that we both find ourselves dependent on these domesticated animals when we were once Skyfather's own pets," Centa said. "I'm longing for a chance to return to a human vessel."

"I don't mind," Perpetua said. "This dog has a simple, uncomplicated relationship to the world. I can retreat from the mess of my own thoughts. I expected the vine would bring an end to it all. I wanted an end to it all. Do you think anyone suffered?"

"It was peaceful for me once the fear had passed."

Perpetua's despair was infectious. Centa wanted to concentrate on facts, not feelings.

"Have you come across anyone else from Aceso?"

Perpetua averted her gaze. "I'm not certain. I was in insects until only a day ago. I know you'll be looking for Disciple Ben."

Centa ignored the comment and the disapproval Perpetua was unable to hide. She couldn't let the oppressions of Father's Law continue to hurt her. She switched her attention to Merlin as he and Lucy led Pixie through an opening in the side of the building. Shards of illuminated dust fell from holes in the roof and onto androids lined up between concrete pillars. Disarticulated arms, legs, torsos, and heads littered the floor.

She returned to Perpetua. "I met a disciple who left Aceso in the early years before we were generated. Her name is Disciple Quinn. She was in the body of an old man."

Perpetua frowned. "So, there's no escape?"

Centa hadn't thought of it as a situation they would need to escape. She did miss the ease of communication between her mind and body, the exquisite pleasure of water in a parched throat, the crunch of fried bugs between her teeth.

"I'm fading again." Perpetua held out her arms and looked down at the molecules that flew from her like smoke in a breeze.

They both returned to the dogs to re-anchor. Centa was happy for the break. Perpetua was dragging her into the undiluted solution of misery she always wallowed in. Any generous feelings Centa had towards her sister-worker always faded with prolonged contact.

Pixie had stumbled into a small windowless room at the back of the warehouse, furnished with a chair and a cot with a pile of rags on it. Cobwebs hung from the roof, and there was messy writing all over the walls.

The dogs crowded around the pile of rags and the smell of infection—bacteria multiplying and flesh putrefying—filled Merlin's nose. A sweaty face emerged and pulled a dusty blanket up under their chin.

Pixie fell to her knees and embraced them. "Wolf!" she cried, over and over.

The dogs tried to work their way into the hug, and Centa revelled in Merlin's joy at the touch of these loved ones. She remembered how the small hairs all over her body had stood on end when Ben touched her. Would she ever feel that again? Experiencing reality through another's body wasn't the same.

Wolf and Pixie spoke haltingly through their pain and sickness. With shaking hands, Pixie opened her pack and dug around, pulling out a metal tin about the size of her fist. She opened it slowly, and it smelt like a kind food to Merlin but not one of his favourites. Centa recognised the dried mushrooms.

Pixie stammered something about easing their passage, but while in the dog, Centa couldn't put together what she meant. She returned to the void where it all made much more sense—the two women were dying. Wolf had been attacked by people she called Mother Feeders two days earlier and now a wound on her back was infected. They were ingesting a fungal fruiting body, probably the same kind Mab had taken, to help them have a good death.

The urge to heal was strong. She had no attachment or investment in the woman and, after all the death she'd seen on Aceso, one more wasn't going to trouble her. Yet it wasn't just the opportunity to be in a human again that called to her. The healing itself was what her new form was made for. She'd felt that when she'd healed both Merlin and Mab. It had been a kind of metamorphosis, like the biology of butterflies and caterpillars that Ben had told her about. The caterpillar consumed and, in large enough numbers, could damage an ecosystem, but once it became a butterfly, it was a pollinator that gave life. Her form on Aceso had been a caterpillar. On Earth she could be a butterfly.

Two glimmering paths unfurled in the void. A change in consciousness had opened the women up, just as Quinn had described.

Centa called for Perpetua. "This is our chance. We can heal the women and then be free of the limits of these dogs. In human bodies, we'll be able to think more clearly."

Perpetua became hazy. "I don't know if I want that... to be human again. Thinking more clearly will mean feeling more clearly. I want to feel nothing."

"Don't you have the urge to heal them?"

"The last time I followed an urge, our whole settlement was destroyed." Perpetua began to fade.

"Wait." Centa reached out as though she could grab hold of her before she returned to Lucy. "You once said my rebellion didn't benefit anyone other than myself. Now you're the one who won't help others. These humans will die if we don't repair them. Please. Just try."

But Perpetua was already gone. Centa couldn't waste any more time. Her sister-worker would make her own choices, despite anything Centa said. They were both equally stubborn.

Centa leaned into one of the paths and left the primitive confines of Merlin behind. The damage to Pixie was widespread. She didn't permit herself time to get comfortable, test her new extremities, or stretch into the limbs that reminded her of her own lost body. She headed straight to the spongy brain, full of holes, and got to work. She disintegrated and cleared dead and dying cells, pushed other cells to regenerate, and repaired torn membranes and sheared DNA. She felt at peace. She was where she was supposed to be.

She knew that she could remove all traces of Pixie's memories and personality and take the body for herself. It wouldn't be the body she considered her own, but it would be better than sharing with another, more dominant consciousness. But to steal a body for her own use would make her no better than Skyfather and the masters. It would make her a caterpillar again.

18

A dog nudged Pixie's hand with its wet nose. Fuck. She was dying. What a stupid way to go. If only she'd listened to that... jizz woman. Why couldn't Pixie remember her name? The folk at Fairy Park must be getting sick now too. They were mostly good people, if a little annoying. It would take longer if they weren't bitten. If they hadn't had a huge dose of disease injected into their bloodstream by pig saliva like she had.

Her memory was as holey as well-fermented sourdough, but the affectionate contact from the dog popped the empty bubbles in her head. His name was Merlin. And there, looking like a dead body beside her own dog Lucy, was Wolf. If Pixie hadn't happened to be so close to death herself, stumbling unexpectedly on her crush would be the luckiest moment of her life.

For once she didn't push Merlin away. She was glad she wasn't alone. Could be they'd all end up together in the afterlife. But what kind of afterlife? The mamas had been split on specifics. The most terrifying version had been the idea of nothing, a total absence of everything, like a snooze without dreams or the assurance that you'd wake up. Some folk found that heartening and restful. The older folk seemed to accept it more. It sounded like a claustrophobic, inescapable boredom to Pixie. The disease had wiped so much from her mind, yet it had left her with these horrors.

The only way she'd been able to keep the fear of death at bay throughout her life was to tell herself that it was something that happened to other folk. Now fear was hatching all over her like lice in the seams of her clothes.

She hoped the shrooms would kick in soon.

Tremors rocked her arms all the way from her shoulders to her fingertips, and her brain fragmented and bounced around the inside of her skull like wattle seeds in a hot pan. She'd always pictured her life as a tall tree that she was clambering up from branch to branch. Each branch represented a year. She could peer back down at the ones below, all the way to the ground where they were blurred by distance. The top of the tree had always been shrouded in cloud, and she couldn't see where it ended. Now, the tip of the tree was being buffeted by gusts of wind under a dark and endless sky.

Tears streamed out of her eyes. She wasn't the kind to cry. She'd never seen the point. But she didn't even have control of her tear ducts anymore. She didn't know what she was most sad about—Wolf's death, her own, or those of everyone at Fairy Park. She might even have spread it to Tadpole.

It was all sad and stupid. She'd supposed Wolf was invincible. A kick-ass traveller who knew what to do no matter what shit she was in. She'd supposed she was invincible too. She'd pictured herself annoying folk and always doing exactly the wrong thing until she was old and officially barren.

After a while, the effects of the shrooms intensified and a calm came over her. Her corpse would feed the Earth just as the Mother Feeders had always claimed. Could be they were onto something after all. Everything was as it was supposed to be, good and right. She opened herself up and remembered everything from the moment she was born and all the lives she'd touched—Snow and Wolf and Merlin and all the folk at Fairy Park. That was what it was all about. She even felt a connection to Mama Rosamund.

Something poked at the edges of her peace. A truth she'd hidden behind clumsiness and troublemaking. A truth she'd never even admitted to herself. She wished she'd been useful. She wished she'd given back to all the folk of Earth and somehow relieved their suffering. Even more than that, she wished she'd never hurt anyone with her actions.

She'd run out of time to find her purpose. Mama Gretel would roll her eyes at her ambition and tell her to get off her high horse, or one of her other weird sayings. She always said not everyone was special. Some folk were put on Earth just to contribute small things, to roll up their sleeves to keep their communities fed and safe, and that should be enough for someone as incompetent as Pixie. Even that was a form of love. Mama Gretel had been trying to make her days easier.

Memories of her life blurred with memories of dreams she'd had and memories she'd invented from remnants of both. The boundaries of reality were leaky and vague, a whimsy of the human mind.

Then someone was there with her, telling her everything was going to be all right. Not a one-with-the-universe kind of all right. Instead, she would be cured. The voice was unfamiliar, dredged up from who-knew-where by her messed up brain.

"What's going on?" she asked. "Who are you?"

"My name is Centa. I'm repairing you. The damage was extensive, but soon you'll be completely restored."

Was this a fever dream? Pixie had no idea. It felt so real. Her mind buzzed and hummed. Gradually her thoughts cleared. She didn't know how long she lay there, but through the haze the voice kept talking as it cleared away what it called misfolded proteins and restored function to her brain cells.

Pixie supposed this wasn't a bad way to die, with the hope that she was being cured. She could accept her fate. Wasn't that what the shrooms were supposed to give to the dying? Would death be worse after this hope? She'd be dead though. She wouldn't care.

"Who are you?" she asked again.

Centa told a wild story about shooting through space from a planet across the galaxy—the planet Aceso. Was that the one that Wolf had told her about all those months ago when she'd still thought she had decades of life ahead of her? Centa had bounced from Merlin to Pixie and before Merlin, she'd been the supposed demon who'd possessed Mab.

Mab who Pixie had given shrooms to and had never taken responsibility for. She'd never taken responsibility for anything. She'd never said sorry or tried to change her ways to help anyone or anything but herself. Her death wasn't supposed to be like this. Shrooms were supposed to make your passing as psychologically easy as possible. That's what Mama Goldy always said.

Centa lulled her with stories of the strange planet that she had come from and a creepy vine that grew there. She settled next to Pixie in her body, their edges melting together like butter and honey in a saucepan. Centa pushed Pixie's torso up from the dusty floor with a burst of delight.

"Is this the afterlife? Am I in heaven?"

"No, you're repaired." Centa opened Pixie's eyes.

Pixie was lost for a moment until she wrested control back from the alien. Moonlight shone through holes in the ceiling. Merlin thumped his tail on the floor and dragged himself forward on his belly to lick her face. They were in the old android factory. The place had been a no-go zone for years—ever since a scavenger had tried to activate one of the solar-powered machines with his palm print and the android had shot him through the head with a weapon stashed in its shoulder.

Lucy yipped and Wolf opened her eyes. "Are we dead?" she asked, her voice far away. "We're not dead, are we? The strangest thing." She sat up and twisted to make out her wound. "It *is* healed. I thought I was dreaming."

Pixie stood. Her body was strong and free of pain. She unwound the dressing from the pig bite on her hand to reveal smooth, intact skin.

"You're not going to believe—"

"I think I might."

• • • • ● • ● • • •

Pixie and Wolf sat cross-legged on the floor in the back office of the old android factory. Centa, the alien who'd set up camp inside her, instructed her to hold hands with Wolf. In the short time Pixie had spent with Centa, she'd struck her as stiff, solemn, and bossy. She would have gotten along well with the mamas.

Once their hands were connected, Wolf's awestruck, sceptical, panicked thoughts flooded her mind. The signal travelled through their skin like the vibrations from a tremor beneath the outcrop, up to the very top where Pixie's bed had been.

There was another there too. A quieter voice. Centa introduced them as her sister-worker, Perpetua.

Pixie didn't believe in demons or spirits, and Centa and Perpetua were adamant that they weren't uploads. They'd been scientists on a distant planet, they said, but they'd died there. They couldn't explain how they'd gotten to Earth.

Pixie had no idea about science. Could be why she was more willing to skip the explanations than Wolf. She remembered an old papa, long dead now, who would blah-blah-blah about the meaning of life and theories of consciousness and reality. The mamas had always rolled their eyes and told him that pondering didn't put food on the table.

All Pixie knew for sure was that she'd been close to death and Centa had cured her.

"Just fuck off out of my head for a minute," Wolf said. "I need to think." She dropped Pixie's hands.

The alien women's voices ceased, but Pixie could still feel Centa inside her, quiet as if she were holding her breath.

Wolf lifted her shirt to wipe sweat from her forehead. "Maybe those shrooms you gave me caused a psychosis and I'm hallucinating all of this."

She didn't blame Wolf for having difficulty believing. They'd been saved from death in a way not even the most shroom-addled youngster could concoct. Pixie unzipped her pack and yanked out her metal spork.

"Watch." She stabbed herself in the back of the hand. "Argh!" It hurt like childbirth. Small beads of blood welled in the puncture marks, much neater than the pig bite had been.

Wolf reared back. "What the fuck?"

"Why would you do that to yourself?" Centa asked, scandalized. Pixie hoped she wouldn't turn out to be as annoying as having a mama in her head twenty-four hours a day.

"Do your stuff," Pixie told her and held her hand up.

"Ah, I see."

The skin knitted together, and the holes closed to leave an unblemished surface with four small drips of drying blood.

"Damn it." Wolf held her hands out to Pixie and the four women connected again.

"There's a good chance this pig disease ROSE has infected all the folk at Fairy Park like it infected me," Pixie said, turning the conversation to what she considered most important. "Do you think you can cure them too?"

"I'm not certain," Centa said. "I've only ever repaired from within a person. I don't know how easy it'll be to transfer from one person to another. An alteration in consciousness is required to achieve it."

"The mamas have lots of shrooms."

"I don't know—"

"We should try," Perpetua said.

Centa stayed silent for a moment. "Perpetua's right. We should try."

Pixie beamed. This was an amazing power. Could even be the most valuable contribution Fairy Park had ever seen. It would make up for all the years she'd been useless. Everyone would respect her and love her. Mama Gretel would be proud.

But the power wasn't really hers. Pure luck had brought it to her. She hadn't studied or practised this skill. She was more like a tool for Centa to do her work, like Mama Alice's axe.

But the life she'd led had brought this to her. Choices she'd made had put her in Centa's path. Could be fate. Or could be she was talking shit, seeing connections where there were none because of the shrooms. None of that mattered. The folk at Fairy Park were in danger. That's what she needed to focus on.

She squeezed Wolf's hands. "I know you were on your way back to Earth Guardians, but the people back home need our help. I'd really like it if you came with me."

Pixie screwed up her face in anticipation. She would just have to get over it if Wolf left her. She was used to disappointment.

Wolf squeezed her hands back. "This is important to you, so it's important to me. There's nothing for me at the Guardians."

Could be Pixie's luck was changing.

Fourth Interlude

They must have looked odd, the professor and child, staring at the towering gingko tree in the middle of the compound, surrounded by the fug of rotting fruit. But plants soothed Rae. They never asked for answers or unreasonable amounts of attention. They fed the Earth and all its occupants, and they fed her soul, even the parts that were vine. They transferred what she needed via some invisible connection.

"This tree was maybe three times my height when I was a child." Rae tilted the professor's head back. Clover-shaped leaves, turning from summer green to autumnal yellow, blotted out the overcast sky. "Now I can barely see the top."

"I remember it too," Ben said through their connection in the forest of nothing. "When I was first brought here as a kid, the smell reminded me of rotting garbage at the bottom of an industrial food waste bin. It fascinated me. That's when Master Helena first noticed my interest in plants."

Rae had found Ben out at the quarantine station, his consciousness sharing the body of a child. It hadn't occurred to him to take over the mind completely as it had to Rae. It seemed years of isolation had made her callous. Now all he had was this unremarkable child named Elly, with her mousy brown hair, hazel eyes, and pale skin.

He told her that once he'd reached Earth, the physical realm had become accessible to him through pores in reality that he likened to leaf stoma. He found himself in the sickly body of an old man. Instinctively he'd flowed through the man like a burst of restoring energy to dispel sickness and decay and make the man whole again. Then he'd returned to the pores and healed all of the six other people in the small wooden hut where the man had lain dying, finally ending in Elly.

The girl was the same age Rae had been when her own life was halted. Elly played with a fallen gingko leaf and clung to a doll named Henny, not unlike Cindy doll. The disease had orphaned her. Both Ben and Rae knew what that was like. Ben could no longer deny that even if his parents had survived that night on Earth when he'd lost them at the factory, old age would have taken them in the years he'd been gone. He had come home to postponed grief.

But while Rae's parents were lost to her and had been for many years, she had somehow found her grandparents after all, preserved in silicon amongst the professor's files. The first time she'd stumbled across them, all of the emotions she'd buried for so many years burst forth and she flung the tablet across the room. The bitter, synthetic taste of their presence was a painful reminder of everything she'd lost.

But curiosity and a lingering ache had drawn Rae back to them, like a scary story she couldn't resist even though she knew it would give her nightmares. Her grandparents had recorded their voices decades before, along with a version of their minds. Ben explained that it was a simulation, that it wasn't really them, but as founders of the first Earth Guardians community, they must have been worthy of digital preservation.

There were things about them she hadn't paid attention to as a child. They'd been moon-mining billionaires—which explained the spaceport at the end of their massive property. Apparently, the view of Earth from the moon was so moving that they dedicated the rest of their lives and bank account to preserving life on Earth—hence the name Earth Guardians.

The silicon versions of them told Rae of how they'd continued their work after her father and his lackeys had left Earth. They'd made technological and scientific advances aimed at preserving the planet and humanity. Their successes had included gene-edited crops, animals, and micro-organisms, efficient renewable power technologies, and improved recycling and waste management. They spoke of seaweed farms, mangrove desalinating ponds, vaccines in carrots, mycoremediation, and on and on.

Rae could feel Ben watching her as she nestled her tablet among the roots of the gingko tree and lowered herself to the dirt. She punched up the program that held her grandparents as Elly danced and played on the lawn.

"We're marveling at how much this tree has grown," she told her grandparent-bots.

"Gingkos are thought to be Earth's oldest living trees," Nanna replied.

"They're resistant to nearly every atrocity humanity can devise, including nuclear blasts," Poppa added.

Rae had missed her grandparents teaching her about the world. All the years they could have spent together. Lost. She had never even properly said goodbye. She hadn't understood she would never see them again. She held onto her precious memories.

Even now, she could picture Nanna leading her by the hand over the soft green grass towards the corrugated metal shed behind the waste disposal building as the sun burnt down from the hazy, grey sky above.

Inside, the shed had been dimly lit by a single bulb, and Rae breathed in the damp earth and rot. It was a good rot. Closer to new life than death. Poppa stood at a bench with his back to them. He turned and raised his thick, crayon-black eyebrows. He held out a deep, rectangular tray. Three round, baby mushrooms, white and plump like marshmallows, grew from a bed of something like sand.

"I don't like mushrooms." She screwed up her face. Nanna and Poppa were forever trying to make her eat the fruits and vegetables they'd grown.

Nanna ruffled her hair. "Don't worry. You don't have to eat these. We're not sure yet if they are good to eat anyway."

"These mushrooms are growing on plastic," Poppa said, swirling a finger around the sand in the tray. "The fungal mycelium, that's like the roots of the mushrooms, will eat up the plastic and grow big and strong in the shape of a brick."

"And then we can use those bricks to build houses," Nanna said. "One day we'll be able to eliminate all plastic pollution."

Rae hadn't understand why Nanna and Poppa were so merry. But if they were, then so was she. She gave them both a wide grin and imagined fairies making homes under all the new mushrooms.

Now, she looked at the compound buildings and wondered if they were made of the fungal bricks Nanna and Poppa had hoped to create. The vine hadn't been able to deliver her to grandma's house, so it had done the next best thing and followed a bread crumb trail of descendants to the professor. She was not the mother Arabella thought she was. But they were related. Arabella, she'd found out, was a descendant of her Uncle Dexter. The knowledge hadn't been particularly soothing. Without her grandparents, it no longer felt like home. Now it was just somewhere she had once lived.

Nothing on Earth was as she'd expected or hoped. It wasn't what the vine had promised. She turned back to the blinking cursor that symbolized her grandparents' life force. The only thing she had left of them. "What do I do now?" she asked. "I'm back on Earth, but you're not here, and I don't know what to do." She wasn't equipped to continue their work, and everyone she ever knew or loved was dead. There was nothing for her here.

"You should listen to your heart," Poppa said.

"How does that help the poor child?" Nanna interjected. "Rae, darling, we created this simulation so that the community would have a touchstone to keep them on mission. Our goal was to find solutions for improving life on Earth for everybody. We didn't achieve as much as we'd have liked, but we hoped that future generations would carry on our work. You, dear child, are the future we dreamed about. You must ensure that our work continues, and not just for the members of the Earth Guardian communities."

They were ambitious goals, and Rae didn't quite know where to begin. Even if she succeeded, her grandparents would never know. Not really. She didn't quite grasp the point of doing something in their memory or carrying on their legacy. Could a simulation be proud?

Tears streamed down her cheeks, and Elly pulled her away from the tree. "Let's eat some blackberries," she said. "They always cheer you up."

The child was in Rae's charge for the moment. And a way to keep Ben close. Over the years she'd fantasized he would be her rescuing prince. But he was no longer the little boy who'd read to her. He was a man. With a whole life lived without her. The heroic version she had constructed of him didn't exist. The only thing keeping them together was a mutual desire to understand the place and time they'd found themselves.

Elly skipped towards the blackberry hedge by the storage shed. The bush had been well picked over, but Rae crouched and reached for a plump berry hidden behind leaves and stems. A thorn pricked her finger, and beads of her blood fell to the ground like Snow White's mother, pricking her finger with a needle. But Rae would be no one's mother. The professor no longer bled from her womb. Rae had never inhabited a fertile body, and now she never would. Another thing that had not turned out how she'd once expected.

Elly sidled up to the storage shed, something mischievous in her eyes. "You know what's inside here?"

Rae sucked her finger. "How could I?"

Elly pulled the handle on the corrugated metal door, and it swung open on well-oiled hinges. Rae startled at a face staring back at her from the shadows. She composed herself and took a step forward, recalling something she'd read in the professor's messages with Arabella. It wasn't a person. It was a tin man.

· · · ● · ● · ● · · ·

A full day and night had passed since she'd discovered the android inside the storage shed, but she'd wanted to dig into the professor's notes before she touched it. Now she was squatting before the blackberry hedge, its leaves glowing brightly green in the sunlight. Yesterday, the fruit had been picked clean. Now the bush burst with blue-black and dark red berries. Under it, a spongy, three-lobed leaf was intertwined with the canes of each plant.

"Are you seeing this?" she asked Ben via their mind connection. Elly was plucking berries from the bush and stuffing them into her mouth.

"The vine," Ben said.

"Yes. Growing from where I spilt a drop of blood."

There was no dust. And instead of ruining food crops, as it had done on Aceso, the vine had bestowed the hedge with vitality. Neither of them knew what it meant. But Rae felt no fear. She'd never feared the vine. Besides, they'd returned to the storage shed with a more pressing task at hand.

Inside, the tin man's body mimicked the contours of an androgynous, muscular human, and the face had been rendered in a pale, sand-like plastic. Rae had found its depleted solar batteries the day before and had left them in the sun to charge, and now she was clipping them into android's metal carapace as Elly and Ben watched from the doorway.

With a whir, the tin man lifted his head and grinned blandly. Rae tilted forward to meet its opening eyes. There was no spark there. The technology to create androids no longer existed, but there was a factory full of them somewhere according to the professor's notes.

They'd been built for human consciousness transfer, though Rae had found no evidence of it ever actually working. But Ben was something different. His consciousness had traversed the galaxy.

And now he needed a body to help him find those he cared about. With each day, it became clearer that Rae was not included in that category. She had accepted the truth. Ben didn't feel about her the way she felt about him. It had been painful at first, but he was ready to go off on a quest of his own. He planned to leave the compound in search of others from Aceso. She consoled herself that she would forever have the stories they'd shared.

"Are you ready?" Rae asked him.

"Yes," Ben answered in the void.

Elly was hopping in and out of the patch of sunlight thrown by the open door, but she paused and closed her eyes. Insects buzzed around the ripe blackberries outside, and someone across the garden laughed.

The grin on the tin man's face widened. "It worked." The voice was flat. Artificial. Ben held up the android hands and turned them in front of his face.

Elly rubbed her head. "He's gone."

"Are you really in there?" Rae asked. "All of you?"

"Yes," Ben replied in his android voice. "It feels cold and hard. Not like a human body."

Elly flung her arms around the tin man's waist. "I'll miss you, Ben."

"I'll miss you too," he said.

"Best if you leave under cover of night. I'm not yet certain what I'll tell the rest of the community."

"You could always come with me."

Rae was afraid to leave the safety of the compound's high walls. She had escaped her imprisonment on Aceso. The tower was unlocked. But fear kept her from straying from the path and into the unknown. She needed time.

"I'll be back later to help you sneak out," she said, steering Elly back outside. "Until then, let's pick some berries to take to the kitchen."

Rae squatted again and brushed her fingers over the vine-entwined blackberry canes. Her blood had done this. A couple of drops had reinvigorated a whole blackberry bush. Who knew what else her blood could do. She would have to ask her grandparents how they would use this tool, but she suspected she already knew.

19

Pixie and Wolf walked amongst nature without any of the fear that Centa and Perpetua had known on Aceso. The leaves of the trees riding the wind and the many and varied bird calls from high in the branches gave Centa a sense of harmony and belonging. If she had her own body, she would have filled her lungs deeply and expelled the last of Aceso and the vine spores that had polluted her cells. For the moment she was content.

She conversed with Pixie as they walked. The earthling was open minded and curious. Nothing seemed to surprise her. She was different from anyone Centa had ever known. The two of them had lived vastly different lives.

Pixie's guileless questions led Centa to speak freely of Ben and the prohibition against relationships that had been integral to social order on Aceso.

"It's a bit like Fairy Park," Pixie said. "The mamas are so obsessed with repopulation and avoiding inbreeding that they control who can and can't be together for the sake of genetic diversity."

Centa wasn't familiar with the social structures Pixie spoke of, but she understood breeding for genetic diversity.

"Ben told me that things were different on Earth. He called our community on Aceso a cult. Are you familiar with that term?"

"I've heard folk say it. Wolf calls Fairy Park a cult because of how the mamas run everything. She says there are villages where people breed with whoever they want. Sometimes couples will commit to each other in a type of ceremony known as marriage and sometimes they'll form exclusive groups of three or four. And sometimes they just move from partner to partner without anyone telling them it's right or wrong. Wolf says you can't have a healthy relationship in a cult. I'm not really sure what that means though."

Those words stunned Centa for a second. *You can't have a healthy relationship in a cult.* Her attachment to Ben had not been healthy. She'd always known it. The truth was that when she could no longer worship Skyfather to keep her doubts and fears at bay, she had transferred her worship to Ben and hoped his touch would banish her doubts and fears instead. Her need for him had been cult indoctrination, just as he had gently tried to tell her numerous times. He had been a constant and important presence and one of the few honest people in her life. But the overwhelming need to be near him had faded. He was a good person though. She hadn't been wrong about that, and she still wanted to find him and know that he was well and had some sort of existence.

Pixie broke Centa's reverie by calling out to Wolf. "Are we going to stop soon? It's bloody hot."

Wolf paused a few steps ahead of them. On her recommendation they'd veered off the road to Fairy Park, due to the risk of encountering the Mother Feeders who'd attacked her.

"According to the Traveller's Guide and Map, there's an outpost up ahead where we can shelter for full sun. Keep your eyes open for a rabbit for our lunch."

Centa wondered if Perpetua and Wolf had been talking the same way she and Pixie had. Had Perpetua told Wolf how Centa had failed her on Aceso? Any contentment she'd felt evaporated at the thought.

Soon they were scrambling down a rocky bank to the entrance of a concrete tunnel high enough for Wolf and Pixie to stand upright. Centa tried to decipher the scrawled words and pictures on the curved walls, but they were too faded and the concrete too cracked and chipped.

They made camp a few metres inside the entrance, where daylight still reached but the temperature was noticeably cooler. The women used fallen branches to sweep away dried leaves and dirt and check for venomous snakes and spiders.

Wolf ventured further into the dark and came back dragging an empty metal drum, blackened from previous cooking fires, then fetched a second that held water, dried foods, matches, blankets, cooking utensils, and basic medical supplies.

"Bit of a rough set up here, but better than nothing." Wolf's voice echoed in the quiet darkness.

They roasted a rabbit over a fire and sat on folded blankets. The dogs padded into the darkness of the tunnel, and Wolf called them back with a whistle.

"What's down there?" Pixie asked.

"Don't know. We can explore it properly one day if you'd like."

"Yeah. That would be tops." Pixie beamed, thrilled at the prospect of future activities with Wolf. She reached for the last piece of rabbit.

"Don't take the last of the meat, Wolf might think you rude!" Centa couldn't stop herself from interfering.

"But I want it." Pixie popped the morsel into her mouth.

Centa had difficulty fathoming this kind of thought and action that flowed straight from Pixie's brain and into being with no examination or consideration. Centa had always presented an obedient and acceptable front, while Pixie cared little for how she was perceived. It seemed freeing though to not be deathly afraid of the repercussions of expressing yourself.

Pixie squished a cockroach with the toe of her shoes and said privately to Centa, "I think Wolf is fine with me as I am."

The whole of Pixie's body blushed, inside and out. She had feelings for Wolf. Centa examined their interactions through a new perspective. There was a definite attraction there. They wanted to be close, and they brought each other joy, but it wasn't primarily driven by sex. Centa thought sexual intimacy was a basic need of all humans. Skyfather had encouraged them to seek out sexual partners so that unfulfilled needs didn't reduce their productivity. Maybe there was more diversity in humanity's needs than Father's Law acknowledged.

"Centa thinks I shouldn't have taken that last piece of rabbit coz you could think I'm rude or greedy. But I wanted it, and I thought if you wanted it then you would have grabbed it first or said something."

Wolf laughed. "Don't worry. I'd tell you if I wanted it or if I thought you were rude. That's something I like about you, Pixie. No games."

Pixie's approach made it easy for her to talk to Wolf. Centa had barely ever told the truth in her whole life. There were no masters now and no Father's Law. She could be whatever she wanted to be.

It was time to talk to Perpetua.

She met her sister-worker in the void. "What happened on Aceso with the master... it was wrong. I'm sorry that happened to you."

Perpetua closed her eyes and looked down. If Centa had a heart, it would have been beating out of her chest. Maybe Perpetua would never be able to forgive her. She wanted to say more, to rush in and fill the silence.

"Thank you," Perpetua finally said.

"I should have said something. I know that now. I know I was wrong. I just—"

"I felt so alone."

"Oh, Perpetua. There was nothing I could do to save you. I had no power. I think that's why I turned away."

"I didn't need you to save me. I needed you to believe me and tell me that what they were doing was wrong."

"I'm sorry. You're right. I don't know why you still want to be near me."

"I can't even conceive of an existence without you."

Centa didn't feel better. She wanted to redeem herself. She wanted to make right all the years she had done wrong by Perpetua. She wouldn't feel better until Perpetua felt better. She just didn't know how to make that happen.

20

After two days of travelling, Wolf estimated they were only half a day from Fairy Park. The sun rose in the sky and a hot wind blew from the north.

"There's another traveller's outpost nearby. I think we should rest and arrive early tomorrow morning."

Pixie rolled her neck to stretch out her tired shoulders. "Fresh and ready to save everyone."

"Exactly."

Wolf led them through the bush to the remains of an isolated warehouse where the victims of the last pandemic earlier in the century had been quarantined. Piles of bones crunched under their feet as they followed the dogs into the high-ceilinged building.

"The skeletons keep most folk out. They think it's bad luck. Same as the android factory. Most traveller outposts are set up to deter random scavengers."

They dumped their packs in a room with a single cot and a stash of dehydrated grub. Wolf poured them both a cup of water from a ceramic container and filled a dish for the dogs who nudged each other away with their noses and spilled most of the water on the floor. They flopped down with their muzzles on their paws. Soon they were both snoozing.

"There's a well out the back. Do you want to have a wash?"

Pixie didn't usually worry too much about hygiene, but she didn't want Wolf to think she was grotty. She didn't usually care what anyone thought of her. Could be Centa's influence. The alien was calm and logical. She nagged at Pixie to think before she spoke and guess the effect her words might have. Centa called it empathy. Mama Gretel would have called it putting yourself in someone else's shoes for a change, you gormless lump.

Practicing empathy left her beat, which could be why she'd never bothered with it much in the past. It also explained why the mamas had gotten so frustrated with her. If she'd seen things from their point of view, she might have been able to give them what they wanted. Even if it was only an act. Centa had told her it was okay if it was only an act. Acting and white lies kept folk around you cheerful and got you what you wished for.

Wolf led Pixie to a well in a sun-blasted clearing behind the building. She hand-pumped water into a pail and handed it to Pixie, along with a rag. Wolf took off all her clothes and ran her own wet rag over her compact, muscular body.

"Don't stare!" Centa scolded inside Pixie's head. "Other people don't like it."

"Duh," Pixie murmured and removed her own clothes.

Seeing Wolf naked didn't kindle the desire in her that she had supposed it might. She still wished to be close to Wolf, but nothing throbbed or tingled around her baby hole the way folk at Fairy Park talked about. She had sexual fantasies, but she wasn't sure she ever wanted to make them real. She couldn't control reality the way she could control her fantasies.

Still, something about Wolf captivated her. There had been a growing tension between them for the last couple of days. Pixie didn't know for sure what it all meant.

Pixie wet her rag and scrubbed at her armpits and between her legs. She'd finally stopped bleeding. Small mercy.

"Maybe we should... fool around." Wolf's dick was semi-erect.

Pixie dropped her rag and straightened up. "Um, I didn't think you..."

"No." Wolf seemed confused. "I don't usually. It's just I have... feelings that I don't know what to do with and I thought if we fooled around—that is if you want to—we could find out if it was the right thing for me and you."

"Perpetua and I are going to retreat and let you and Wolf have some privacy," Centa said.

Perpetua must have told Wolf the same thing because Wolf said, "Thank the Earth for that. I'm not used to being watched all the time."

Wolf had been having a harder time with the lack of privacy than Pixie. As a traveller she was used to being on her own, while Pixie was used to being surrounded by folk she'd learned to ignore.

Pixie crossed her arms over her breasts. "I thought you weren't interested in me like that. You know, because when I told you what happened with Aladdin, you weren't bothered."

Wolf blushed. "I was bothered. A lot. But you don't belong to me. I would never tell you what you can and can't do."

"But sometimes you might have to. I do stupid shit all the time. Shit that hurts people. And I never want to hurt you."

"That's just you, Pix. I'm not gonna try to change you. But how about we tell each other if we're hurting, and then we can decide what to do from there?"

Pixie nodded. A sob was rising in her throat, and she couldn't speak. Wolf was one of the only people, along with Snow, who made her feel understood and not like a complete fuck up who would never be good enough.

Wolf wiped a tear from under Pixie's eye and cupped her cheek in her hand. Pixie rested her face in the soft curve where Wolf's shoulder and neck met, breathing in her scent. She had never held her naked body against another's before. The world around them disappeared.

Their mouths met and Pixie's lips felt huge and swollen. They kissed slowly and their bodies melted together. She could have held and kissed Wolf forever. And for now, that was enough. She didn't think she'd like Wolf's dick inside her. Not at that moment anyway. Being with Wolf was like getting a new set of clothes that were comfortable and whole. She wore out new clothes quickly by snagging them on rocks and sticks or sliding on her knees and ass. She would be more careful with Wolf and consider the damage that could be done by her usual carelessness.

They stood together in a perfect bubble of time and space. This was the completeness she'd glimpsed on shrooms, as though Puff the dragon had finally given her the answers she sought. A jumping spider traversed her foot. Wolf's half-erection waned. They parted and kissed gently with closed mouths.

"Maybe we should keep getting to know each other," Wolf said. "We can think about taking things further when it's not so hectic."

Pixie nodded in relief. Wolf was right. It wasn't going to happen that day, but it didn't mean it wouldn't happen sometime in the future when it felt safe and right for them both.

Pixie reached into her pack for her clean set of clothes. There was something smooth and hard right at the bottom. She yanked out a glass bottle with clear liquid sloshing inside. The label had worn off years earlier, but she knew it was alcohol from the divers' stash. She didn't remember nabbing it, but her memories of that time were a mess. Or could be Tadpole had slipped it in there as a parting gift.

However, it had gotten there, they were going to show the aliens a good old-fashioned Earth time.

21

Perpetua and Centa rejoined the corporeal women just as Pixie presented Wolf with a bottle of something she called real grog, and in return Wolf presented Pixie with an electronic item called a music player.

Pixie pulled Wolf into an embrace. "Those are rarer than clean undies."

"It only has a little charge left. I was waiting for a special occasion."

Their faces lit with smiles, and they jumped around, squealing in vulgar excitement.

"What are you both so giddy about?" Perpetua asked.

"We're having a party," Wolf replied.

Whenever they spoke like this—the four of them connected by Pixie and Wolf's skin—the earthlings weren't actually in the void with Centa and Perpetua. It was more like they were part of the fabric of what the void ran through. The women were trees, while Centa and Perpetua were embedded in the mycelial network in their roots.

Pixie's joy and elation beckoned Centa. She had only ever come close to such emotion when she was with Ben. A warming liquid travelled down Pixie's throat and into her belly, radiating a sense of well-being and relaxation.

The women moved their bodies to the sound coming from the music player. Ben had spoken of music. It was something he'd missed from his life on Earth. He'd tried singing the songs he recalled from his childhood years. His voice had been terrible.

The women drank more of the grog, and feel-good chemicals flooded their brains. The grog was oxidized within their bodies to a poison that made them happy, loud, and carefree. Centa helped Pixie's liver to efficiently metabolize the poison for elimination.

"Don't do that," Pixie said. "It's a waste. You can help me with the hangover in the morning."

Centa suppressed her instinct to repair and optimize and let the euphoria and disinhibition overwhelm her. Pixie sang and danced and laughed, and it was as though Centa were singing and dancing and not caring about anything other than that very second. She had an urge, and she didn't stop to examine it. She called Perpetua into the void with her and took hold of her hands and peered into her eyes.

"You know I love you, don't you?"

Perpetua smiled. "Is that why you've been trying to get rid of me for twenty-five years?"

Centa winced and screwed up her face. "I don't know why I did that. No, I do know. You're irritating, but that's not really it."

A subdued part of her told her to be careful. Her words had power, but she had been careful all her life and it hadn't helped anyone.

Perpetua frowned. "You're not as perfect as you seem to think either."

"I know, I know. But as I said, that's not all of it... I felt guilty. Seeing your face all the time made me feel guilty because I knew what was going on —"

"It's fine," Perpetua interrupted. "I don't want to talk about that anymore. I just want to forget it ever happened." She withdrew from the void.

Centa visualized taking a scythe and slicing off Master Anton's limbs one by one. It had been some time since she'd had such a violent thought. She returned to Pixie.

"Pixie?"

"Yeah?"

"Do you ever think about doing something horrible?"

"All the time." Pixie took Wolf's arm and twirled her around.

"I mean something really evil. Like decapitating a baby. The thoughts just come into your head, and you visualize the whole thing."

"I used to picture stepping on one of the toddlers crawling around Fairy Park. I imagined the sound their ribs would make when they cracked under the weight of my foot."

"Oh! That's awful. What's wrong with us? Why do we think these things?"

Pixie laughed. "You're so uptight about everything. Nothing's wrong with us. They're just thoughts. Everyone has them."

"You think it's normal? Not a sign of evil?"

"Yeah. It's not like you're actually doing these fucked up things. They're thoughts. They're not you."

Wolf howled and screamed into the star-strewn sky and Pixie joined her.

Centa sat with Pixie's words. Her thoughts were not her. It didn't completely make sense, since thoughts were part of consciousness and that was the only part of herself that she had left. But she felt lighter than she'd been in some time. She put all the violent thoughts and urges she'd worked so hard to suppress all her life into a scream and let them go as she joined the women in their howling. For a moment, Worker 9 was completely gone and she was truly Centa.

· · ● ● ●· ● ● ● ·· ·

As the night wore on, the disinhibition that had brought Pixie and Wolf together in the early stages of intoxication devolved into slurred, repetitive conversations that pushed them apart. They both got stuck on ideas they thought were profound and couldn't properly articulate. Centa grew bored and spent more and more time in the void, but she was called back to Pixie, squatting behind a tree urinating for what seemed like the hundredth time.

"Waddaya reckon if I kiss Wolf now?" Pixie asked. "Just plant one on her. Good idea, yeah?"

"I don't think that's a good idea, Pixie. Neither of you are using good judgement right now."

Pixie stood and leaned against the tree as she struggled to get her pants up over her knees and buttoned up. "You're so fucking boring, Centa." She pinched her lips together. "Fuck off back to where you came from, whydoncha."

Centa recoiled and tried to make her presence as unobtrusive as possible. Her relationship with Pixie was tenuous. At any moment, Pixie might consider Centa less of a symbiont and more of a parasite to be rejected.

Lightning flashed in the dark sky, followed by a crack of thunder. Skyfather used to say thunder and lightning were expressions of The Spirit of Aceso's displeasure. What a crock, as Pixie might say.

Pixie staggered back through the warehouse, kicking bones out of her way and mumbling something about having avoided being knocked up only to be implanted with a grown woman instead. She found Wolf lying on her cot, snoring with her mouth wide open.

"Well, fuck," Pixie said and then ran back outside to vomit all over the ground.

• • • ● • ● • • • •

Early in the morning, while Wolf and Pixie slept, the intoxicating effects of the grog gave way to the pain of poisoning. Centa and Perpetua reduced inflammation in the women's gastrointestinal tracts, eased the dilation and constriction of blood vessels, especially around their skulls, and promoted endorphin production. They couldn't rehydrate until the women roused and drank water.

Centa kept an eye on the progression of day to night. Sleep assisted the repair of cells and clearance of toxins, but as soon as the Earth star breached the horizon, she would wake Pixie and urge her to drink.

A shimmer at the edge of her consciousness alerted her to a new individual in the void. Centa found Perpetua already there, her mouth tight and eyes wide.

"Who is that?" Centa said.

They had found only one other refugee from Aceso since their reunion. A kitchen worker, who neither of them had known well, residing in a tiger snake.

"Not who you hope for. I've encountered them before. Best you go alone." Perpetua retreated, her panic palpable.

Centa reached towards the newcomer. They reached back. Both strained against their limits until their forms met. It took her a second to recognize the figure. She recoiled as Master Anton pressed forward to grasp her wrists. They were both incorporeal. He couldn't prevent her from fleeing, but years of obedience and subservience were built into her every action. Perpetua could have warned her before she'd disappeared.

"Ah, Worker 9. What good fortune! I thought I sensed Worker 8 again. I found her several days ago in a lower being. I called out for help. Unfortunately, our connection broke."

How could he be so unaware of Perpetua's loathing of him? Or how much harm he'd done? Centa had foolishly thought she might never have to face him again, that her apology to Perpetua could be the end of her guilt.

"I'm so pleased to have found you. Have you come across anyone else? Other than you two, I've only encountered workers of no importance. How do you think this happened? I have some theories I'd like to share with you."

He spoke on and on, oblivious to her silence. If he couldn't help her find Ben, there was no reason for her to endure his company. Pleasing Master Anton with the quality of her work had been a priority for her on Aceso, and she'd respected his biological and scientific expertise and teachings, but she'd never liked him. Now that she'd confronted what he'd done to Perpetua, she loathed him.

He continued unburdening himself, completely ignorant of her disdain. He still thought of himself as her superior. She pulled her hands from his. He spoke of his human. A killer who wore dirty, white robes. A Mother Feeder.

"The man is a savage." Master Anton shook his head. "There was another in his party when I possessed him. A female companion. Together they attacked a family on a beach. One of their victims slashed the woman's Achilles tendon with a piece of rusty metal. She was having difficulty walking, so my man simply slit her throat in her sleep last night." He shuddered. "He believes she should be sacrificed to the Earth, rather than dying of her wounds. He's preparing the ritual as we speak. I've tried to alter his brain to curb the violent tendencies, but the scars of a past illness are too well established to be reversed."

She would need to warn Pixie and Wolf of the proximity of the Mother Feeder. At least this interaction had yielded something useful.

Anton reached out, took hold of her wrists again and pressed his face near hers. "You must help me find another host. This life is torturous. And now there is a large fire coming and he's refusing to move."

He finally left space for Centa to speak. "So, you haven't come across Disciple Ben?"

He dropped her hands and drew back in disgust. "Have you learnt nothing in your life, Worker? How many times must you be punished for your transgressions?"

Centa recalled the evening before, screaming and dancing. "I'm not a worker anymore, and we're not on Aceso. You don't have any authority over me."

She severed her connection to him before the anger on his face exploded into words that she would have difficulty forgetting.

Perpetua appeared beside her in the void. "Are you going to help him?"

"No! You think I would help him after everything he's done?"

"He's always been your mentor. You spent every day in that laboratory trying to impress him."

Perpetua was right. Centa had looked up to Master Anton. He had given her approval and attention. Part of her still wished for his approval. Part of her had already considered ways to help him out of his current troubles. He had guided her into a passion for science. When she'd handled cells in the laboratory, she'd used skill and a little bit of magic to master nature, and all other concerns had disappeared. Anton had given that to her. And now Perpetua expected Centa's betrayal.

"He's not my mentor any longer," Centa said. She didn't know what she could tell Perpetua that might convince her, so she turned to more urgent matters. "But Anton said there's a large fire nearby, and If he's close enough to communicate, that means the Mother Feeder is too. We have to get out of here."

"We should wake them then," Perpetua said and slipped from the void without another word.

"Wake up!" Centa shouted through the neural corridors of Pixie's mind. "Fire! Mother feeder!"

Centa had learned that Pixie didn't like being told what to do. Despite their mostly friendly interactions, Centa knew that if it weren't for the biological repairs she carried out, Pixie would have tried to expel her.

How long could they continue this semi-symbiosis where they both gained something and lost something too?

22

Pixie's eyes popped open. Her throat was parched, and her head pounded. She whimpered back towards sleep.

"Stay awake!" Centa shouted. "I woke you for a reason."

"You woke me?" Pixie sat up and winced against the harsh daylight.

"Yes. Hold hands with Wolf please."

Wolf blinked and groaned her way into a sitting position.

Pixie yawned and rubbed her sore head. "I really gotta get a bit more of a snooze. You said you were gonna give me a hand with this hangover."

"I did my best, but you need to rehydrate. First, though, hold Wolf's hands. It's urgent."

Wolf crossed her legs and held her hands out. "Perpetua and Centa have something important to tell us apparently."

The aliens could be as annoying as the mamas with their *gotta do this* and *don't do that* all the time.

"There's a Mother Feeder nearby," Centa said, once they'd joined hands.

"And a fire," Perpetua added.

Centa explained their connection to the other Sky Human nearby and the Feeder who'd sacrificed his traveling companion.

"Sounds like the pair who attacked me," Wolf said.

"What should we do?" Pixie asked. She had no experience facing Feeders on the road. She'd known they were around, but when her brain was being wrecked by ROSE, they hadn't been much of a priority.

"The bloke's fairly old." Wolf began to gather up their supplies. "They only got the best of me through surprise and teamwork. We could maybe thrash him if we struck first." She raised her eyebrows at Pixie.

"Don't look at me," Pixie answered. "I can't fight."

Fighting had always been someone else's job. She was searching for something to be hers, but warrior wasn't it. She would rather avoid any skirmishes. Mother Feeders were one of the mysteries of the world that she was cheery to take other people's word about, like labour pains or the deadly thirst caused by drinking straight from the ocean, or even finding what you thought were shrooms in the bush and then shitting yourself to death.

Wolf frowned. "Then we should leave now and stay ahead of him."

"I'll keep track of his movements as much as I can," Centa said.

They walked out into the pale dawn light. Pixie sniffed the air, then stopped and breathed more deeply. She'd been too busy worrying about the Mother Feeder to take Perpetua's offhand comment about the fire seriously.

"You smell it too?" Wolf said.

"Yep." Summer had been long, hot, and dry, and the undergrowth had recovered from the fires a handful of years before. They had all known the flames would come again eventually.

"Is this fire something to worry about?" Centa asked.

"I don't know what it's like on your planet," Pixie said, "but fire's always something to worry about round here."

Pixie wasn't afraid of much. But fire had lots of ways to wreck you and none of them were easy or peaceful. She'd seen the blistered hands and faces of those who'd fought spot fires at the edges of Fairy Park with nothing but blankets, buckets of sea water, and a hand pumped hose in the lake. And she'd lived through the hungry months of rebuilding afterwards.

She let Centa view the memories that rose through her mind. Night come early as the fire closed in and smoke obscured the sun. Writhing sheets of flame. Kangaroos, rabbits, birds, and feral livestock fleeing the fire front and screaming in a way you never knew animals could scream, some of them alight like candles. The pop of trees exploding. Flames jumping fire breaks and leaping up the outcrop. Youngsters stamping out embers with their bare feet or hiding under blankets, struggling to extract air from between particles of ash and smoke. The heat rising until you passed out, waking later with singed eyelashes and tender, red skin. Lying next to a youngster who hadn't been as lucky.

The dogs wound around their feet. Wolf yanked on Pixie's arm and led her back to the warehouse. They scrambled over a pile of rubble at the rear of the building and clambered three storeys up a metal ladder to the roof.

To the west, a plume of dark smoke dwarfed the treetops. Underneath, an orange glow oozed along the ground like liquid heat. Leaves and branches flailed as if the trees knew what was coming but their feet wouldn't obey their wish to bolt.

"It's heading this way pretty fast," Wolf said. "Which direction is the Mother Feeder's camp?"

"According to Centa, it's between us and the fire." Pixie pointed to a collection of shipping containers amongst the dense bush about two kilometres away.

"If the wind keeps pushing this way, it could reach Fairy Park."

So much for her luck changing. Mama Rosamund was convinced fire was driven by vengeful spirits. It thrashed and consumed with a passion usually seen in the living. But Mama Gretel had taught Pixie that it was just a chemical reaction. Fire had no mind or heart to take joy in the harm it caused.

"Let's go," Wolf said and gave her a shove. "There's not much we can do except get ourselves out of the way."

Wolf was right. One of the worst things about fire season was waiting to see if nature had it in for you on that particular day. They grabbed their packs and headed towards the ocean's edge and, with any luck, out of the direct path of the fire.

After almost an hour, they reached the beach and travelled for another twenty minutes along the shore before they found two-and-a-half walls of a structure made of solid concrete and breeze blocks.

They sheltered from full sun and took turns to nap and be on watch. Pixie was too uneasy to sleep. Wolf fell asleep on cue—a skill she'd likely honed during her months as a traveller.

Pixie watched Wolf snooze and threw chunks of plastic at an imaginary target on a nearby rock. "What's the Feeder doing now?" She asked Centa.

"A ritual for his sacrificed companion."

Pixie pictured the divers' bodies arranged on the beach and shuddered.

"He's still at the shipping container camp and the smoke's thickening." Centa continued. "Master Anton's quite distressed."

By the afternoon, smoke blanketed the beach, and distant flames beat the air like a cyclone. Luckily no embers had come their way. If their luck didn't hold, their last resort would be to retreat to the water and tussle with the stinging jellyfish. A few stings hurt like childbirth, but lots of stings could kill. Even the curative powers of Centa and Perpetua would be stretched in a sustained jellyfish attack.

Wolf woke coughing and they took a walk together to the water's edge to wet some cloths.

"How long do you think this is going to last?" Pixie rubbed a cloth all over her face and then tied it over her mouth. Every moment the fire delayed them could be critical. The pig disease moved fast and killed fast. Some higher power, could be one of Mama Rosamund's demons, was determined to make it difficult for her to save Fairy Park. But she wouldn't give up because it was too difficult. Not this time.

"I don't know." Wolf stared up through the smoke haze at the sky. "Our best hope is for a storm to come through —"

"My master... ex master. He's... very... distressed." Centa cut in. "It's like he's screaming in the void. It's just like you showed me. The flames are everywhere."

23

Bushfire was a new kind of threat for Centa. On Aceso, fire had been a tool wielded by humans to cook their food or battle the vine. These earthlings had lived with fire throughout their lives, and they were alert, anxious even, but not yet panicked. Centa tried to take her cue from them.

She kept track of Master Anton and his Mother Feeder while Pixie and Wolf sheltered on the beach. Perpetua stayed silent. The least Centa could do was be a buffer between them.

Anton strengthened their connection in the void, bright and hard.

"What are you doing?" Centa reached for the flickering flame he'd brought with him. She'd never seen such a thing. A psychic energy she didn't know was possible.

"Help me."

"What's happening?"

Anton propelled her into his experience. The Mother Feeder cowered inside a metal room that warped and shimmered with heat. The dark orange-red air ravaged his lungs and eyes. Sweat streamed from the Feeder's pores only to evaporate instantly. He doubled over, coughing. Anton scrambled to repair the heat and smoke damage as cells burst with abandon.

"He's not going to survive. Let me come with you. We can share your host."

She hesitated. "I don't think that's a good idea."

"There's nothing close enough to transfer to," he whined, frantic. "Not even an ant. They've all fled or are dead or dying themselves. If you leave me here, you're killing me, and I know you're not a killer, girl."

But she wasn't killing him. She was letting him die. On Aceso, the masters killed the workers compromised by the vine. On Earth, the billionaires poisoned the sky and water and sea and then left the planet or retreated to bunkers. The powerful had always wielded violence with impunity. And now that power was hers.

"Goodbye, Anton."

"You would turn your back on me, your master? After everything I've done for you?"

"What did you do for me? I was your servant. I did everything for you. You used Worker 8 in terrible ways. You didn't even see us as human."

It would be too much of a mercy for him to die thinking he had been a good and righteous person. He had to die with the facts of his crimes in the forefront of his mind.

"You're speaking nonsense."

The Mother Feeder made a run to escape the unbearable heat in the shipping container. Outside, flames leapt from treetop to treetop over his head.

The roar nearly drowned out Master Anton's voice. "I know how to find Disciple Ben. I can show you."

Centa hesitated. It was most likely he was lying to save himself. Even if he wasn't, she would never forgive herself for picking Ben over Perpetua yet again. She let go of their connection. The shock and censure on his face would persist in her memory. His disapproval, when she was doing something righteous, was more satisfying than his approval when her actions served only the masters and Father's Law.

A weak trail to Anton persisted in the void. Then flame flared brightly and Centa shielded her eyes. The void bloomed green, then faded to its cold and empty state. All traces of Master Anton were gone.

· · · ● · · ● · ● · · ·

Pixie and Wolf huddled on the shore, each sharing their fears of death and fire with Centa and Perpetua but not each other. Beyond healing the smoke damage as it occurred, Centa didn't know how to help. If enough fire and smoke came for them, they would be overwhelmed as Master Anton's Mother Feeder had been.

On the horizon, dark clouds rumbled towards the shore and bled water into the ocean, bringing a briny, decaying smell that chased away the smoke. Rain drenched Pixie and Wolf like a dam had burst in the sky. The women stood with their faces upturned and let the water wash away dust and soot from their skin and clothes. Wolf reached out and held Pixie's hand.

The storm passed and the downpour slowed to a drizzle and then stopped completely as the afternoon sun dipped in the sky. The red of flames above the trees gave way to the white and grey of smoke as the fire was doused.

"Is it safe now?" Centa asked.

"I don't know about safe, but yeah. We got lucky," Pixie said. "I hope Fairy Park got lucky too."

Centa felt Pixie's worry about the fire diminish, only to be replaced by the return of her worry about her village. "Humans have so little control," she mused. "On Aceso we thought we could tame a whole planet."

Wolf handed Pixie a piece of mutton jerky. "If we leave now, we can get to Fairy Park before full dark."

They headed east through scorched patches of undergrowth, and soon the land was completely black and smoking. Charred tree skeletons stretched into the distance, smouldering trunks and hollow butts draped in soot like black capes.

Centa fixed the smoke damage in Pixie's lungs and eliminated toxic particles. Merlin and Lucy scampered ahead and sniffed at animal carcasses. The bottom halves of their bodies were smeared with ash. The bush was gloomy without the calls of bugs or birds.

Every now and then, when the back of Wolf's hand brushed against Pixie's, the woman would feel a moment of calm and optimism.

The wheat field on the outskirts of Fairy Park was reduced to ash and the blackened ground extended all the way to the edge of the lake. Centa was heartened to see that the trees closer to the outcrop seemed bushier and greener. Perhaps the storm had come through in time.

She called out for Quinn in the void, but there was no answer.

Pixie had noticed something strange about the lake though. She stepped closer. The water was clear and free of the stink of algal bloom. The dogs stood on the muddy shore and took cagey sniffs before lapping the water up with their tongues.

"What the hell has happened here?" Wolf squatted next to Pixie at the water's edge. They both scooped cool, clear water in their cupped hands and let it drip between their fingers, too wary to taste or drink.

"What's that?" Pixie walked towards a tree whose trunk was striped bright green.

Wolf shaded her eyes with her palm. "Looks like kudzu. Not even singed."

"That's not kudzu," Centa said. It looked like the vine. On Earth. But how could it be? "Get closer, but don't breathe! I want to see."

"Calm down, Cent. You're carrying on like a youngster who fell into a bull ant nest."

The earthlings had no concept of how dangerous the vine could be. Pixie wouldn't be telling her to calm down if she did.

Through Pixie's eyes, Centa traced the path of the vine through the trees and around the lake to about three quarters of the way up the outcrop. It seemed to have sprouted from Jack's house, where Isaac and Quinn had lived. At Centa's request, Pixie rubbed a bright, shiny leaf between her fingers.

"There's no dust," Centa said. "But the leaf shape, colour and texture are unmistakable."

Wolf put a hand on Pixie's shoulder so that they were all connected.

"I don't understand," Perpetua said. "Have you seen this before on Earth? Perhaps it's a species common to both planets but adapted differently."

"I can't say I ever have, and I've travelled a fair bit," Wolf replied.

"I've never seen it either." Pixie pierced the leaf with her nail and sniffed her fingertips. "I'm no plant expert or anything, and I haven't travelled much, but it is weird. Real spongy for a plant. Smells nice. Can you eat it?"

The woman had no common sense. "Only if you want to hallucinate," Centa said.

"I usually do. But not right now." Pixie let the leaf fall to the ground. "Do you think it cleaned up the lake?"

"I really don't know." The vine had done many things on Aceso, but she'd never seen it clean up a lake. "That's the old papa's house that it's sprouting from, isn't it?"

"Yep, home of all the saggy-sacked retired travellers." Pixie squinted up the outcrop.

Centa began to form a hypothesis. "One of them, Isaac, had a Sky Human with him, Quinn. I haven't been able to make contact with her since we came within range of Fairy Park."

"Let's push on and do what we came here to do." Wolf stood. "We can deal with the vine-thingy later."

Centa bristled. There would be no point saving people from the prion disease only for them to be consumed by the vine. But it did seem different on Earth. Less menacing. It didn't provoke the terror she'd felt on Aceso. She'd always thought it lured people in with lies so it could consume their bodies. She'd thought it killed for simple survival. But its promises of Earth were real. She didn't fully understand its motivations. If its purpose was to protect Aceso, then why was it on Earth?

They walked past the beehives and pit latrines and up the path to Ticket Booth House. One of the park dogs sprinted towards them, its ears low and tail between its legs. Merlin and Lucy lowered their heads and hair rose along their spines. Further up the path, another animal stopped at the sight of them, its shadow long in the fading light, and grunted.

"This fucking pig again," Pixie said.

Wolf ripped her machete out of her pack. Taking it as a signal to attack, the dogs sprinted forward, teeth bared.

"No! Lucy... STAY!"

The dogs were in too much of a frenzy to listen. Wolf took off after them and Pixie followed, one step behind the safety of Wolf's machete. As they ran, her typically scattered thoughts speeded up too, dashing from one panic to another, until the scene took on a disjointed, screaming quality. Centa anchored herself inside Pixie, visualizing her own breathing, even though she no longer had any lungs. If only she could have convinced Pixie to do the same.

The pig flung Lucy away with one powerful toss of its head, and she landed with a crunch several metres away, her leg at a strange angle.

"Hey!" Pixie shouted, waving her arms. She picked up a fallen branch and tossed it at the pig. While it was distracted, Merlin lunged and fastened his teeth to the animal's ear.

The pig pitched its head and sent Merlin skidding across the ground with a chunk of ear in his jaws. The scene was exhilarating. Centa inhabited Pixie's senses completely.

Merlin and the pig faced off again, teeth bared and blood dripping from their wounds. Pixie held her breath as Merlin growled and inched forward. The pig grunted and tossed its head and then seemed to lose its footing. It staggered in a misshapen circled and collapsed onto its side.

Centa's exhilaration drained away until only blood, gore and disgust remained. Pixie was right. Centa's violent thoughts were not her. And without the cruelty of the masters and Skyfather, she no longer had an appetite for violence.

Pixie fanned herself and sluiced sweat from her brow, and her own breath and heartbeat settled. Prions streamed from the gasping breaths of the fallen pig and into her bloodstream. Centa calmed herself by neutralizing them. The pig was no longer a monster, just a sick animal.

"Lucy's dying," Wolf said, kneeling where she lay with blood-matted fur and a compound fracture. Merlin whined and limped around Lucy in one direction and then the other, licking at her face.

"Can you do something?" Pixie asked Centa.

"I don't know. One of us would have to transfer into her I think." Centa knew it was selfish, but she feared being confined in Merlin once again.

Wolf cradled the dog's head in her lap. "Perpetua is going to try to heal her." Wolf's tears fell on Lucy.

Meek, unadventurous Perpetua? Although her defiance on Aceso had been spectacular, she'd hastened the ruin of the settlement with one act.

Lucy lifted her head and licked Wolf's hand, and Wolf whispered to her in a low, consoling voice.

Centa found Perpetua in the void. "How are you going to do this? You could get stuck in the dog again. Maybe I should..." Usually Centa was the pioneer and Perpetua the beneficiary of her newfound skills.

"No. I know this dog. She sheltered me when I had nowhere else to go. It should be me."

"Fine, but how?"

"I'll try to keep part of me here while I reach out to her."

Perpetua faded and became smaller. "I'm trying... I'm half in the dog now... knitting blood vessels and bone back together... I need to concentrate." Her voice came from far away.

She rushed back. "It's working, but I keep slipping. I don't want to lose my link with Wolf. You were right about it being better in a human. I can't go back to not being able to think and not knowing who I am."

"Let's try something." If they could repair without transferring from their humans, it could change everything.

Centa asked Pixie to touch Wolf.

"All right with you, Wolf?" Pixie asked.

Wolf nodded and Pixie rested her hand on Wolf's shoulders. The link between them was instantly stronger.

"I'll anchor you here in the void. Try now."

Perpetua made her way back into Lucy, and Centa held part of her on the path to Wolf.

Several minutes later she returned. "She's repaired."

Centa relaxed her grip. Lucy pushed onto her feet, planted her paws on Wolf's shoulders and licked her all over the face. Wolf laughed and cried and embraced the dog around its middle.

"Let's fix Merlin too," Wolf said through her tears.

"All right," Pixie answered. "He's not my dog, but he's been hanging around me for as long as I can remember." Pixie's heart thundered in her chest, and she put effort into remaining outwardly calm.

"I'll do this one," Centa said. "If Perpetua can manage, I should have no problem."

To heal felt right and good, an antidote to all the violence and fear.

Nearby, the pig gave an agonized moan.

24

Lucy and Merlin pranced around the outside of Ticket Booth House as though they'd never been injured. Silly old things were as hard to get rid of as she was, Pixie thought.

She glanced up the outcrop. Sometimes she thought that the village folk would all be okay and that she'd hurried back to Fairy Park for nothing, but then an instinct inside her would scream that something terrible had happened and they were all already dead. It was all bullshit. Her good and bad feelings meant nothing. Her body had no magical, psychic power. Whatever had gone down at Fairy Park had gone down, regardless of her feelings about it.

How would the mamas react to her return? The exile order had been as permanent as a tattoo. To be fair she had been a pain in the ass a lot of the time. Bloody Centa and her ability to see things from other folk's point of view. Could be better if she sent Wolf up ahead to gauge the welcome.

Nah. Stuff that. She'd help them whether they wanted her to or not. It was for their own good, like yanking out a rotten tooth.

Pixie prodded the pig with her boot. Froth bubbled from its snout and blood dribbled from the dog bites. Crusted over wounds from previous battles covered its flanks. It squealed, low and raspy. Wolf knelt and put her hands on its side. It raised its head and snapped in her direction before collapsing back down.

"What're you doing?"

"We either put it out of its misery or we heal it."

"Fine. Let's make it quick. I need to find Snow." Pixie put her hand on Wolf's shoulder so Centa could anchor Perpetua. She hated the fucking pig, but she knew it wasn't its fault. It had been the victim of the disease just as she had. She expected folk at Fairy Park to give her a second (third, fourth?) chance. So it wouldn't be right for her to deny another, even if they were just a pig.

The dogs approached with the heads and tails low and hackles raised. Pixie shooed them away and picked up Wolf's machete with her free hand.

"I didn't start biting folk when I was infected. Could be it's just a nasty bastard."

"All the old reports said only a small percentage of the infected became aggressive. They reckon some of the aggressive ones who survived had completely different personalities when they recovered and went on to become Mother Feeders," Wolf said.

"Perpetua has found the damage to the brain and it's fresh enough to be reversible," Centa said.

The process took a bit longer with the pig than it had with the dogs. Centa said it was because the pig was bigger, and the prions had caused intricate and widespread damage. While, in contrast, the dogs had suffered straightforward wounds and the prions didn't seem to cause damage or proliferate in the same way. Sometimes Centa spoke like she'd swallowed one of Mama Gretel's medical textbooks.

When Perpetua told them the healing was complete, Pixie and Wolf stepped back slowly, ready to defend if the pig attacked. The animal rose and grunted at them before heading for the scrub behind Ticket Booth House. The dogs sniffed it from a distance, their hackles replaced by wagging tails.

They started up the outcrop. Pixie had only been away for a handful of days, but the park was smaller and more faded than she remembered. It was also worryingly quiet and still for early evening. The only light came from the night-glowing plants and mosses that slowly brightened as night fell.

Merlin, Lucy, and another park dog sniffed at the pig-mauled remains of one of their old pack in the dirt outside the dining hall. There was a faint tang of human waste and decay in the air. Not everyone had pulled through. Seeing the park in such a mess only heightened Pixie's doubt in the might of the mamas. They could fall just like the neoliberal civilisations they scorned.

They would later learn that many had fled when the first tremors of illness had shaken their neighbours. Over the coming days they would return, some with stories of burying loved ones in unmarked graves. Some of them would bring the prion back with them and would require cleansing.

Flies swarmed the preparation benches and unwashed dishes in the kitchen. A single youngster staggered around, licking bowls and plates. She stared as they approached. Her name was Muffin. The only other thing Pixie could remember about her was that she had a relentlessly snotty nose.

It wasn't the first face Pixie had wished to see. When she'd pictured curing at Fairy Park, she'd seen Snow and not much beyond that. If she thought really hard, she saw Mama Gretel and even Aladdin. On the plus side, if Muffin were still alive it meant others could be too.

She started up the outcrop. She couldn't stand not knowing for a moment longer if Snow was alive or dead.

"Oi, Pixie. Back here. We should start with this one." Wolf had Muffin by the shoulders and was reassuring her that they were going to make her all better.

Pixie took a long glance up the outcrop for any sign of Snow then headed back.

"Don't worry. We'll get to Snow," Wolf said. She always knew just what Pixie was thinking.

Muffin shuddered and stuttered, and her eyes rolled back in her head as Centa and Perpetua began. Wolf made soothing sounds and said soothing words, and Centa told them of empty bubbles in the youngster's brain and pneumonia in her lungs.

An aunty that Pixie only knew by sight, staggered out of the water condenser shed and into the kitchen.

"What... are... you doing?"

"We're curing her. We'll get to you next," Wolf said.

Pixie winced. Snow could be dying that very minute and the aunty looked like she had a couple of days left in her.

The woman glared at her. Could be thinking Pixie shouldn't be back there. She'd be thinking differently, they'd all think differently, when they realized Pixie could be useful after all.

Once Muffin and the aunty were cured, they pointed them over to the barricaded laundry. Inside, they found three aggressive infected, huddling amongst shredded sheets and snarling, though barely able to move from their wounds and sickness. None of them was Snow, and Pixie waited impatiently as Centa and Perpetua did their work.

"I need to find Snow," Pixie said once they were outside again. Further up the outcrop, rats roamed freely and sniffed at sun-dried puddles of vomit and human faeces on the unswept paths. Pixie dragged Wolf past the other mamas' shelters and straight to Mama Gretel's surgery.

Inside, Gretel lay on the table in the middle of her clinic. Jars of herbs and powders and unguents were smashed all over the floor. Piss spilled from the table. Threaded through it all was a scent of shit.

Wolf stood in the doorway behind Pixie. "I think she's dead."

Tears clouded Pixie's eyes. Could be from all the fumes and dust in the air. She'd supposed Mama Gretel would be around forever. Even with all her medical knowledge, she hadn't been able to save herself.

What would it be like if the mamas all were gone? Fairy Park could be different. It would be sad, but it could also mean there'd be a place for her and others like her who didn't want to breed.

Pixie cleared her throat. "Snow's not here."

Mama Gretel turned her head and moaned. Butterflies rose from low in Pixie's abdomen and lodged behind a sob in her throat. She rushed forward and put her hand on Gretel's forehead.

"It's okay. We're going to cure you."

The first thing Mama Gretel said when she was able to talk again was, "Pix. You're a sight for sore eyes. I had a strange dream that a woman was fixing me from the inside."

Pixie was glad she wasn't yet questioning her return from exile.

"It's true, Mama. Everything she said to you was true. They're humans from another planet and they've got special powers."

She sat up. "What? My brain's still a bit scrambled, I think." She smoothed down her hair. "I must look like I've been dragged through a bush backwards. Traveller Wolf? Did you bring medicine from the Earth Guardians?"

Wolf glanced at Pixie and frowned. "It was the women from another planet. Just like Pixie said."

"That's ridiculous. Don't go telling everyone that nonsense. They'll think you're a few sandwiches short of a picnic... or, even worse, possessed."

Pixie pictured Mama Rosamund rising from her death bed and proclaiming that she was demon possessed. Pixie could never be herself at Fairy Park. While the mamas ruled, it would never be her home. She had a skill now. It was really Centa's skill, but she had the body to transport it. She would be a travelling healer. If she was lucky, Wolf would travel with her.

Mama Gretel swung her legs off the table and held her head. "Still a bit woozy." Wolf gave her a hand down. "This place looks like a dog's breakfast."

Soon she would be bustling about and organising everyone and pretending she hadn't just been a sperm's width from death. Nothing ever really changed at Fairy Park.

"Where's Snow?"

"I don't know. We had a barney before we all fell ill." Mama Gretel opened a trunk and yanked out a set of clean clothes. "So much to do," she muttered. "Now tell me about this medicine or treatment. And no more fantasy stories."

"Was the barney about you sending me away or about the baby she's been forced to carry?"

"Both. She doesn't know what's in her best interests." Mama Gretel tutted. "There's no time for this conversation. There are sick folk everywhere who need tending."

Pixie clenched her fists, but Wolf took her hands and pulled her back to the door. Gretel tutted. "You can complain until the cows come home. You know this is the way things have to be."

"We need to keep going," she said quietly. She turned to Mama Gretel. "We'll take care of treating the sick. You can concentrate on getting yourself, and everyone else, cleaned up."

"Who are these roaming cows anyway?" Pixie muttered as Wolf guided her out of the shelter before she could waste time on a pointless argument about a stupid way of life that she was powerless to change.

They bounced from shelter to shelter curing the residents of Fairy Park wherever they found them. Many of their minds and bodies had been wrecked by the prion. Some staggered around in confusion, others cowered in corners, and many of them lay in their shit-stained beds.

At each successive shelter, Pixie was disappointed to find no sign of Snow.

Most of the villagers had been lucky. Their damage was reversible, and the death toll wasn't as bad as she'd feared. Amongst the not so lucky were Mama Wendy, three breeders, two newborns and two sperm-sacks. Taking the dead newborns from the arms of their barely conscious birthmothers could be the worst thing Pixie had ever had to do, even worse than having to walk away from Fairy Park after she'd been bitten by the pig.

The youngsters had suffered the mildest symptoms. Once he was well, Aladdin sat up from the pile of rags that was his bed and gave Pixie a hug.

Pixie pushed him away. "We still have more people to treat. Do something useful for once in your life and round up the others to start cleaning this place out. It stinks even worse than usual."

"You really are possessed."

Pixie cuffed his ear.

The first aunty they'd cured brought Pixie and Wolf grub. "There's nothing hot to eat yet, but we're getting things going in the kitchen."

They drank the water and scoffed the jerky, then headed up to Jack's house, where the elderly papas lived. It was almost dawn. They'd been curing people all through the night, and they still hadn't found Snow.

"Where is she?" Pixie fretted. "Do you think she ran away? Could be she set out searching for me and got sick somewhere. Or ran into those Mother Feeders."

Wolf took Pixie's hands in hers and they touched foreheads. "We'll keep searching until we find her, okay?"

Pixie took a deep breath. "Okay." She wouldn't give up on Snow. The stubborn strength inside her that had kept her from becoming a baby factory these past few years pushed her on.

They came to a building that Pixie called Jack's House after an old fairy tale character. The concrete beanstalk that jutted from its front wall was now bursting with bushy, green vine. More stems shot from the doors, windows, and a hole in the roof.

"Be careful," Centa said. "There doesn't seem to be any dust, but it's still dangerous." Her unease was like the shadow of a heart beating rapidly in Pixie's chest.

Pixie pitched over a lump outside the front door. Her solar lamp revealed four papas splayed on the ground. The vine had grown around them as if they were below its interest. Wolf knelt and checked their pulses. One of them was dead, but the other three were alive.

Pixie and Wolf held hands so they could converse with Perpetua and Centa.

"Why isn't the vine devouring them?" Perpetua asked. "On Aceso you only had to stand still in a patch of vine for it to start twining up your body and attaching suckers."

"I'm not sure, but I think it works with a purpose," Centa said. "Is one of them Isaac?"

Pixie rolled one of the papas onto his back with her foot and Wolf turned the other three over gently.

"Nah," Pixie answered. "I'll check inside for him."

She pushed through the leaves that curtained the doorway. The vine became thicker the further she went. She followed the stems to the point where they converged just below the dead face of Papa Isaac. She tried to push the vine aside to reveal his body, but the vine *was* his body now. It had erupted from his chest like he was the soil in which a seed had been planted. Pixie rose and stepped back beside Wolf.

"Bloody hell. It's like the story Mama Goldy used to tell about the youngster who swallowed the stone from a plum and grew a tree from her belly."

She'd seen a lot of gruesome things, many of them just in the last couple of days, but this was the most bizarre. Beautiful too, though, like his body had transformed into something lofty and meaningful after his soul had ascended.

Wolf steadied her. "Why did it attack him and not the others?"

"It didn't attack him. It grew from him," Centa said. "Disciple Quinn must have brought it with her from Aceso and it took root within his DNA."

"Huh." Pixie had no idea what that meant. By the time they'd finished with the papas, Fairy Park bustled with activity. Nobody mentioned the aliens who'd come with Wolf and Pixie to cure them. There was too much to do. Pixie knew there would be gossip soon enough. She didn't want to be around to have to explain it to folk who likely wouldn't be convinced anyway.

She caught lots of glances of fear and suspicion thrown in her direction. She'd saved their lives, yet she could be banished again the moment things settled down.

The sun was almost up, and they still hadn't found Snow. Pixie told herself that the absence of a body was better than a dead body and then immediately countered that she was full of shit. A locust swarm of dread built in her innards.

"Is there anywhere else Snow could be?" Wolf asked.

"Could be she fled with some of the other folk." Pixie had been ignoring the possibility. She couldn't help Snow if she couldn't find her.

The dogs ran barking down the path from the summit, then turned and headed back up.

"Worth a check," Pixie said and headed for her old shelter at the sun-blasted, windswept pinnacle of Fairy Park.

Inside, someone was curled up on Pixie's mattress with their face turned away from the door. Matted brown hair was pasted to their head and neck with sweat.

"Snow?" Pixie whispered.

The person turned their head slowly. Kind brown eyes settled on Pixie. *Snow.* She was here. She was alive.

Pixie fell to her knees and gathered her sister into her arms. Her relief was short-lived, though, like rain on a hot day that soon turned to suffocating steam. What if Snow was too far gone for Centa and Perpetua to cure?

"I'm so thirsty," Snow moaned.

Wolf wet Snow's lips with water from her condensing bottle while Pixie stroked her forehead. "You'll be all better soon," she said. "We're here to cure you."

The sun bathed them in morning light as Centa began. Pixie had day-dreamed through many of the other curings, but she watched Snow closely for signs of health.

Gradually Snow's skin smoothed and cleared, her breath eased, and the dark circles underneath her eyes receded. A tear dripped from the tip of Pixie's nose and onto her sister's forehead. Snow pushed herself up and glanced down at her stained clothes and the sodden mattress.

"You worried about my mattress being a health hazard before," Pixie said, drying her cheeks with the back of her hand.

"Do you think being sick stopped the pregnancy taking?" Snow cupped her lower belly with a hand. She'd been inseminated with Wolf's sperm only a handful of days before.

"A healthy blastocyst has implanted in her uterus," Centa whispered in Pixie's head.

Pixie didn't understand all the words, but she got the gist. "Looks like you've been knocked up."

Snow's cheeks flushed with misery. "But how do you know?"

"Centa told me. You met her while she was curing you. Remember? She had a good tour of your innards." Pixie brushed hair back from Snow's clammy forehead.

"I thought that was a dream. How did you fix me? I don't understand."

Pixie sighed. This felt like the thousandth time she'd had this conversation. "Do you trust me?"

Snow bit her bottom lip. "Yeah."

"Then go with it. You've been cured, and you're having a baby."

Snow's face crumpled. "I don't want to have a baby. I thought the disease might have fixed everything for me." She lay back on the disgusting mattress. "I don't want to be a breeder. I don't want to give birth again. I don't want any of it. I've heard every single breeder screaming on the childbed. It's the hormones and everyone cooing over the baby and telling us that they were worth it that makes most folk forget. But I can't."

Pixie rocked back on her haunches. "Is there something you can do, Centa?"

Centa was quiet for a moment. "Yes. Put your hand over her uterus."

Epilogue

EARTH

Year 2338
Three months later

Centa initiated rapid cell division along the lining of a fallopian tube, one epithelial cell after another. They multiplied and spread across the divide to seal up the lumen. Ova would no longer make the journey to meet with sperm. Instead, they would be reabsorbed by the body. This cheerful, round-cheeked woman named Maudie would never again fall pregnant, exactly as she had requested. According to Mama Gretel, tubal ligation was the resurrection of an evil procedure performed by selfish neoliberals. Pixie had found that hilarious.

Centa had spent most of her years in a laboratory trying to generate life. Now she travelled the Earth bringing health and reproductive services to the scattered population. Some people needed help to have the children their bodies had denied them, while others wanted the choice to never have children at all. Choice had never been valued on Aceso or at Fairy Park. Now she was a potent instrument of it.

The acts of cell repair and manipulation calmed her. She was still a cell biologist, only now she no longer needed a pipette to complete her work. The vine had taken those tools from her and given her new ones. She could get right amongst the cells and know them intimately.

Every piece of healing made Centa stronger. The mycelial network of the void was like a system of tunnels through reality that carried the metaphysical: information, thoughts, consciousness. Even what some might call the soul. When these tunnels connected to the physical world, some aspect of the metaphysical became physical for a brief time. *She* became physical for a brief time.

She returned to the void where Perpetua anchored her and then back into Pixie.

"You're done," Pixie said to the woman, smiling.

"Bullshit. It's that easy?" Maudie looked down and rubbed her belly.

They'd received a mixed reception everywhere they'd travelled. At Pixie's insistence—and to alleviate the guilt she carried—Tadpole had been the first outside of Fairy Park that they'd repaired. He'd been in the last stages of the prion infection when they'd found him, and once cured, he'd offered them their choice of items from the coveted divers' stash. He'd also asked Pixie to stay with him, but thankfully for Centa she hadn't been interested.

From there they'd been denounced as demons and chased out of one of the more fundamentally religious villages. Luckily, most of the subsequent communities had been convinced by the results, especially when the wounds or infirmities had been visible and obvious.

Pixie held one of her hands up in front of Maudie's face and cut the end of her thumb with her machete. She'd found sticking a spork in the back of her hand hurt too much to be repeated with any regularity. Centa knit the edges of her cut together at once.

"That is impressive," the woman said in awe.

"Trust me," Pixie replied. "We'll be back this way sometime next year, and if you've gotten knocked up in the meantime, I'll let you cut my whole thumb off."

Maudie laughed. "I'll hold you to that. Or maybe you could just make it up to me with some of your tattoo work."

Maudie was the last of that community to seek their services. They tended to the most life-threatening conditions first, such as metastatic tumours, heart failure, pneumonias, and infections gone systemic, and then they worked their way down through venereal diseases and yeast infections, toothaches and rashes, until finally they performed reproductive services.

To those whose bodies and cells were too damaged or who were ready to move on from this life, they gave a peaceful, painless death.

"Will you be staying another night?" Maudie sat up on her cot and swung her feet onto the floor. "You'd be welcomed."

Centa and Pixie had developed ways to keep their thoughts private from each other, yet Centa could still read Pixie by the chemicals that ran through her body. She was tempted to stay. She and Wolf had been fed well and had slept in soft beds beneath a tarp on the deck of the ship the community called home.

They declined the invitation. They wanted to be on their way to the next place on their route. They had developed the ability to tell what the other was thinking without even speaking. Centa had never been that way with anyone. Not even Ben.

They still hadn't found him, though they'd come across other Sky Humans on their travels. On the rare occasion there was more than one of them inhabiting humans in a village, Centa and Perpetua taught them how to anchor each other to make biological repairs.

Wolf reassured her that there were many more communities to visit. Centa wanted to know Ben was safe, but she wasn't in love with him anymore. She wasn't sure she ever really was. She'd been in love with what he represented and the feeling of defiance that being with him had given her. Perpetua was conspicuously silent on the topic.

Centa still felt the weight of her role in Master Anton's death. On her worst days, she thought she was the most depraved and arrogant human on Earth, wielding power over life and death as she saw fit. On her best days, she believed she'd redeemed herself by putting Perpetua first for once. Regardless, that decision was in the past. She would just have to find a way to live with it. She couldn't let Master Anton continue to destroy her. The violence had to end or else his death would have been for nothing.

Maudie handed Wolf and Pixie packs filled with food and fresh water, and they climbed down the knotted rope that hung from side of the ship, past round windows that resembled eyes weeping rust, and into a small rowboat. Maudie rowed them ashore while Lucy and Merlin ran along the edge of the water barking with excitement. The pig ran with them. Without the prion warping her brain, she was a different creature, sweet and affectionate. Now she was part of their nomadic family.

Pixie dipped her hand into the clear water of the bay. Below the surface, a seaweed-like strain of vine swayed and reached for the light of the Earth star.

Over an evening meal, community members had told them of a metal man with a plastic face and a fierce-looking woman who had passed through before the strange plant appeared. The vine had digested all the plastic on the beach and then retreated to the water and purified it.

It was the third time they'd come across the vine on their travels. Everything Centa had known her whole life had been turned upside down. The vine had been a constant threat on Aceso, the enemy that had united them and given them their purpose and, ultimately, their ruin and salvation. There, it had been an immune agent, a phagocyte that worked to rid the planet of its alien invaders by engulfing them.

Its role on Earth was different. Humans had done so much damage, yet the Earth had accepted the vine as a gift from another planet across the galaxy, not to annihilate the detrimental species, but to help them undo the damage they'd done. The Earth had forgiven its destructive children. She hoped its faith in them wasn't misplaced.

"Next time we come here, I'll bring some fertilized fish eggs from the aqua farms of the Earth Guardians so you can reseed these waters," Wolf said as Maudie dragged the boat ashore and Pixie and Wolf climbed out. Besides medical care, they also carried information, tech, and resources from one place to another.

"That would be ace," Maudie replied, dragging the boat back into the water and waving them goodbye.

"We're not far from the android factory," Wolf said as they set out across the beach in the fading daylight. "Let's stop there tonight."

"Sounds good." Pixie chewed on a piece of dried seaweed from her pack. "You up for that?" She asked Centa.

"Wherever you go, I go."

Centa appreciated Pixie's acknowledgment of her ideas and desires, but she controlled the biological repairs she made, her own thoughts and not much else. She took as much joy from this life as she could. Her only other alternative was complete disintegration in the void. She wasn't dejected enough for that yet. While she still existed, the possibility of finding a way to be independent also existed.

For now, she would travel with these women across a planet that for once felt like home. There was bliss in the swaying of the trees, the burbling of a stream, and the thumping vibration of an unseen kangaroo passing nearby. Nature had not been calming and soothing on Aceso. They'd cringed from its native lifeforms, with mesh screens for the bugs, traps and poison for the lizard-pigs, and fire for the vine. They'd only been content with the organisms they'd brought from Earth and knew how to control. But it wasn't possible to live in harmony on a planet while suppressing all other life.

She wondered if Skyfather had ever yearned for Earth and regretted leaving. She would never understand how he could give up on such a beautiful and generous planet.

Earth possessed an intelligence that humans didn't recognise, yet felt the consequences of every day. It spoke to those who were paying attention. Plants were its words, rocks its story, and weather its mood. It crooned to them in flowers, shouted in trees, grumbled in fungi, and whispered in grasses. The creatures they crossed paths with were, like humans, nothing more than brief daydreams. Humans had the arrogance to believe that they had the power to destroy or save the Earth. Centa was certain they only had the power to destroy or save themselves. The planet would recover from their abuse with only scars, given enough time. It would take back all their corpses to feed itself until even the memory of humankind had long since disappeared.

For now, as the sun set, the women would make camp in the android factory up ahead and light a fire to hold back the Earth's dark, nighttime thoughts. They would dance and sing and scream, and Centa would pretend that she was truly free.

• • • • ● • ● • ● • • •

To the south of the android factory, Rae and Ben weaved their way through hundreds of derelict cars crouching in the long grass, like crocodiles with jagged metal teeth waiting to slice unwary flesh. Throughout the remains of civilisation, plants had found weaknesses and openings in metal and concrete, as though they'd been waiting patiently for decades under the thin layer of human activity.

Rae wondered why Earth had created humans when it had such perfect children in plants and fungi. Were they a dangerous addiction? An experiment out of control? The fateful indulgence of a bored planet? They were Earth's unexpectedly sociopathic offspring.

She paused in the shadow of a derelict farmhouse and sliced open the scab on the tip of her index finger, squeezing drops of blood onto the shattered glass that was sprinkled across the soil. The vine was part of her body at a molecular level now, and it purified the land and broke down toxins to something the Earth could use again. She knew little of science or medicine or the workings of chemicals, cells, or atoms. But the vine did. And it had travelled with her across the galaxy. The blueprint of the vine was in the DNA of every cell in the professor's body, and it took root with every drop of blood that touched the Earth, healing the planet but not in the way it had healed Aceso. Humans were not a toxin to be expelled but a vital presence to be nurtured.

Creating the vine on Earth with drops of her blood had allowed Rae to continue her grandparents' work after all. That was what the patch of vine beneath the blackberry hedge had been trying to tell her—that she needed to venture out, to leave the safety of the Earth Guardian compound and spread the vine far and wide. On the road, she slept during the hottest part of the days and the darkest part of the nights while Ben watched over her. She was hobbled by the limits of her flesh. All he needed was the energy of the sun.

They reached the android factory as the sun dipped low in the sky, and inside they found a row of the machines identical to Ben's own in a rack that ran down the centre of the wide, dusty factory floor.

"These could be the way to help others from Aceso who have no bodies of their own," he said.

Rae had kept her knowledge of the factory from Ben at first. She thought it would be a distraction from her work. But he had become more and more despondent with each Sky Human they'd come across. To her the idea of an android body was horrible. Cold metal and plastics where warm flesh should be. Never sleeping or eating or feeling the breeze on your skin.

But Ben maintained that his android body was practical. He thought it fitting that his flesh had been recycled and given a new purpose on Aceso. And in a machine, there was no pain or hunger. Sensors gave him access to sight and sound, proprioception, and touch. He derived his energy directly from the sun, almost like a plant.

Rae took a deep swig from her water condenser bottle and consulted the professor's tablet while she tapped on the keypad beneath the chest plate of one of the androids. She'd been wrong to think that she and Ben were close. It had become obvious that he hadn't thought of her as anything other than a symbol of Father's Law in years.

Still, she had enlisted him into her plans, the way her father had all those years ago, except now he wasn't a child and there was nothing to keep him walking away whenever he wanted.

"Cross your fingers," Rae said and replaced the android's chest plate. She lay her hand on the palm panel in the centre of the chest.

The panel glowed green, and the android lifted its head and opened its eyes.

Ben stretched his plastic skin into the shape of a smile. "Now when I find the souls of Aceso, I can offer them more than pity." All he ever thought about were those workers.

One day his part in her story would end. She couldn't keep putting her love into people who wouldn't love her in return. Now her only love was for the Earth. And it loved her too. Just as Aceso had wanted them gone, Earth had wanted them back. It had called to her from across the galaxy, and she had brought the vine with her as a gift. This was the love story that she was part of now.

As the Earth healed, perhaps she too could heal. Forgive those who had kept her from her path. They hadn't understood the curse they were placing on her. She feared the story of her imprisoned years would take on an aura of importance and romance in the telling, in the way fairy tales were shaped over time into something more palatable. But she was not a sleeping beauty. She had changed. Rae's time trapped in her body had taken all joy and hope from her, but nurturing the Earth could give back what she'd lost.

She didn't know how this story would end, but one day her work might be done. When that time came, perhaps she would have room in her heart for other humans once again.

And perhaps, when the Earth was restored, humans would no longer scorch their fingertips reaching for the stars.

About the Author

Melissa is a scientist and Aurealis Award nominated author who writes fiction about Neandertals, cyborgs, cults, future science, evil scientists and infectious diseases. Her debut novel, The Shining Wall, is available now. Her eco-punk, science fantasy novel, Star-Scorched Fingertips will be published by Android Press in 2023.

You can connect with her on twitter @melissajferg or on Facebook: Melissa Ferguson

Also By Melissa Ferguson

THE SHINING WALL (Transit Lounge, 2019)

www.ingramcontent.com/pod-product-compliance
Lightning Source LLC
Chambersburg PA
CBHW060905210726

48293CB00006B/1965